# THE CAMBRIDGE CURRY CLUB

## Saumya Balsari

BLACKAMBER BOOKS

Arcadia Books Ltd
15-16 Nassau Street
London W1W 7AB

www.arcadiabooks.co.uk

First published by BlackAmber
an imprint of Arcadia Books, 2004
This B-format edition first published in 2008

A catalogue record for this book is available from the British Library.

ISBN 978-1-905147-69-4

Typeset by RefineCatch Limited, Bungay, Suffolk
Printed and bound in Finland by WS Bookwell

Arcadia Books gratefully acknowledges the financial support of Arts
Council England.

Arcadia Books supports PEN, the fellowship of writers who work
together to promote literature and its understanding. English PEN
upholds writers' freedoms in Britain and around the world,
challenging political and cultural limits on free expression.

To find out more, visit www.englishpen.org or contact
English PEN, 6-8 Amwell Street, London EC1R 1UQ

*Arcadia Books distributors are as follows:*

*in the UK and elsewhere in Europe:*
Turnaround Publishers Services
Unit 3, Olympia Trading Estate
Coburg Road
London N22 6TZ

*in the USA and Canada:*
Consortium Book Sales and Distribution
1045 Westgate Drive
St Paul, MN 55114-1065

*in Australia:*
Tower Books
PO Box 213
Brookvale, NSW 2100

*in New Zealand:*
Addenda
Box 78224
Grey Lynn
Auckland

*in South Africa:*
Quartet Sales and Marketing
PO Box 1218
Northcliffe
Johannesburg 2115

Arcadia Books: *Sunday Times* Small Publisher of the Year 2002/03

*For Sudhanshu,*
*Sárica Robynn and Sanna Linnéa*

# Prologue

THE SLY OCTOBER wind tore through Cambridge, boldly lifting the prim skirt of the Junior Bursar as her court shoes, indignant at a male colleague's promotion, clicked briskly through a college archway to meet the waiting porters and bedmakers. It scattered the papers of the student vaulting fluidly over the rhododendron bush near the Buttery, and waltzed through the hoary trees of the College Backs, rocking *Venezia*, a derelict punt on the river. It tousled the hair of the Japanese tourist posing in front of the Victorian pillar box and the lamp-post outside King's College. A few yards away on King's Parade, a passerby lingered inexplicably in front of a Bible in the display windows of the Cambridge University Press, and the bells of Great St Mary's chimed grandly as a bird wheeled through St Edward's Passage, past *G. David, Booksellers since 1896* and over the Fen farmers unloading produce at Market Square.

The wind paused to reflect on its own past glory; in its time it had circled the Roman settlement at Castle Hill and rattled the round-headed Saxon windows of St Bene't's Church. At Christ's College, it had swept the

1

conversations of Charles Darwin and John Milton, two centuries apart; at Corpus Christi it had been Christopher Marlowe's whirling Muse. The wind also shook the trees in the orchard of Isaac Newton's family home in Lincolnshire. An apple fell.

The wind had been the harbinger of revolt urging the students fleeing the Oxford riots in 1209 towards Cambridge; it had hastened their staggering steps to the medieval brothels in the area surrounding Magdalene College. It knew where Oliver Cromwell's head was secretly buried in the chapel of Sidney Sussex College. Centuries later, it still whispers envy to townspeople pausing to watch new graduates in gowns and hoods file through the streets towards the Senate House.

The bird perched on the segment of missing stone ball on the parapet of Clare Bridge until the wind whipped its wings, whirling it into the autumn sky. Together, bird and wind sailed jauntily through the Gate of Humility in the Master's Garden at Gonville and Caius College, departing humbly through the Gate of Honour and soaring high over Parker's Piece and Fenner's Ground to seek the homely pleasures of Mill Road.

Colourful Mill Road bore no resemblance to the shops of elegant Magdalene Bridge, nor, for that matter, did Covent Garden, a side lane of Mill Road, recall its London namesake. No riverside café served steaming latte and mozzarella panini here, no leafy towpath walked the sluggish dog or mind; instead, a daily brigade of bargain-hunters sniffed their spoils, their hard noses pressed against the display windows of the charity shops. With its rows of small houses, ethnic food stores, hair salons, curry houses, Internet cafés, bookmaker, health shop and dry cleaners, Mill Road was the city's pumping heart.

Spotting a homeless drunk lying outside the bookmakers, the wind swooped, tossing the shivering man into dreams of Salvation soup and death. Next, it flirted with a large Asian woman bent over a black bin bag on the pavement outside the charity shop called IndiaNeed. Lasciviously lifting her blue silk sari, it revealed sensible men's socks above sensible women's sandals. The large woman's neck showed traces of talc. A white van halted at the traffic lights opposite the shop. *Wish my wife was as dirty as this van* was scrawled on its dusty side. The driver leaned out of his window and whistled at the bending woman. She straightened hastily, feigning indignation, but a smile hovered over her lips at the moment that the bird circled above. Plop, plop, plop. Everything auspicious was always in threes; it must have been an Indian bird in a previous life. The green-white slime slithered down a rolling mountain of flesh, splaying rivulets over the plains of her unsuspecting back.

The bird hopped away, and the triumphant wind scampered back over Silver Street and across the Bridge of Sighs to slip into the waiting willows nearby.

# CHAPTER ONE

# Many hands make light work

SWARNAKUMARI WAS BENT, innocent and ungainly, over a black bag lying on the pavement outside the charity shop IndiaNeed, her posterior turned heavenward like an overturned duck scrabbling in the shallow brook that runs along the Botanic Garden overlooking Trumpington Road.

She hauled the bag from underneath the vandalised sign that read *Do    lean bicycles against the windows please* and dragged it into the shop. Watching her from the windows of Flamenco, the salon opposite, the hairdresser James alias Juan slipped warm Mediterranean vowels into his Glaswegian accent and waited near the Rexine customer chairs. Once inside, Swarnakumari bent over the displays in the shop window. Three amused women watched from the till as she carefully placed a pink china plate depicting a grinning bulldog next to a framed Jubilee photograph of the Queen.

Heera leaned with both elbows over the counter. 'Just look at Swarna, how that woman bends . . . she can bend for England! You know, Durga, my grandfather used to go to the village temple and feed the cow there every day. He was such a naughty man! One day he pretended to be blind and he patted a fat bending woman as if he was stroking a cow, and then he pulled her long plait just like a cow's tail. She thought he was blind, so she didn't get upset, but when she bent again to remove her slippers, what d'you think happened? He did it again!'

Heera dug an ebullient elbow into Durga, chuckling into the folds of her chin; her body shook under the shapeless black sweater and elasticated trousers she wore, and her short hair bobbed in mirth. Swarnakumari straightened, patted the flower in her neat bun and retrieved her handbag, calling over her shoulder as she headed for the Staff Area behind the green floral curtain, 'Window display is done now. Just going to wash my hands, *hanh*.'

Hunched over the till, Durga twirled a strand of shiny shoulder-length hair. She was slim in jeans and a cream turtleneck. Sudden laughter had creased the solemn lines of her face, skimming lips ashamed of their fullness. She observed, 'Every time she touches anything in here, Lady Macbeth washes her hands over and over with her Sainsbury's soap dispenser, but the damned charity shop spot remains like a turmeric blob on a white English hob, staining her Brahmin sensibilities.'

Eileen muttered, 'Sixteen times. Swarna washed her hands sixteen times last Thursday.' Eileen had been a gifted mathematics teacher; she knew her numbers. Born in Armagh, Northern Ireland, she was tall and wiry with wispy grey hair, and was dressed in a long black skirt and matching knit cardigan accompanied by a silver cross around her neck and silver bracelets on her wrist. Her mother had been a hungry seamstress raising a family of six children; the exhausted father ran away and jumped aboard a ship called *Providence* bound for New York. Young Danny Watts of Cambridge met the twenty-year-old Eileen on a camping holiday in Cork and was entranced by her dark eyes and hair, creamy neck and ready laugh. The smile had faded first; her black hair followed twenty years later.

Swarnakumari's handbag contained the soap dispenser, a tiny towel, a prayer book, a tortoiseshell comb and the distinctive red Shantiniketan hand-crafted leather money purse. The colour of the folded towel was different every week.

On Thursday nights Swarnakumari lay in bed, eyes turned upward and away from her sleeping husband, Shyamal Chatterjee. On her bedside table stood a tube of Neutrogena cream; an application after dinner ensured that her fingers had shed the chalky film covering shop rejects and other rejections unnamed. Once the ceiling above her bed no longer reflected the passing lights of street cars and desire, unguent calm had been restored.

Swarnakumari was a charitable woman, and her thoughts, like her puja table for the gods, faced eastward. She had initially read fiction every Wednesday to Jean Ward, a blind woman in a Cambridge nursing home, but her strongly accented English proved too much for her elderly listener, who promptly fell asleep each time. Swarnakumari had enthusiastically recited an entire novel, unaware that her listener had not progressed beyond the first page. Jean Ward passed away peacefully in the Prologue of the second novel.

The charity's name, IndiaNeed, led Swarnakumari to volunteer in a shop whose proceeds benefited deserving villagers in a desert region of Rajasthan in Western India. The director on the Board of the charity, Diana Wellington-Smythe, was mockingly nicknamed 'Lady Di' by her staff. Her hyphenated surname had found immediate approval with Swarnakumari's husband Mr Chatterjee. A link with a village project in West Bengal would have been ideal, but a Cambridge charity shop had its limitations, as did Mr Chatterjee, thought Swarnakumari.

Heera played idly with a basket of small leather purses. She wondered why Swarnakumari had volunteered at IndiaNeed; she had the look of a pukka Bengali madam in a paisley silk sari presiding over a sitar soirée, and on the first day of the shop orientation meeting with Lady Di and the volunteers two months ago in that very spot, she had known Swarnakumari would be a strange one – she simply didn't belong. Those silly Korean student volunteers didn't belong either, and were there to practise their English one afternoon in the week, but in the end they jabbered away together in their own language, and if a customer approached, they pulled out a superfast translator to slowly make a sentence and a sale.

Heera sighed and rearranged the brooches on the jewellery shelf. What could be cured in life was little, whereas what had to be endured was a coiled snake around the neck, her Aunty Buddi Mai used to say. Durga with her clever remarks was another strange one, thought Heera, and Eileen was even stranger. Those two were both so secretive about their lives that getting any masala – any juicy bits – out of them, was like trying to make a stubborn camel move. And why did those two *eediots* Bitter Butter Betty and Quite

Contrary Mary volunteer four days a week if they were going to complain all the time?

Swarnakumari returned, deposited her handbag on the table and held out a small plastic Tesco box sporting a humous label. Inside was a powdery concoction of sugar, ghee and roasted flour.

'My hands are washed now. Today is Her Holiness, my Guru Ma's birthday. I am also fasting today. *Cholo cholo*, come, come, hold out your hands and take *proshad*. Take more, Eileen,' she urged.

Heera, Durga and Eileen dutifully held out their palms and licked off the crumbs as she continued, '*Bhalo*. Good. We are all blessed now, and today will be a good day, so now we shall start sorting the bags that came this morning.'

They approached the long wooden sorting table directly behind the curtain that concealed the Staff Area. Above it was an oversized notice: *Sort out any bags stored under the table. Put all rejects into bags and onto skip outside. Do NOT take home, or throw away in bin. Remember to check the pockets of all clothing and contents of all purses, wallets and handbags. Do NOT take away contents, especially money or jewellery.*

Two entwined hearts and the words *Pamela and John forever* had been anonymously etched into the table's far right corner; eternity was evidently to be seen in a grain of wood.

The area under the large table was the depot for the black bags arriving from the pavement outside. The bags were wrung tight with yellow string, startled plump chickens strangled at the neck by their donors. After dark, the wind rummaged the other bags left in an alleyway outside the shop, and the crumpled plastic morphed into flapping ghouls of the night. Black bags and charity shops were an inseparable pairing, like 'chicken' and 'egg', 'honour' and 'killing'. Like Pamela and John, forever.

Swarnakumari opened the first bag with suppressed excitement, gingerly retrieving lingerie and men's tweed trousers. She dropped the trousers in horror. '*Chee, chee*, I am not going to check another man's trousers; that too, the backside pocket. So dirty, *na?*' *Na* in Swarnakumari's speech was a statement of finality rather than a search for validation.

Holding the offending trousers by their waistband, Heera twirled them slightly. 'Yeah, they are quite manky. By the way, girls, did you know one in four Englishmen never washes his favourite underwear?'

Swarnakumari emitted an exaggerated wail on cue. 'You are always teasing me. You know I do not like touching unwashed clothes of others. What would my people in Kolkata think of me? Oh, look at this swimsuit, so transparent – you can see everything!'

'If you hate all this touch touch, then why so much rush rush to open the new bags? *Arre*, I know all your tricks. If there's something new or nice to buy, you'll say you saw it first.'

As the shop's manager, Heera could have vetted the goods first, but an Indian deference to age had prevailed. Swarnakumari was fifty-seven; Heera was forty-seven. Eileen was three years older than Swarnakumari, but showed little interest in the bags, only in the arrangement or disposal of their contents. The previous week Swarnakumari had profited from the delivery of a manufacturer's bag containing new sweatshirts in S, M and L sizes. After pricing them herself, Swarnakumari purchased six for her favoured Kolkata nieces. Durga intervened; black sweatshirts would not find favour in India. Swarnakumari had hesitated, but in the end, the words *Cambridge University* emblazoned in red had settled the matter favourably.

'And by the way, this isn't a swimsuit, it's a teddy,' explained Heera.

'Teddy?'

Heera continued, 'Yes, teddy. Listen to this, Swarna. On Ritu's anniversary, Raj went home with one yellow and eleven red roses and two plane tickets; he made her pack her bags in one hour. First he gave her a flower, then he gave her one hour.'

'That's flower power,' interjected Durga.

'She told me they went to the Moulin Rouge. So romantic, can you imagine? He bought her a teddy in Paris,' Heera gushed.

Swarnakumari was perplexed. 'Why buy all the way from Paris? Ritu comes to the shop so often, and she could have bought the teddy bear cheap from here, *na*.'

'Not teddy bear, *teddy*. You really don't know what a teddy is, do you? *Arre*, can't you see it's so transparent, how can it be a swimsuit? It's lingerie. Underwear. Honestly, Swarna, sometimes you're worse than those Korean volunteers.'

'These young English girls are wearing anything nowadays, how was I to know? Shameless girls. Their clothes for wearing outside look like underwear, so *baba*, I am confused, *hanh*.' Swarnakumari fussed, 'Are these garments washed? Heera, I am asking you the same thing again and again – remind Mrs Wellington-Smythe, we must have gloves when we are doing the sorting.' She retrieved further items in haste and distaste. 'And what is this, now?'

'A blond wig and a whip,' said Eileen flatly.

'And such tiny white knickers! They've got *Punish Me* embroidered in black. Let's write a note for Lady Di: *Awaiting instructions*. Then just watch the fun, because the knickers will disappear, poof, into the air. Like the inflatable doll that came in two weeks ago,' laughed Heera.

The inflatable doll had not mysteriously disappeared; it had been sold by the Korean volunteers to a dejected young man swathed in a black scarf. He carried it home for target practice and shot several toy arrows of rejected love into its plastic heart. As the doll collapsed, the air oozing out of its red duck lips, the student had opened a celebratory bottle of beer and slashed his wrists on its broken glass.

'What doll? I never saw it. You should at least have shown it to me. I love dolls; I used to buy so many. Heera, such good things have started disappearing from the shop: new video recorder, antique brooch, necklace, watches, camera. And tell me, what is the thief going to do with my reading glasses from Vision Express? Why did he steal them? Can it be he has the same prescription?' demanded Swarnakumari.

'One can only speculate, Swarna. Why don't you arrange the teddy, the blond wig, whip and knickers in the window? We could pull in a few more customers that way. And where's that magazine we got the other day, Heera? It could go into the display, too,' suggested Durga. 'It had a double-spread of a punk hunk who was once a monk.'

'I threw it out,' said Heera curtly.

'Fascinating, isn't it? The monk became a gay hunk. Maybe the pay was better,' continued Durga.

Swarnakumari was curious. 'What private talk is going on?'

'It's about a gay magazine. And don't pretend you don't know what that is,' teased Durga.

'Of course I know about these things. So unnatural, but anyway, thank God this problem is not there in good Indian families.' A practised angler, Swarnakumari fished in the black bag. 'Look, a fur coat. Fur. Can it be real?'

Eileen gave the coat a brief examination. 'Fake.'

Swarnakumari continued as she found a hanger for the coat, 'So many people have so many problems in this world; look at these poor villagers in Rajasthan for whom we are raising money. They have no running water, no electricity. Guru Ma says we must always remember there are many more who have much less.'

Durga mused, 'My former supervisor here in Cambridge was gay, and he had more than most. Termtime tutorial visits were only between one and three in the afternoons. Whenever I left at three, I saw a Lebanese student bounding up the stairs for "happy hour". And I could tell you a story or two about the Formal Hall dinners. Some female students at the tables wore more or less nothing under their gowns. You might say those who had less had much more.'

Swarnakumari looked shocked as Heera asked, 'Really? I always wondered what went on behind those college gatehouses. What's a Formal Hall dinner?'

'College dinner in an echoing hall a few times during term. Stern portraits on the walls. Sherry in the Fellows' Drawing Room. Grace in Latin followed by dinner of warmed tart of broccoli and red onion topped with Emmental and watercress, escalopes of beef, dauphinois potatoes, apple and cinnamon flan with vanilla ice cream, finishing with coffee and Cambridge mints. Everyone waits until High Table departs, and then the fun begins.'

There was the sound of a drill. Heavy boots crossed the floor overhead.

'There he goes again,' cried Heera in irritation. 'Vroom vroom. One of these days, I am going to ask that man what he is doing in the room upstairs.'

'Perhaps he could use the blond wig and whip?' suggested Durga.

'Who?' asked Swarnakumari.

'The man upstairs, who else could we mean?' replied Heera.

'What do you want to do with these crutches?' demanded Eileen. 'They were lying next to the same bag.'

'Crutches and whip from the same donor? Which of the two gets a person walking faster?' wondered Durga.

'Heera, why should we keep these crutches in the shop? Can we not offer them to Ritu's mother-in-law? You told me she has recently broken her leg, *na*,' proposed Swarnakumari kindly.

'Has she really broken her leg, or has her son broken her heart by marrying Ritu?' Durga was intrigued. 'Anyway, who is this ever-ready to beddy, teddy-wearing Ritu?'

'She lives on Fendon Road. Her husband Raj always looks deep into her eyes. He squeezes her waist like a lemon all the time,' sighed Heera wistfully.

'Juicy stuff,' was Durga's comment.

14

'How is it that they can always be so romantic, even after so many years? It must be all those dates they ate when they were living in Dubai,' concluded Heera spitefully.

'Fake,' repeated Eileen before disappearing to replace a roll in the till machine.

Raj was inseparable from Ritu's waist at parties, and as soon as the women disappeared into the kitchen and the men held their whisky glasses aloft in the living room, he challenged other husbands into true confessions. When was the last time they had sent flowers or chocolates to their wives? He, on the other hand, knew the gift for Ritu's every mood. Her favourite bouquet consisted of eleven red roses and a single yellow stem. Wispy teddies were her undoing, he admitted with a wink. Mohan Karnani bent forward in bluff incomprehension. What were 'teddies'? Raj roared, patting Mohan's shoulder affectionately as he described the garment. It was short and didn't stay on long, he said, with another wink, as the other men shuffled with guilty feet.

'If only Raj would escort his mother to the Moulin Rouge instead, voilà, she would ditch the crutches and kick the stick habit,' said Durga.

'So what do you want to do with the crutches?' asked Eileen doggedly, as she reappeared clutching a book on mountaineering in the Balkans.

Every object handled by Eileen had its place, a number, a weight, a size, a shape and a space at IndiaNeed – and in her ordered universe. Chaos belonged to scientific theory, not in a charity shop.

'How many are there?' inquired Swarnakumari.

'It's a "Buy one, get one free" deal,' teased Durga.

'Two. Do you think we all need crutches, metaphorically speaking, that is, to get through life?' She gazed at the passersby bent against the curling wind. 'Perhaps crutches can never be given up or away. They are the desire and the dream that keep us breathing. And from walking. Away, that is.'

Durga was accustomed to the silence that invariably followed her observations. Eileen hovered until Heera spat impatiently, '*Arre*, just put them anywhere.'

'And what is this, now?' demanded Swarnakumari, retrieving a large box. 'Oh, it says on the cover that it is a machine for checking blood pressure.' She forced open the lid.

'It's a toy gun,' said Eileen with her usual grim composure as Swarnakumari recoiled at the contents. 'What do you want to do with it?'

'Scare the Korean girls? Price it and put it in the window?' mocked Durga.

The shop bell tinkled, and Heera emerged from behind the curtain as a young woman entered.

'Oh, hello, where are the children's bicycles?' asked the eager customer. 'I'm looking for one for my little girl, a pink Barbie one.'

'I'm sorry, but we don't have any.'

'You did have one. I saw it outside your shop last week,' insisted the woman.

'Yes, but we sold it, madam. You can see for yourself, there are no more bicycles here.'

Heera returned to the Staff Area as the customer departed. 'If we get one bloody bicycle in six months, does this mean we've become Halfords?'

'We could rename the shop Wellington's Wheels and Deals, or Smythe's Bikes for Tikes,' quipped Durga.

As she returned to the table, Heera continued, 'Girls, today's black bags are very strange. First manky trousers, then blond wig, knickers and teddy, then whip, crutches and blood-pressure kit with a toy gun inside.'

'Send the whole lot to Rupert darling,' Durga drawled.

'It is rude to talk about the husband of Mrs Wellington-Smythe like that,' admonished Swarnakumari.

'D'you know, the Heart to Heart shop got a 1917 diary the other day?' revealed Heera. 'A woman had sent love letters to her soldier fiancé, and she kept writing to him even after she knew he was dead. It was in the papers, didn't you read about it? And look at us – when we got a decent oil-painting two weeks ago, those stupid Korean girls sold it while it was waiting to be valued.'

'You mean the portrait of the dimpled heavenly cherub? Its hands were a bit fluttery. I'd get rid of it in any language,' Durga ventured.

Swarnakumari was defensive. 'We do get good things in this shop. Otherwise I would not be working here, *na*.'

The shop items passing through Swarnakumari's keen hands underwent a primary test of usefulness to the Chatterjee family, other volunteers at the shop and selected members of the Cambridge Indian community, after which time-consuming procedure she reluctantly considered the items for window display. A consignment of red and black porcelain mugs with *Mad Cow Mother-in-Law Disease* inscribed above the face of a scowling woman left Swarnakumari unmoved despite the magic words *Made in England* on the underside.

Durga used one for coffee breaks at the shop, but the rest lay neglected on a shelf until purchased by a taciturn Bulgarian language student who was brilliant at mathematics but struggled with his English. Eileen had silently pointed to the words *Mad Cow Mother-in-Law Disease*, and he had merely nodded. The meeting of minds over mathematics never took place. It was one of those encounters bursting at the bud, like the thousands in the lifetime of an individual, that, but for chance or fate, lead nowhere.

Heera moved forward to answer the insistent telephone. 'IndiaNeed . . . Yes, Mrs Wellington-Smythe, it is Heera here . . . No, I'm sorry, I was a little late today because I wasn't feeling . . . It was only ten minutes after ten . . . Yes, the shop should be opened on time, I am very sorry. Next time I'll . . . Yes, it is important for the customers . . . Yes, they come first . . . No, we haven't heard anything new about the missing items . . . Yes, of course I shall let you know . . . You've found a new volunteer to join us? That's very good . . . Yes, goodbye.'

She stormed back to the sorting table. 'How many times does Lady Di need to ask me about those missing items? *Arre*, once they're gone, they're gone. Is the thief going to come back and say, "Here, you can have them back, I'm having a bad hair day, now please arrest me?" And making such a big fuss over my coming late this morning! I wasn't feeling well, and I almost didn't come at all. Everyone has his or her problems, right? And every time I answer the telephone, why does she ask me who's speaking? Shouldn't she recognise my voice by now?'

A female pensioner entered as Eileen continued to

count the pieces in the cutlery boxes. Despite her record as an inspiring mathematics teacher, Eileen had been dismissed by the Village College where she was Head of the Department, as soon as she crossed her sixtieth birthday in June. A number had been the final betrayal. Her husband, a plumber, had recently discovered his body's tendency to spring leaks of its own, and so the pipes were no longer calling 'Danny Boy' as he retired, driving Eileen out of their home in secret desperation.

There had been a child once; an engaging curly-haired boy of six, struck down by a speeding van outside the school gates as Eileen watched. For days she stayed in his room, rocking back and forth on his bed, hugging his clothes close to her chest. Mathematics and the Catholic Church had provided succour, and she had plunged gratefully into the worlds of numbers and rosary beads.

Eileen had been the shop's first volunteer. Every Thursday, she bustled quietly, her bright eyes inquiring of the objects she constantly rearranged whether life was an endless equation. The shop items became mathematical digits to contemplate in endless combinations: she placed a bunch of yellow recycled pencils at five pence each along with elephant key chains and beaded pens and colourful Rajasthani cloth puppets and McDonald's Happy Meal toys in a wicker tray near the till, returning almost immediately to remove the pens and look anew at the configuration.

Heera continued to fold the clothing in silence. She had been appointed the manager of IndiaNeed ten days after her seventeenth wedding anniversary, and sought solace in work with fierce dedication, a quality Diana

# CHAPTER TWO

# A trouble shared is a trouble halved

IT WAS 15 AUGUST, the anniversary of India's Independence and of their marriage. Heera Malkani Moore still celebrated the first of the two with pride. She looked at her husband, Bob; he was sprawled across the bed, his mouth slightly open in sleep. How thin his lips were, she thought, a gingery grey for a sunny day.

'Adam!' he had called out gruffly, and she awoke instantly. Who was Adam? she wondered.

Heera's transparent, bubbly exterior concealed an edgy sexuality; she was a forgotten kettle boiling over. Only once had she known real passion, at eighteen, with lithe Javed in his tight blue Terylene trousers. He had exuded an animal vigour, demonstrating clever stealth in their assignations. Heera cherished a velvet memory; they had watched the teen romance *Bobby* in the back row at the local cinema in Hyderabad, and Javed's fingers had splayed interrogatively across her breasts while he popped peanuts into his mouth with his other hand. He had retained a last peanut for the moment when the lights came on, despatching it with studied nonchalance as other couples leaped to their feet to shuffle demurely out of the hall.

Bob's contribution to the anniversary was a generous Marks & Spencer gift voucher. On the advice of his aunt he had presented Heera with English cookery books to mark the first, and Heera had dutifully noted the recipes for Yorkshire pudding and mince pies. On the second anniversary he took her to a caravan site in Cornwall. Heera now used the vouchers to buy white six-pack tummy control undergarments.

On every anniversary and several times through the year, Heera entertained the local Asian community as well as Bob's friends and colleagues in their spacious semi-detached house on Tenison Road. The front door was decorated with an Indian floral garland from which a green chili and lemon were suspended. The men huddled over the whisky and the women flocked to the large floral Chesterfield and overflowed onto the red Persian carpet. The guests departed at midnight with a lover's lingering touch of Indian spice in their hair, coats and eyes. 'I should call this house "Heera Hotel",' complained Heera. 'I get absolutely knackered with all these people coming and not going.' It never occurred to her that she had a choice.

Once inside the door, her overnight guests succumbed to the languorous air, moving from one calorie-laden meal to the next in a stupor, too soporific to consider the red Cambridge sightseeing bus that departed hourly from the station. Bob frequently returned to slipper-shod strangers wandering with easy familiarity in his home. Standing on his doorstep one evening a few years ago, he was welcomed by a large woman in a shimmering red salwar kameez. She giggled coyly. Several perspiring strangers were executing various dance poses on his carpet, a large woman whacked a *dholak* with podgy fingers and her listless companion sang tunelessly to the strains of a wheezing harmonium.

Another woman and her bowed daughter were straining over the guests' outstretched palms, squeezing intricate mehndi patterns with weary flourish through tiny cones.

'*Arre jaan*, where did you come from?' cried Heera, aghast. 'You had said you were coming home late. We are having a mehndi party. No men allowed.'

The large woman gushed, 'Poor man, let him be. He can be the gora Krishna, our white Krishna among the gopis. Come, come, *chalo* Bob, you must also dance!' She dragged him into the circle of giggling women. A shrill Bollywood tune sprang to life on his stereo system operated by a hard-faced stranger with a diamond stud in her nose, and the large woman shook her hips suggestively, hiding her face behind her shiny dupatta. The women tittered as Bob ducked like a diver in a scuba suit wandering into a May Ball by accident.

'Come, Heera, I will read your hand before you have your mehndi put,' offered a large woman in a purple sari, who fanned herself vigorously. Bob watched as Heera was led to a couch.

'Heera, you give only happiness wherever you go. It is in your bhagya, in your destiny,' declared the woman. 'Your husband is a very lucky man.'

Heera smiled.

'But what is this?' queried the woman in deliberate tones. '*Hai*, what is this? You are blessed by the Goddess Lakshmi herself, but you were not meant to have any children?' Deliberately ascending an octave, she repeated, 'There is no line at all in your palm. How can that be?'

Heera glanced at Bob in the silence. She had looked stricken, he thought later, as he stood in front of the mirror, removing his tie. Unfathomably stricken, for he recalled his question to her in Hyderabad: could she contemplate a life with him and without children? She had appeared not to hesitate in accepting his proposal.

Their announcement to Heera's flabbergasted family led to the appointment of a lynx-eyed chaperone waiting for gora Bob to make an unlicensed move. Cinema visits were conducted without peanuts and in the company of curious relatives eager to behold Heera's white fiancé in the dark.

Tonight, on the evening of his seventeenth anniversary party, Bob felt constricted by the tight collar of the white sherwani he wore, although a frail little man in a black sherwani holding a whisky glass appeared to suffer no such discomfort.

'Brahma-ji, you are such an expert in English Literature, and we haven't heard your recitations for a long time. Why don't you give us all a demonstration?' prompted Heera gaily.

'Su-er,' assented the little man in a pronounced Sindhi accent. He handed his whisky glass to Heera and moved to the centre of the room to sit cross-legged on the carpet. There was a hush as, arm raised to render a qawali, he announced, 'Hamlet'. It sounded like 'omelette'. His voice boomed:

*To beeeee* (he paused overlong, looking meaningfully around the gathering)

24

*Orrrr* (long pause)
*Not to beeeeee* (he shook his grey locks), *that is the qu-ushtion:*
*Whether 'tish nobler in the*
*Mind to suffer*
*The s-lings and arrows of outrageous fartune,*
*Orrrr* (meaningful look) *to take up arams against*
*A sea of troubles,*
*And by opposing end them?*

There was a thin ripple of applause. Brahma Mansukhani was a retired doctor from Bradford, who had once been travelling in a minicab that was blocked by a red Ford Fiesta. Three young men wearing balaclavas sprang from the darkness, brandishing knives at the driver, wrenched the car door open, punched his face, took his money and vanished. They failed to notice the tiny terrified doctor slumped low, cowering in the back. The next day his son, a locum at a pharmacy, appeared before the Royal Pharmaceutical Society, charged with the unlawful sale of prescription painkillers. The combined shock could have rollercoasted the little doctor to drink, but he had turned to the Bard instead.

His mentor's birthday on 23 April filled him with a religious fervour of such potency that he undertook an annual pilgrimage to Stratford-upon-Avon. Then he read of the controversy over the Bard's precise date of birth in April. A cautious man, he now celebrated at home for an entire month.

The chance discovery of an anagram website that had rearranged the letters 'William Shakespeare's birthday' into 'April's skies: we may hail the Bard' filled his days with activity as he created his own anagrams from various Shakespearean plays to post on the Internet. His attempt to rearrange his own name 'Brahma Mansu-khani' concluded abruptly after the emergence of the embarrassing configuration 'Bra Man Khan'.

While 'Shakespeare' trilled in the centre of the living room, Bob stood on the patio, a large, bluff man like a farmer without his wellingtons. He thought again of Heera's wounded glance. Charlie (Chandru) and Barry (Bhagat) called out goodnaturedly for whisky refills as they admired his artificial Japanese garden. A few min-utes earlier, Bob had slipped upstairs, crossed over to the window and looked out onto the street, deliberat-ing before he dialled. 'Adam Russell,' answered a man's voice. Bob replaced the receiver without speaking. His palms were sweaty as he descended the stairs to serve apple juice to the owner of a London frozen food com-pany who urged his sympathetic listeners, 'We need more burial sites in this country, and we must have burial within twenty-four hours.'

'Have I ever introduced you to Lord Bijlani?' asked Heera, linking her arm in Bob's, guiding his reluctant feet across the room.

'A peer?'

'*Arre* no, *jaan*, his first name is "Lord". What clever parents – why didn't they call him "Lakhu"? This way, everyone thinks he's an MP sitting in the House of Lords. Anyway, he's in the manufacturing business, he makes leather seats for luxury cars. He was also in some insurance scam. His bossy mother lives with him and everyone knows she sits on his head, so he can't find a wife,' whispered Heera in a tumble of words.

Lord Bijlani wore a black leather jacket and tight leather jeans; his fitted shirt was unbuttoned to display a gold chain. He squealed and kissed Heera soundly and roundly on both cheeks. Was the leather of his jacket the same as the fabric of his car seats? wondered Bob, as he offered him a drink, aching to hear the cool voice at the other end of the telephone. On his way upstairs, he was stopped by a man with greasy hair and piercing eyes. 'I am Dr Sridhar T. I cure incurable illnesses,' he announced, thrusting a visiting card into Bob's hands. He moved away, but returned an instant later. 'Slight spelling mistake in card. Printing was done in India, but do read.'

Bob read obediently: *People loose valuable things in life. Without Health life is nothing. Patient cured includes many Business magnets, many M.PS, M.L.A's. Successful treatments by Dr. Sridhar T for Intestine disc's, gynaecological disc's, sexual disc's, baby of choice.*

Dr Sridhar was a 'world-renowned miracle doctor' visiting England. His previous surgery had been conducted three evenings a week at a school hall in his Indian hometown. A new patient entering the hall was presented with a token and seated among a few hundred people in perpetual motion. The newcomer was then sent to men and women in white coats in a tiny room, and Dr Sridhar stepped forward. As the patient opened his mouth for a mandatory inspection, several heads peered in as one, notes were taken, glances exchanged and little white pills prescribed by Dr Sridhar, to be taken twice a day after meals. Despite the fact that only the tongue was on display, the patient came away feeling undressed.

Dr Sridhar's wife, Manjula, was a tall woman with a face the shape of the full moon. Placid and calm, she bore her sister-in-law's harassment with equanimity.

Radiant in her third month of pregnancy, she initially dismissed a mound of curly human hair, red chillies and a doll stuffed with pins on her pillow as a childish prank. When she gave birth to a deformed child, Manjula shrieked it was the hand of voodoo, but remained unsupported in her conviction. The baby died within days, and a year later Manjula became the wild-eyed mother of a healthy boy, but still slipped into post-natal depression, a condition that remained undetected by her husband. She attempted suicide, mistakenly swallowing the pills he prescribed to his patients instead of the sleeping pills purchased for the overdose, but survived, recovering the calm of thin ice. Manjula was living testimony to both the failure and success of her husband's little white pills.

Bob slipped away from the doctor, excitement driving him upstairs.

'I know it's you, Bob,' accused the voice.

Bob stared silently out of the window, telephone in hand.

'We can't go on like this. You know that. Tell her. Tell her now.'

*O Romeeeo, O Romeeeo, wherephore art thou Romeeeo,* wailed the cross-legged 'Shakespeare' as Bob wandered in a daze into the hallway and into his study. Eight children were on the carpet watching a Bollywood film in a room overflowing with laundry baskets, books and a computer on a tiny table. A photograph of Heera in a bridal sari stared back at his shuttered eyes as a plate of tikkis and chutney hovered over his shoulder. 'There you are, *jaan*,' chided Heera. 'Why are you here? There are so many people you must meet – how can you neglect your guests? Come outside, come look after them.'

A voice yelled, 'Heera, forget your *bak bak*. Talk later, go to the kitchen, your kebabs are going to burn.'

Heera peered into the oven and retrieved a steaming tray of kebabs. 'This is Sam. She works at Smith's. You know, the curtain shop on Burleigh Street. She's the one with the tattoo on her thingy,' said Heera on her way out to serve the kebabs.

'Shall I show you my tattoo?' challenged the girl called Sam.

'That's entirely your decision,' replied Bob.

Sam swiftly unbuttoned her blouse for an instant to reveal a black rose tattoo nestling between her Wonderbra-enhanced breasts, before turning to the aloo tikkis in the microwave. 'I used to work in a salon on Green Street. I do hair, nails, mehndi, threading and facial. I used to do full body wax also,' she continued archly. 'You know – *full*. Where does she keep her pickles?'

The young woman hunted in a cupboard. She walked closer to Bob, scrutinising his face. 'You need to look after yourself. If you don't, who will? Anyway, I'm saving up for a boob job now.'

Bob felt no obligation to respond.

'What's that about boobs? Take some of mine, they're too big.' Heera turned to Bob, who was perched on a kitchen stool. '*Jaan*, again hiding? Sam, what magic are you working on my husband? Leave him alone. Come, *jaan*, look who's here – it's Manoj Daryanani!' she announced flirtatiously.

Manoj Daryanani was a tall, slim man with an unlined face. Dressed in a spotless white kurta pyjama, he greeted people from afar with folded hands, backing away as if from contamination.

'*Jaan*, look after Manoj, give him some pakoras,' advised Heera.

'No fried things! He has a problem, you know, with his digestion,' warned Manoj's wife, a silent fellow sufferer.

Charlie and Barry waved their whisky in wobbly unison. 'And do you remember what Karnani said at the end of the shareholders' meeting?' asked Charlie. 'That he must thank people "on the backside".' The two men roared at an old joke, the ice in their glasses rocking in merriment. Another voice roared from the carpet, reaching a crescendo:

> *The evil that men do lives after them;*
> *The good is oft interred with their bones*

An elderly Englishman declared as he waved a kebab in his listener's face, 'I do agree, without Asian medical personnel, the NHS would collapse.'

> *When shalla we three meet again*
> *In thunder, lightning,*
> *Orrrr in rain?*
> *When the hurrrlyburrrly's done,*
> *When the battle's losht and won.*

Heera hurried over to 'Shakespeare'. 'Brahma-ji, you must be so tired, dinner is served on the table.'

'Su-er.'

Bob turned to leave the room. 'Where are you off to, Bob? Aren't you going to cut the cake?' cried his sister Sarah.

'You're a lucky man, Bob,' observed his cousin Jonathan.

'Heera's a lucky woman to be married to my brother,' contradicted Sarah. 'Let's raise a toast to the happy couple.'

'Speech, speech!' clapped a woman with flaming henna-dyed hair and blue clanging bangles on her wrist.

Bob put his arm around Heera and addressed a speck on the floor. 'She's everything to me.'

A murmur went round the room. 'Ah, bless.' Heera sniffed, before twisting herself out of his embrace to cry, 'Who wants tiramisu, who wants apple crumble, who wants ice cream and who wants rosogulla?'

'Mustn't be naughty!' vowed Sarah, a hand fluttering over her abdomen, as she greedily surveyed the desserts. 'Ooh, shall I give in this once?'

'Wouldn't you rather have the cake and eat it, too?' asked her husband Brian sourly.

Sarah always surrendered to her sweet tooth, but rarely to her husband. She had persuaded him to exchange their house in Royston for a dilapidated farmhouse outside a Tuscan village, hoping to convert the barn and stables into luxury tourist apartments. The legalities of the transfer of property deeds were as much a nightmare for Brian as working the ancient water pump and cleaning out the well. He harvested the grapes and olives and struggled to find a match for broken kitchen tiles. She never wanted sex, only olives by the truckload to sell in the local market. He was ready to return to England, but Sarah refused. He wished he could write an autobiography with the title *My Grapes of Wrath*.

'Anyone for coffee?' Heera approached Manoj

Daryanani, who asked for a glass of hot water. His wife explained, 'For his voice.'

'Why, what's wrong with it?' queried Heera.

'He sings.'

'*Wah ji*, you are a gayak, you are a singer, and you did not even tell us! That means you must perform for us right now. Yes, yes, I'm not taking a "No" from you. It's my anniversary, you have to please me. Come on, *ji*,' cried Heera persuasively.

Manoj Daryanani, who needed a straight-backed chair, now occupied the carpet so recently vacated by 'Shakespeare'. Heera carried out a harmonium and a pair of tabla, but he looked disdainfully at the instruments and waved them away as he cleared his throat. '*Hari, meri itni suno*,' he intoned. It was the first line of a devotional song.

'Why don't you sing a film song instead? How about "Yeh Shaam Mastani"?' suggested Barry, now on his third Scotch and viewing the world through heavy-lidded eyes. Barry was recovering from a disagreement earlier that day with his teenage son. The drink would dull the pangs of parenting.

He ached to leave it all and return to India. Perhaps he was not too old; he might still find a job in an Indian company. Life wouldn't be the same, of course, none of the luxuries they took for granted in England, but at least he would never again feel the fear, the black pounding of his heart as he discovered the cannabis hidden behind his son's physics textbook. It was still not too late to take his son back to India. Ari was a good boy in bad company, but what would Shanti say? It would kill her, the way she pampered that boy, as if he were a prince from Patiala. It was all her fault, spoiling him, letting him think he could do whatever he wanted, money from his mother any time, so what if Dad didn't give it to him, the manipulative little bugger went to Mummy. 'Come to Mummy, son, Mummy understands her *beta*.'

He had told Ari from the very beginning, 'Yes, it is hard to live in this British society. You can't be mediocre if you want to be accepted here, you have to show you are the best at something – swimming, maths, science, computers, something at least – then they will admire you. But instead you have become a zero, a nothing, a charsi, a drug addict, and what do you think, just because you can fool your mother, you can do the same with me? You will know what your father is made of if you ever touch that stuff again.'

'Yes, why don't you sing "Yeh Shaam Mastani",' repeated Barry jovially, as he hitched his trouser waistband.

Manoj Daryanani frowned at Barry's levity. Thirty minutes later, during his rendition of 'Raag Bageshree', the bolder members of the audience had already escaped via the conservatory door. Those who remained trapped leaped with unapologetic haste after the last prolonged note and scattered, beads of a strung note onto the carpet.

The guests disbanded at the moment that the Trinity College clock struck midnight over Great Court. Heera surveyed the empty living room with satisfaction. She had already guessed Sarla's gift by its contours; always the same Indian wrapping paper bought in bulk and the same box of chocolates without an expiry date or manufacturer's label from a shop in Wembley. Sarah and Brian's gift was olive marinade.

Bob was lying on their bed, staring at the ceiling. What was it that ridiculous little man 'Shakespeare' had recited about a tide in the affairs of men taken at the flood, and was this such a time, to submit, release the torment and anguish within and allow it to take its course, let it take him to good fortune or to defeat? Or would he regret it forever afterwards, and would the shame be a torment far greater? Would he be forever damned, or should he plunge, surrender?

*This above all: to thine own self be true,*
*And it must follow, as the night the day,*
*Thou canst not then be false to any man.*

The crumbling sensation in his throat all evening turned to fuzzy warmth as he remembered. The meeting had been in a small conference room. As the executives streamed in, Bob's secretary hurriedly handed him a copy of the Finance Director's memo before the heavy oak door closed. Bob nodded to his colleagues, his eyes roaming the room, a swelling bubble of excitement as he recognised the dark, bent head of a man reading by the window. The man turned and looked at Bob, eyes a cool smoky grey that clashed and tumbled into his own, and Bob turned from the flint of the other man's gaze to take a seat at the table. As the diminutive Finance Director talked, a powdery thirst invaded Bob's throat, and he reached for a jug of water, staring involuntarily at the golden hair on the wrist of the man beside him. The lights dimmed as they looked at the first chart in the PowerPoint presentation on the wall at the far end of the room.

Bob felt tingling heat on his thigh as the brushing

movement of a hand left its searing imprint. He continued to stare at the wall. As Adam teased Bob's ankle with his own, Bob grappled this new, daring reality while tortured angels tumbled and frolicked in a forbidden fountain, resisting banishment. At the end of the meeting, he hurried towards the door. A cool voice behind him asked if he would like to stop by at the pub. Without meeting Adam's eyes, Bob mumbled that he had to get home. 'Another time, then,' Adam had said smoothly, turning away. 'No, wait!' flung Bob. It was a strangled, torn sound.

As Heera entered the bedroom, she knew something was wrong, something far worse than unwrapping stale chocolates from Sarla for the third consecutive year. She had found Bob pacing the room, a half-empty whisky glass in his hand. He never drank upstairs, and usually shared a pot of Chinese green tea with her before retiring. He told her he had something important to say, but that it could wait until she was ready, and she had looked at him, wordlessly taking her perspiration-stained pink nightgown and matching robe from the room, returning drawn and anxious a few minutes later.

Afterwards, she had asked Bob in the dim bedroom light why he had chosen their anniversary to tell her. All he could say, standing ridiculous and pale in his faded blue striped pyjamas, was that big occasions made his decisions seem smaller. He had finally found the handle to the door of his closet, and he was coming out. He could no longer conceal, only reveal; he would not hide, he would announce with pride – he was a bisexual.

Then Bob crumpled at the hurt she would feel, the

disgust and repulsion, her accusations of trickery and fraud. He had never meant to deceive or dissemble, he beseeched, he was fragile and frail.

If he was frail, so was she, Heera thought fiercely. It wasn't only her depleted hormones that needed replacement; she needed implants of reassurance. He had never really been by her side, she decided; she had been living with a phantom, hollow, filled with straw, lit and brought to life by another. What had he expected her to say? she thought dully, head exploding, as she lay awake in the dark. What did he think she would do with his revelation? And it had to be a coincidence, one of those amazing ironies of life, that her cousin had told her of Javed's divorce and of his forthcoming visit to England.

Bob had a dream that night; he was a boy in his father's cottage near the moors, running home through the heath to his mother, who was wearing a blue and white floral dress. She scooped him into her arms for a warm embrace, and he hugged Adam back. Heera responded sleepily. As suddenly, his arms fell away from her, and he turned on his side again, heart thumping in the darkness, afraid that she might be awake.

It was Adam who banished Eve from the Garden of Eden.

# CHAPTER THREE

# The customer is always right

THE WIND PROWLED for new victims as cyclists wobbled, their nostrils filled with the sniff of fresh bread snaking out from the bakery on Mill Road. The smoke from its blackened chimney was whirled away over the grey rooftops, and three doors down from IndiaNeed the handpainted sign *Wright and Sons, Bookbinders since 1930* flapped noisily above the entrance to the shop. A young man in a black leather jacket and merino russet scarf announced his arrival; inside, an elderly man shuffled towards him in the dim light, weaving through stacks and piles of theses, glue, buckram, bookbinding tools and overalls. The young man took delivery of a Cambridge thesis bound in black, pressing it proudly to his chest as he left.

The blonde florist arranged the blooms in buckets on the rack outside the Sunflowers Florists shop, waiting for her boyfriend to propose. The wind spotted two Pakistani women walking slowly past the solicitor's firm towards IndiaNeed, and playfully buffeted the elderly lady and her stick into the shop. Abandoning her mother, the younger woman swooped on the soft toys, gathering armfuls of teddy bears that were as suddenly dropped back onto the shelves.

'One ear or two – does it really make a difference? *Arre*, tell the child that they are special designer teddies. Doesn't that expensive Steiff teddy always have a button only in one ear? See, I am giving these to you at a special discounted price. One for a pound,' urged Heera.

The young woman needed little persuasion; the one-eared toys were shiny and new. Shabbier toys were always removed by the volunteers and despatched to the skip, along with the reject clothing that often only missed a button or a thread. A firm regularly collected the contents of the skip and paid the shop fifty pence per bag. Heera's neighbour was an airline manager, who offered to send the reject bags to any charitable institution in India free of charge, but Diana Wellington-Smythe's grey eyes had narrowed at the suggestion; she was convinced the contents would be distributed or even sold among Heera's relatives and friends.

The elderly Pakistani lady examined a furry black monkey lying in a basket next to her chair. Its giant tail had been mistakenly sewn on in front, and she looked at the freak toy in silence. Swarnakumari frowned and whispered, 'This is not good, Durga. What will that lady think of us? I thought we had thrown that dirty thing away. Who put it there again?'

'The Korean girls?' suggested Durga.

'Auntyji, this is not for you,' appeased Heera smoothly, attempting a seamless exchange with a blue Beanie Baby teddy announcing *It's a Boy* across its chest. 'Take this, only two pounds.'

'Who put that blue teddy there again?' asked

Swarnakumari, perturbed. 'I had thrown it into the rejects bag.'

'I did; there was nothing wrong with it. Why did you throw it away?' Eileen was surprised.

Swarnakumari remained silent; some secrets were best kept buried, like the stories the black bags never revealed.

The elderly lady held the monkey firmly in her grasp, waving Heera away with her stick as the daughter spotted the sign *IndiaNeed* and the photograph of the smiling Rajasthani villagers on the wall.

'Does the money you make go to India?' she probed.

'Yes, of course.'

'And only to India?'

'Yes,' repeated Heera, surprised.

The daughter catapulted her protesting mother out of the chair. The monkey tumbled onto the floor, where it lay brazen, its furry tail on display. They left without a purchase.

'We are all the same here, the same brown skin fighting for respect in this society. Why carry on India–Pakistan enmity here? Even the leaders of both countries have started peace talks now, so what's the problem with these two? The daughter was pretty, though. She reminded me of Nafisa,' observed Heera. 'You know, Swarna, Nafisa coolly sent her mother-in-law back to Lahore, and I hear the room has been given to three Japanese students. Of course, it's not far from the Bell Language School, so the room must be in demand. She's making good money, but how do those poor students all fit? I know Japanese girls are tiny, but still, three? By the way, her sister Razia is with Nafisa's neighbour's husband now. He was helping Razia build her extension.' Heera chortled. '*Arre*, if you ask me, he should have looked after his own extension, if you know what I mean. Anyway, long story, some other time.'

Eileen bent to pick up the monkey. 'I'm off to rearrange the soft toys,' she announced, her quick eyes noting their disarray. She placed the monkey on the shelf next to a blue-eyed china doll. The story of *Beauty and the Beast* had always been a favourite with her.

'Girls, why are the English so mad about their teddy bears? Teddy waiting on their beds, telling Teddy their secrets . . . Bob has a teddy called Charlie, you know. Such a shabby teddy! Only one eye. When I first met Bob, I actually offered to sew the other eye on.' Heera chuckled. 'You know how it is in India, those dhobis wash the clothes so carelessly sometimes, the buttons become loose, so my mother had a huge collection of assorted buttons, all colours, all sizes, in a big biscuit tin. I could have found an exact match. But Bob said he preferred Charlie with one eye.' She called out, 'Four out of four Englishmen don't wash their teddies, Swarna!'

Two startled elderly ladies sifted through the pile of net curtains, eavesdropping with bright bird eyes. 'Are you all Alsatian, then?' chirruped one, turning to Swarnakumari. 'I have a lady next door who is Alsatian. She's very nice, very nice, very well-spoken indeed. Lovely dark eyes. Dear, when you're ready, could you measure up this curtain for me?'

Swarnakumari turned to Durga in bewilderment.

'Forget it. Asian or Alsatian, what does it matter? No point trying to explain to these sweet *buddi* biddies,' whispered Heera. 'Half of them can't hear, half can't see, half can't walk, half can't talk.'

'Dogs and Indians once had to use the back door,' mused Durga.

'The Irish too,' added Eileen as she disappeared down an aisle. She was fiercely proud of her heritage. Annoyed by Durga's appropriation of the Diaspora to signify Indian sub-continental migration alone, she usually remained silent. Some things were felt, and not always said.

A middle-aged woman had been standing uncertainly in a corner; she rummaged in her bag and removed a plain gold band and a platinum ring studded with a large ruby. 'There, you can 'ave 'em both and good riddance,' she rasped, flinging them on the counter in front of Heera. 'Me old man's done a runner, gone an' left me, so I took me engagement and wedding rings to the jeweller's down the road.' She jerked her head sideways to indicate the location of a Mill Road shop. 'An' what d'yer know, they're worth no more than five quid after all these years. Five quid, I tell yer!' she repeated, her voice rising. 'I been with 'im all these years, and the bugger couldn't even give me a decent gold ring. So I says I'll take 'em down to the charity shop and get rid of 'em. You can do what yer want with 'em,' she told Heera. 'Don't never want ter see 'em no more.'

Heera handed the rings silently to Eileen, who placed them on a little velvet fold and slid them onto the jewellery shelf below the till counter.

A wedding ring always reminded Durga of Pooja, the popular, leggy prefect at her school in Bombay, now Mumbai. Pooja and Anil had married, won a *Wills Made for Each Other* couple contest and a new car. A year later, Durga had sat uncomfortably in a living room in a

41

Cuffe Parade apartment overlooking the bay, witness to a marriage rotting twig by twig. Pooja had initially turned a blind eye to Anil's affairs and embarked upon revenge romps of her own. Her husband's Malayali chauffeur with jasmine oil-greased hair was startled, but willing. It was her discovery of the maid's gold earrings tucked under Anil's pillow that impelled a dramatic confrontation between the couple. He must choose, Pooja said imperiously. Anil obeyed with alacrity and stayed with the maid; humiliation sent Pooja out of her marriage and house into obesity. Durga had heard later that a week on a health farm in Bangalore had restored Pooja's holistic balance. Two months later, she wedded the masseur and flashed a new gold ring on her finger; jewellery was both the bane and balm of her marriages.

'They're new, don't you want them?' asked Eileen, handing a pile of net curtains to Swarnakumari.

'I have already got net curtains, *na*. Your Uncle says our house must look English from the outside.'

Swarnakumari never referred to her husband by name, oblivious to the confusion caused by 'Your Uncle' as the substitute. She had initially refused to arrange the display when asked to 'do the window', and announced with a vigorous shake of her head, 'I am not here to clean. Your Uncle would not like me to do that.' Diana Wellington-Smythe had merely arched an eyebrow, enunciating in slow English thereafter to Swarnakumari and the Korean volunteers.

'White wisps of respectability,' commented Durga, examining the net curtains. 'Give the immigrant net curtains and he simply blends, like the tea packet labels that say *Product of more than one country*. But to blend or not to blend into the diasporic cuppa – that is the question.'

Swarnakumari picked at a loose thread on the curtain. 'Durga, my Mallika is not listening to me at all nowadays. See, she is now twenty-two. She has finished at Emmanuel College and she wants to do postgraduate also, but I am thinking if she settles down with a good Bengali boy, she can also continue her studies, but she is not agreeing. Early in the morning she was fighting with me when Your Uncle was not there. Tell me, if your parents find an intelligent boy from a good family for you, you will agree to see him, *na*? At least you will not say "No" straight away?'

'What's this got to do with me?'

'You both are similar – see, you are twenty-nine, your studies are over, now you are doing this research on charity shops for the television, and soon you are going to London for your new job. But you must also think of marriage, or it will be too late. That is what I keep telling Mallika.'

Heera bent to pick up a basket of baby clothes. 'Too late? Too late for what? You know, girls, when I was eighteen I was in love with a boy called Javed. He was our neighbour. He used to write beautiful Urdu love poems. Then my parents found out. Usual Hindu–Muslim problem and both the families immediately stopped it. Javed was sent to Dubai; he owns a big construction company now. Three days before he left, we met for the last time and we went for a walk on the beach. He suggested a camel ride, and we sat on the same camel, but the camel wouldn't move. It just sat there in the sand. People were staring and laughing and suddenly there were many stalls there – peanut-seller, balloon-seller, coconut-waterwala. People even threw peanuts at the camel to make it move. Then the owner told us to get off, and he kicked the camel hard on its bottom.'

Heera paused; no one said anything. She continued, 'We went back home. Javed didn't say a word to me again, and he left for Dubai. For many years, I refused to see any of the boys my parents showed me. After all, if you fall in love, you fall in love, right? The heart remembers its broken song for ever. Then Bob came to Hyderabad. He knew one of my brother's friends, and that's how we met. There was such a big fuss when Bob proposed – you know, how could I like a gora, an Englishman, how could I leave India forever and go to England and all that – but we got married anyway.'

'Your Bob is a good man, just like Your Uncle,' confirmed Swarnakumari.

'Yes,' replied Heera, 'he is a good man, otherwise why would I follow him to this country?'

'Javed was a Muslim, and you a Hindu. *Baba*, it would not have been possible. Love is blind, I know, but I am telling you, such marriages are very difficult,' Swarnakumari said sagely. 'There is too much difference. Too much adjustment for both parties.'

'And your esteemed opinion is based on . . . ?'

Ignoring Durga's sarcasm, Swarnakumari persisted earnestly, 'See, in arranged marriages, quarrels about basic things are not there. Everything is matched. That is why these marriages work, *na*?'

'Work. Marriage is work,' muttered Eileen, who had been listening with interest as she returned with an armful of boy's clothes, looking as if she would hold them forever.

'Tell me, Swarna, do you love your husband?' asked Heera moodily.

Swarnakumari was surprised. 'Of course. You always give your love to the man you marry.'

'I didn't mean that. What sort of love is the love for a husband?' said Heera.

'A mistake,' said Durga.

Swarnakumari continued patiently, 'A marriage should also be blessed by the gods, but it is the woman who has to make sure everything is in its proper place. Then only it works. She must accept that there are things she wants but cannot have. The tragedy is our young girls these days don't know themselves what they want. They are confused, and they feel pressure. They are trying to be like these English girls. Parties and clubs, drink, wearing those clothes showing everything, and they want—'

'Wild sex with white blokes,' interrupted Durga.

Swarnakumari was shocked. 'My Mallika needs—'

'Wild sex with black blokes? Oh, of course, sorry, these things don't happen in good Asian families.'

'What dirty talk is this? It does not suit you, Durga. Take my advice, and let your parents help you get married. They can easily find an intelligent boy, good personality, same values, same social background.'

'Leave my parents out of this. And what's with you first-generation Indians, anyway? You came here thirty years ago with a suitcase you never unpacked. It's all about tradition, family, culture, honour, isn't it? Why are you so keen on carrying on tradition? It's as if you're scared – you have to obey, or else. But does tradition exist? Is it real for us to taste, smell, feel and hold?'

A customer approached the till. 'Er, could you . . .'

'Anything wrong with what I said? One day when you girls become mothers you will understand your own mothers. Each generation will not listen. It will understand only later. That is the tragedy of life. Tell me, Durga, who are you without your roots, *hanh*? It is because of our roots that we can survive in this society. Why do you want to deny our Indian culture, that's what I don't understand.' Swarnakumari matched Durga's passionate outburst with one of her own.

'Don't you see that you seize upon "Indian culture" out of desperation and fear? Fear of erosion and erasure of identity. Why not welcome the churn of East–West encounters instead, take the plunge into the flow and see what happens? Diaspora isn't only about displacement; it's a progression, a moving to a new location of the liberated self.'

'*Baba*, I do not understand this high talk of yours. What I am saying is there is nothing wrong if parents guide and advise children even when they are older. That's all. Your parents must surely be telling you the same thing.'

'Blankets,' interjected the customer.

Durga cried, 'Leave my parents out of it!'

'My Arthur used to say—' reported the customer unsuccessfully.

'Why, your parents should not worry about you just because you are grown up?' pursued Swarnakumari.

'I said, drop it.'

The customer grew bold. 'Could I just . . .'

'Yes, madam?' inquired Swarnakumari, noticing her for the first time.

'Do you have any electric blankets, dear?'

'No, madam, but do look in that section there. We

have some new Edinburgh wool blankets,' replied Swarnakumari as the customer moved away.

She continued, '*Baba*, forget it, why are you getting so upset? You know, so many things have changed for the better from twenty-five years ago. You must have heard how we used to buy baked beans to make an Indian dish, and in those days we could not even get coriander. What could we teach our children about India, living here in Britain? That is why I am thinking there is nothing wrong at all if youngsters like these Bollywood films nowadays.'

'Did you understand anything I said? Oh, and about Bollywood, let me tell you, the only reason you welcome those films is because at last there's something much bigger than a bunch of coriander to reflect your "Indian values". But I think Bollywood has stereotyped us further in this country, shut us all in a cage called "Asian". One size fits all, so my Asian bum doesn't look big in this. Do the J. Kumar grocer and I have anything in common? No, but we're all Asian, so let's party.'

'I don't understand—' Swarnakumari began.

Durga interrrupted sharply, 'At last, Mr and Mrs Jones next door know the real me. I'm Asian, right, so *of course*, all I do is I boogie my belly and bounce my bosom to the bhangra beat. Jerk and jhatka, ooh, that's hot, that's Asian cool! Swarna, the future is so bright it's not orange, but brown.'

'Durga, what are you talking about? Everything is so easy for your generation now. Let me tell you something. Mallika's father and I got married in Kolkata. He left, and I came later to England. In Kolkata my family had five servants – *five*. And first day in England, he gave me an empty milk bottle in my hand and told me, "Roll out chapattis with this!" The kitchen window must be kept shut also. "No Indian cooking smell should go to the neighbour," he warned me. You cannot imagine the shock; it took me such a long time to forget my Kolkata, to like this country, even other Bengalis, the weather, even my own house . . .'

The eavesdropping customer agreed. 'Don't blame you, dear. I still don't like the weather. No good for me bones – got arthritis you see, just like me sister Maud. She's the younger one, holidaying in Spain at the moment she is, but our poor Edith was buried with her pacemaker she was, and ooh, what a problem she used ter have going through metal detectors in airports. She went on a holiday to Rome and those Italians thought she was a terrorist. Bleep, bleep, bleep, the detector went off and poor Edith got such a fright, I can tell yer. My Arthur used to say—'

'How can we help you, madam?' prodded Swarnakumari.

'Er, well, yes, I wanted an electric blanket, you see, but you don't have any, so I thought I'd donate these ten pounds. Mary did say to me ter make sure the money goes ter those wee cats. My Arthur always said—'

'I think you mean the cats' charity next door, madam. It is called Catnap. This is IndiaNeed. Our money goes to poor Indian villagers.' Swarnakumari shook her head vigorously. 'No cats here.' She pointed to the photograph on the wall behind her of the group of smiling Rajasthani villagers. A larger photograph of Diana Wellington-Smythe shaking hands with the Duke of Edinburgh hung adjacent on the wall.

'Oh, but we do have one,' contradicted Durga. 'Her name is Mrs Well—'

Swarnakumari frowned.

'Well, dear, I'll be off, then. Goodbye. You too, dear, goodbye,' sang the customer, opening the door. 'My Arthur always used to say . . .' The traffic outside drowned her voice.

Durga wanted to call her back, ask about Arthur. What did he always say? Who was he? Husband, lover or son? He was dead, or perhaps he was alive and now said something different, something he had never said before. And what if everything Arthur had ever said was gone, washed away like the ashes and flowers floating on an Indian river, and one human being had the power to keep his spoken word alive in an echoing universe?

The customer returned, popping her head through the door. She paused, lost in thought. 'There was something I had to remember,' she announced amiably. 'And I've forgotten what it is. Never mind. Goodbye.'

Memory was a capricious tool; it airbrushed the cavities of time. Javed no longer wrote Urdu love poems – he wrote invoices. After a successful career as a builder in Dubai, he had recently purchased a plot of land in Harrow, north-west London, for the development of offices and residential flats. His wife had custody of the children, for whom he felt affection but no pangs of separation. Javed was now a new man, and he intended to behave like one. 'Freedom by fifty' was his new life slogan.

He had never sat on a camel again, although fate had

confidently despatched him to the land of camels. As long as he was within sight of a dromedary, it was clear that his marriage to Shabana would remain doomed. Shabana was a Pathan, fair and loose-limbed, with light grey eyes and silky brown hair; she was also a deeply religious shopaholic. He had indulged her excesses, and even when her two younger sisters and mother joined a household already bursting with servants, his protests remained benevolent and mild. With the sunlight pouring onto his desk one afternoon, he stumbled upon her latest bank statement. Blinded by the intensity of the light, he misread the digits and decided that Shabana had stretched both her credit and credibility too far; he had reached his limit. In a moment of insight, Javed discovered his was a marriage by numbers.

His thoughts turned to Heera pickled in time, and of her soft arms and bubbly optimism. He had heard she had married an Englishman. His lip curled. What did an Englishman know of love, of its obsessive sweep, rain-drenched passion, mystic couplets of yearning divided by immeasurable distance? Of the glance like a sweetly poisoned arrow and the tender curve of lips, of the dusky, honeyed surrender of being and soul, of the tortured wait for an answering echo of devotion? What ardour could an Englishman produce in that miserable weather, when the rain and the cold could only dampen the blood to congeal into colourlessness? He tried to recall the poems he had written to her more than two decades ago, but remembered nothing. He wondered if a fragment was what his life was, she the other; together were they meant to be whole, for what had driven her to an Englishman, revenge or indifference?

She had haunted him. She could not be happy with an elegiac Englishman.

He looked at the slip of paper on which Heera's disapproving cousin had reluctantly written the telephone number and address of the charity shop. He was driven by dread; would she be as he remembered? A man needed a dream, a passion to live and die for, or what was life worth? He had made a mistake once in relinquishing her love. Far worse to yearn and ache, never knowing, than to try to make it happen and fail; far better to reach for the dream than pluck air.

Despite his roguish looks, Javed was in torment as he glanced in the mirror at his dyed black hair, the tiny wobbles of flesh fanning his cheeks and the portly frame. He was forty-nine, and dissipated. The doctor had warned him about his cholesterol. He took three tablets twice a day and had to remember the large white pill was to be taken first, before the smaller two. His lips twisted ruefully. Romance had to be more than a weak-hearted, pill-popping middle-aged man, who couldn't chase a bus any more, asking a lost love if she had ever thought of him again. Then the image of the jeering crowds and the camel arose before him, and he was filled with new resolve. The camel had not moved then, but today he would move mountains with his hope. He would go to Mill Road to see Heera.

The telephone rang. 'Sir Puzzle', who had been standing near the till, jumped like an electrocuted cat. Every Tuesday and Thursday the elderly man wandered into the shop, lifted his cap with gallantry to greet the women and request new jigsaw puzzles. The harder the better, he pleaded with a twinkle in his eye, preferably with a piece missing.

'Good morning, IndiaNeed,' said Heera. 'Heera here . . . *Heera* . . . The wheelchair? For the Arthur Rank Hospice? Yes, I'll keep it ready for collection this afternoon . . . Yes, I'll remember what you said earlier . . . No, it won't happen again, Mrs Wellington-Smythe . . . Goodbye.'

Heera returned to the Staff Area and brought out a wheelchair from behind the curtain to park near the till. She noticed a video cassette lying on one of the smaller sorting tables.

'My little nephew loves *Thomas the Tank Engine*,' she confided amiably, 'but I'd better check the tape first. Those Korean girls sold *Snow White and the Seven Dwarfs*, and that *eediot* customer complained after a whole week that it was an adult video. She bought it for her toddler's birthday party, she says, and the children saw some hot Russian babe called Nikita with seven LittleJohns. What does she expect? This is not Block-buster. But she kept the video a whole week, so how many "children" watched the Russian babe Nikita "by mistake" is what I'd like to know. *Arre*, I also found a video once, and it was called *Birds in the Bush*. So I nicked it from the shop for a day, and it really was about some rare Australian birds, but I didn't com-plain,' divulged Heera with a chuckle. 'Anyway, girls, sad news. Meera Patel's husband died last week. Massive heart attack. He was watching *Jerry Springer*. Don't tell anyone, all right? Meera told me she's telling everyone he was watching *Newsnight*.'

Looking shocked, Swarnakumari moved to a table to arrange children's books. 'Poor Meera,' she murmured sadly. 'Who will colour her hair for her now? Terrible, *na*.'

Discovering a second pair of trousers and a tweed cap in another black bag, Heera continued, 'Her sister Madhuri was mixed up in some dispute with her English neighbour fifteen years ago. There was a common blocked pipe, and they wouldn't decide who was going to pay for the repairs. Anyway, things got really bad between them and the neighbour called Madhuri a "black bitch" in front of her in-laws from Surat – can you imagine, during the Diwali days, that too! And then Madhuri said that during the night this *angrez* woman's dog had done a wee over her rangoli pattern on the ground near the garage. She said it must be on purpose, naturally, because English dogs are so well-trained, they never do their business just anywhere, so how else can it happen? But of course, who knows the truth? The English neighbour may not have been to blame, but anyway, one thing is clear. I would not like to be called a "black bitch", either,' concluded Heera firmly.

'Nor "fast colour",' added Durga, enjoying Eileen's puzzlement.

There was a twist to the story: Madhuri had garnered her children's support during Diwali to enthusiastically etch traditional Diwali rangoli patterns using white powder on the path near the garage. The English neighbour's elderly father was visiting that year, and took an evening walk with his terrier in the fading light. The moon was already visible among the bare branches of the tree-lined street as he noticed what appeared to be a ghostly white Nazi swastika shining on the ground. A war veteran, he returned unsteadily to

53

his daughter's home, incoherent and disoriented. Convalescing on his bed, he pointed wordlessly with a trembling finger in the direction of the window. Later that night there was a sharp passing shower, and the rangoli patterns were washed away, leaving the ground dry by the morning. The rest was history.

'Look, girls, how is it that all the manky trousers and tweed caps in England land up at Lady Di's posh shop only? The more she wants to impress her friends, the more rubbish we get. Funny smell in here.' Heera sniffed. 'Smells like cat pooh.' She thrust her hand into the bag. 'It *is* cat pooh!'

Swarnakumari wailed. Heera dragged the offending bag away and commanded, 'Give me your soap dispenser, Swarna!'

Swarnakumari removed it with reluctance from her handbag. 'I will also go and wash my hands,' she said. 'Dirty, dirty shop. Much better for me to go and help in the old people's ward at Addenbrooke's Hospital. When I see those poor helpless people I tell myself, I am not staying in Cambridge when I am old, but Your Uncle has got so used to life here, he likes this English law and order. Just the other day he showed me the Cambridgeshire County Council blue library van. It had stopped outside old people's flats so that elderly people could climb into the van to borrow books. Your Uncle told me so proudly, "See, Swarna, this is why I like this country. I can see where my tax money is going." No, Your Uncle will not leave England.'

At the precise moment when Heera marched towards the telephone to do battle with her employer, 'Your Uncle' folded away his newspaper. Two hours earlier, Mr

Chatterjee had embarked upon his daily trek to the newsagent next to the Methodist Church, bought his Bengali newspaper and savoured the headlines. As he walked away from the till, he sneaked a ritual glance at the covers of the girlie magazines that Mr Patel, a family man, placed on the highest shelf and always upside down.

Peering sideways, Mr Chatterjee wondered about Newton's law of gravitation and whether the falling apple could ever have remained suspended in mid-air.

# CHAPTER FOUR

# All cats are grey in the dark

MR CHATTERJEE TWITCHED the net curtains at the bay window of his semi-detached home and peered outside. It was 8.13 a.m., and as always, Mondays to Fridays, the woman emerged, wheeling her bicycle out of her doorway. A freckled toddler sat stoically on the child seat, and the woman bent over the strap, displaying exposed breasts to an expectant Mr Chatterjee. With a flash of black fishnet tights and the twirl of her skirt, she was gone.

Every weekday morning, the sight of the woman was as wholesome as a portion of tropical fruit in a breakfast of toast, juice and tea. Growing up as a boy in Calcutta, as the city of Kolkata was then known, he had been accustomed to the British legacy of thick white bread, and as a creature of unswerving habit he rejected new-fangled wholemeal, wheatgerm, organic, rye, poppy seed and barleyseed varieties. The white slice emerged every morning, lightly browned from the toaster. The popping sound soothed his waiting ears, and, thick and respectable, the bread stared up at him from the white and green patterned Johnson Brothers plate, waiting for the corners and edges to be carefully buttered.

Thin-cut marmalade came next, followed by a single slice of mild Cheddar cheese and his cup of Earl Grey; not for him the nostalgia-inducing vapours of ginger tea laced with cardamom.

Mr Chatterjee was a man of method, and order his only god and guru, although he dutifully accompanied Swarnakumari once a year to the Bengali community's Durga Puja celebrations in London. Mr Chatterjee surveyed his household with pride; everything was in its place, and all the clocks obeyed the same master, as did the weeds.

He had perfected a daily regime that started with the head, not the heart. Every Saturday he vigorously massaged coconut oil into his receding hairline. The oil seeped into every corner of his being, soothing away self-doubt and dandruff. It coated every thirsty, curious hair until it lay down satiated and limp. Yoga face massage followed, as he slowly pinched his sallow forehead, cheeks and nose to nervous life.

On Thursdays he walked from his neat front lawn to the Rock Road Library, reading the newspapers there for hours. Mr Chatterjee followed British politics closely, and was informed, if conservative in his views. On Wednesdays he strolled to the city centre and spent the afternoon at Heffers, Waterstone's and Borders, often browsing through the old books outside the Fisher Hall. Once a month he accompanied Swarnakumari to the Sainsbury's at the Coldhams Lane roundabout, and every Tuesday he drove her in their white Vauxhall to the local Tesco at Fulbourn. The trolley always carried the same brand of soap, detergent, juice, cornflakes and honey.

On Mondays he wrote letters of complaint to the

local authorities and sent readers' views to the newspapers. He always wrote each note in a neat, rounded hand with a blue Parker fountain pen. *Respected Sir/Madam*, he would begin, drawing attention to the overflowing bin in the park, the litter left by schoolchildren walking on Queen Edith's Way and the pupils smoking in the quiet lanes.

He wrote to the heads of various schools, accusing them of moral turpitude. In his view, despite their school uniform, their female pupils looked like young women of dubious character. He listed a number of suggestions: skirt lengths well below the knee, stockings thick and opaque, shoes flat and sensible and the hair neatly tied back with school ribbon. No cosmetics or jewellery, nor smoking in uniform or 'mingling' between boys and girls outside the school gates.

Overhanging boughs on Trumpington Road were a danger to cyclists and walkers, he wrote to the City Council, and the bus service down Queen Edith's Way was disappointingly irregular.

Peering through the net curtains, he hurried to the door. Habituated to Mr Chatterjee's simmering excitement, the postman ceremoniously handed him the post on an imaginary silver salver. The sight of the buff envelopes filled Mr Chatterjee with nervous suspense; he opened each letter with care. Those from the Inland Revenue were sharp and advisory, others from the credit-card companies and retail outlets relentlessly unforgiving. It was the latest stern summons from the DVLA local office for repeated road offences that captured his attention. He penned an immediate response:

*Respected Sir/Madam,*

*I have received an envelope containing Summons Section 29 – Unlicensed Keeping – requesting the defendant to appear at 10.00 hours on 25th November at the Magistrates' Court to answer the information that on 23rd August at the A14, a mechanically propelled motor vehicle was kept on a public road for which a licence was not in force, contrary to Section 29 (1) of the Vehicle Excise and Registration Act 1994.*

*I have noted there is an accompanying document, which outlines the full nature of the offence concerning the expiration of driving licence and continued driving of the vehicle without displaying trade licence plates. I have noted that despite being told the offence would be reported, the offender made no attempt to respond. This indifference is not surprising. It comes from the man Langley Tonner, who repeatedly uses this address for reasons I cannot fathom. He has never resided in this house, of which I have been the owner for the past three decades, and he is completely unknown to my family and myself. I do not know why he continues to evade the long hand of justice and the law in this manner, causing such inconvenience and harassment to my family and myself. I receive Inland Revenue tax bills and summons to bailiffs' courts at this address on a regular basis because of this man.*

*I have repeatedly contacted Royal Mail, urging them not to deliver mail to him at this address, but have been informed that it is not possible to take any action in the matter. Apparently, a letter with an address and stamp must be delivered. I urge you to find the offender without delay and prevent him from using this address henceforth.*

*Yours faithfully,*
*Shyamal Chatterjee*

Despite his failure to convince the DVLA and other authorities of the misdeeds of the elusive Langley Tonner, Mr Chatterjee had engineered a more recent coup of which he was proud. New kitchen units had been ordered from a leading local DIY firm; they were delivered with five items missing, including the new sink tap. Incensed, Mr Chatterjee telephoned the company.

The girl at the other end loved her vowels less than her nail extensions, but he understood that Customer Services could do nothing, for Customer Services was not the same as Sales, and Sales Orders were at a Norwich number. After listening to Vivaldi's *Primavera* four times, he was transferred to a queue with Westlife easing the pain. Sales had little contact with the factory near Basingstoke that delivered the items, and the factory recommended he try Customer Services instead.

Mr. Chatterjee wrote an irate letter to the company director, sealed the envelope and carried it to the post office, where the friendly woman recommended 'recorded delivery'. His further purchase of a weekly stamp booklet was a secret indulgence, producing the excitement generated in lesser beings by a lottery ticket.

Seventy-two hours later, the missing units had arrived safely, although Customer Services had been unable to specify a time of delivery.

Mr Chatterjee took the new items of unsolicited mail to his garage with an air of quiet achievement. Tying a fresh bundle, he placed it on the existing stack. It was thirty inches high and consisted of five hundred and seventy-one letters and leaflets and brochures, weighing sixty ounces. Ever since he had heard of a retired gentleman whose photograph had appeared in the *Daily Mail* displaying seventy ounces of junk mail, Mr Chatterjee had been determined to compete, ambitiously setting his sights on a two-year record. Swarnakumari never visited the garage, and it was yet another of her husband's secrets of which she was unaware.

Having completed the important business at hand, Mr Chatterjee turned to the *Victoria's Secret* catalogue that arrived with regularity in the post, requested by the rascally Langley Tonner at Mr Chatterjee's address. He stared at the bold eyes of the models on the pages, their flirty posture as they slung their fingers casually over a bare hip or a bikini strap, bronzed bodies sheathed in tiny garments of lace and crochet. He felt unease tinged with self-disgust meeting the gaze of the young girl with the golden beach skin. She looked fourteen.

Shortly after his retirement, Mr Chatterjee had begun to surf the Internet. Reluctantly discontinuing his subscription to the *National Geographic*, he now attempted to find material online on the tigers of the Sundarbans. His search for 'wild animals' led him directly to a website of girls clad in faux fur bikinis. Surprised but not unappreciative, Mr Chatterjee decided on further explorations with a click. He was confronted next by a *Teen Lusties* live video with free sound and chat, no credit card, no hidden charges, and was to regret his mistake once he was flooded with regular offers on *Beach Babes* and *Barely Legal Sluts* along with guaranteed breast and penile enhancements. Puzzled over his automatic transfer to an *Asian Babes* Home Page, he was annnoyed that his ethnic origins had become public knowledge on the Internet. The pneumatic images of a girl called 'Shonali' were particularly disturbing; the name sounded Bengali, and he wondered why an Indian girl would bring such shame upon her community. Disgusted, he resumed his search for a heater for Swarnakumari's conservatory, which, in turn, led to a flood of intriguing adult inducements ensuing from the word 'heat'.

World news occupied centre stage several times a day; he listened to the radio and watched television until the headlines were as familiar as a shloka or mantra. He hastened to share the information with Banerjee, who made clucking noises of disbelief, shaking his head at the evil in the world that had so narrowly missed Cambridge and the Banerjee and Chatterjee households. Together, they mourned the old days, each tragedy serving to highlight and underline their present wise life choices. Banerjee began listening to the news himself on his new digital radio, ahead by two additional bulletins while his friend took a nap. He was thus able to refer to items in the afternoon bulletin of which Mr Chatterjee was as yet unaware.

Mr Chatterjee took his constitutional twice a day; the benefits of regular exercise were balanced by the opportunity it provided as the Neighbourhood Watch Co-ordinator to observe his neighbours, their homes and their habits without embarrassment. Mr Chatterjee firmly believed that a Bengali man's home was his castle, and he its commanding military officer. Mondays to Fridays, Swarnakumari served him macher jhol, corchori, posto, sukhto, macher tok, mutton kosa, begun baja, chingri macher malai curry, amer chutney, dal, chapattis and rice. On Friday evenings, he had a gin and tonic.

62

On Monday evenings he and Swarnakumari visited the Banerjees on Nightingale Avenue for a game of bridge. He drank malt with Gaurab Banerjee, who had made the mistake of nominating his wife the commanding military officer of his castle. A fiery woman with a stentorian voice, Mrs Banerjee always glared menacingly at her husband as he poured a second whisky and announced, 'That is enough.' At this, Banerjee would subside without protest into his leather sofa. Mr Chatterjee, who never had a second glass, watched the public humiliation of his friend with disapproval; a woman should know her place, and if she did not – well, it was up to the man to firmly escort her there.

Gaurab Banerjee's daughter Madhumita had married an Albanian classmate at Columbia University and now lived in San Ramon, California. That was like losing your daughter forever, thought Mr Chatterjee sadly; how often in a lifetime would and could the Banerjees meet Madhumita in San Ramon without the Albanian son-in-law in tow? At least, ventured Banerjee in hesitant defence, Heinz would learn Bengali. Madhumita had promised. Their children would have a fair complexion, he added.

The Albanian son-in-law from Tirana went by the name of Gjynejt. His parents called him 'Gjelosh', while his friends called him 'Haxhi'. Madhumita called him 'Ferrok'. Banerjee was bewildered. As Gjynejt-Gjelosh-Haxhi-Ferrok was addicted to ketchup, he had been nicknamed 'Heinz' by his American classmates. Banerjee was relieved. Heinz was a German or Austrian name; it could even be Swiss. It sounded respectably Western and European. San Ramon was full of Indians, added Banerjee; there were plenty of temples and Indian restaurants all over California. The latest craze was for Chinese-Indian food, he said – spicy Chinese food with a touch of Punjabi. Mr Chatterjee shuddered.

Shyamal Chatterjee had always been of a serious bent of mind. As a boy, he had preferred books to the company of other children and adults; as a teenager, he profited from the hours spent at Durga Puja, Shivratri and Saraswati Puja learning logarithms instead of flirtations with his doe-eyed cousins. Like several young men of his time, he was sent to London to study law, a subject for which he had no interest but much aptitude. He spent his years and money wisely as a lodger with his landlady Rosie on Tottenham Court Road and complained about the biting winters before returning home carrying both the china teapot for his mother and his virginity intact.

Swarnakumari Mukhopadhyay had lived a sheltered and exemplary life in Calcutta as the youngest of four children. The family doctor had been convinced it would be a boy; her father concealed his disappointment over a fourth daughter, and Swarnakumari rewarded him with sweet renditions of 'Rabindra Sangeet' in gratitude. A product of Brahmo Girls School, she was shy and reticent; her sisters Devika, Menaka and Madhulika were the fiery rebels who married wealthy landowners and heirs to tea plantations. Swarnakumari liked needlework.

Her father consulted the senior Chatterjee in all his legal affairs and for advice in a wrangle over the eviction of tenants. Barely home from London, Shyamal Chatterjee was despatched with papers to the rambling Mukhopadhyay mansion. Swarnakumari's father was impressed by the manners of the earnest, neatly dressed young man who refused to share a glass with his host. Work and drink never mixed, he asserted firmly, also politely declining the sweets brought to him on a silver salver by Swarnakumari. Padding gracefully across the room, she sent him a shy glance, one that he intercepted and took back with the dusty legal files he carried that evening. Swarnakumari's father needed no further persuasion; Shyamal Chatterjee's honesty and humility would be suitably rewarded.

If Swarnakumari found Mr Chatterjee dull, she would have been incapable of expressing those sentiments as she settled into life in England. They moved to Cambridge, where he commenced employment with a reputed solicitor's firm. He was always sensible, never spontaneous but always reliable, and Swarnakumari had few complaints after the renovation of the kitchen with its stainless steel double sink, the building of the conservatory and the landscaping of the garden. Swarnakumari had nevertheless received the news of her husband's retirement with alarm and discovered her spiritual guide and mentor Guru Ma at the moment when Mr Chatterjee discovered mould in the bathroom. For Swarnakumari, Guru Ma was the equivalent of headphones.

Swarnakumari firmly believed that a prayer recited with increasing frequency became a living truth. Guru Ma's little book of homilies for daily happiness was a clarion call to right action and non-action, resistance and endurance. Truth stood naked, but physical intimacy was no longer an option for Mr Chatterjee; his wife's permission and participation had been withdrawn years earlier. Swarnakumari had taken a private decision under the influence of cloudy sandalwood incense and pious prayer; he sensed a steely resolve in her that would not be easily challenged. Battling her resistance silently, he was annoyed that he had not been consulted on a matter of such importance. He could not be certain, but he suspected that Banerjee was in a similar situation of choicelessness. Women had their secrets, their eccentricities and unfathomable rituals, Banerjee had once intimated with an air of such resignation that Mr Chatterjee had clung gratefully to his words as evidence that he was not alone.

Swarnakumari had been an exemplary wife and mother, he thought; she had been content to settle in England, displaying a quiet support of his every suggestion. Conscious of her sheltered upbringing, Mr Chatterjee had ensured her protection from the evil influences of British society, endorsing her reluctance to venture out of the home.

Her desire to work in the charity shop was applauded by him as a noble, altruistic effort. The impulse purchases were another matter; he was somewhat unhappy with her gift of a grey Marks & Spencer cardigan from the charity shop. Englishmen appeared to be of an entirely different build, even if the size was S. It was difficult to ascertain whether it was the shoulders or the chest or the sleeves that were the problem, for no full-length mirrors were to be found in the Chatterjee household, a move initiated by Swarnakumari after she had read Guru Ma's homily on vanity. A mirror reflection, decided Swarnakumari, was merely an illusion, not reality.

They did not need any more bone china cups, saucers, plates and bowls, egg slicers, rattan magazine racks, vases, recycled pencils or lampshades from the shop, thought Mr Chatterjee. The small television set she acquired for the bedroom had, however, been useful, and after Swarnakumari fell asleep he turned down the volume and watched until late into the night. His dreams were lurid, and, feeling revulsion and distaste, he wrote letters of complaint to the television watchdog protesting against explicit programme content.

Swarnakumari was garrulous every Thursday evening as she recounted the day's events, described the customers and the arrival of new items. Mrs Wellington-Smythe was a fine, aristocratic woman, with a strong sense of authority and command, decided Mr Chatterjee. He mentioned her name several times in conversation on his walks with Banerjee, who in turn narrated Heinz's stories of barbecues in the San Ramon backyard and a trip with Madhumita to Yellowstone National Park in their black BMW five series car. Banerjee had somehow formed the impression that Swarnakumari and Mrs Wellington-Smythe were good friends.

Mr Chatterjee had noticed an increasing yearning in Swarnakumari for India, for Kolkata and for her relatives, but he deliberately refrained from comment. He was of the view that the past should remain the past. There was no future in the past, and as for the tense, it was present perfect. At an early age, Mr Chatterjee had learned the wisdom of the haiku he had read: *When sitting sit/When standing stand/Above all, don't wobble.*

Mr Chatterjee never wobbled, although the breasts of the woman in No. 32 opposite the quiet square did. He had noticed them and their owner from the moment she had moved into the house with the blue door on 24 June 1997. She lived alone with two cats that were entirely house-trained and remained indoors. Two days after her arrival at Newton Square one of the cats had leaped out of the window and was seen wandering disoriented and distraught over the lawn like a blindfolded inmate released at midnight from a high-security prison. By a happy coincidence, Mr Chatterjee was tweaking the net curtains at the time. Despite a strong aversion to cats, he gallantly gave chase. Rachel Chesterton explained that she had lived in a London flat and was obliged to relocate after her divorce. She expressed her gratitude with an offer of tea, patting his arm gently with rose-pink nails to propel him into her kitchen. He had stared in wonder at the wooden flooring, the cosy bright curtains and the cheerful furniture of an IKEA world.

Rachel was lonely; she had recovered from skin cancer three years ago, but it was her divorce that was her undoing. Her chronic alcoholism led to a court decision awarding custody of the child to the father. She found Cambridge provincial and dull, as dull as her little Indian neighbour, who looked at her with inscrutable eyes and transparent thoughts. Conscious of the proprieties, he had declined further offers of tea, choosing instead to chat on the street. If he passed her in the company of Banerjee, he merely nodded briskly from afar.

On his Neighbourhood Watch rounds one winter's evening he saw a twisted bicycle abandoned near Rachel's house. He knocked on her door, noticed it was unlatched and waited. He knocked and rang again before gingerly calling out her name. He found her crying on a sofa in the living room, wearing only a dressing-gown, an empty bottle of vodka by her side.

Between sobs she told him that her ex-husband had moved the courts to prevent her visits to her child on the grounds that they were disruptive.

Absorbing the impact of her words, Mr Chatterjee found the sight of her gown open to the waist even more disturbing, as she leaned across and rested her head on his shoulder. He patted her reassuringly, but suddenly felt warm, naked skin instead, as the gown fell away. She began to kiss him with urgent, desperate passion. Then a furry living snowball scratched his arm and landed with lightning speed on Rachel's bosom. The sight of her ballooning breasts swinging under the weight of a clinging cat clawing them in jealousy was one that Mr Chatterjee never managed to erase. He fled, remembering to shut the front door firmly behind him, and on reaching home rang the local police station about the twisted bicycle. He was a good Neighbourhood Watch Co-ordinator.

Rachel Chesterton had moved home shortly after the incident, carrying no recollection of her last encounter with Mr Chatterjee, a detail sadly unknown to him. For years thereafter, Mr Chatterjee had suppressed a thought couched in rhyme that gnawed at his insides: what would he have done, with the dress undone, had the cat not won? Searching for the answer, he drove solitary in the silent winter dusk down Lime Kiln Road to gaze at the city of spires below. The branches of the bare trees were wagging, censorious fingers in the sky and the frost on his neat patio garden was the ice in his heart.

Over the years, Mr Chatterjee slowly convinced him-self that he was not to blame, that her breasts were, in fact, thorny, wrinkled pineapples that should have stayed on the stem, and that encounters of this nature were as much an occupational hazard for a Neighbourhood Watch Co-ordinator as for the engineer called out to inspect a gas leak.

Mr Chatterjee had recorded a private image of English life in the neighbourhood with his customary powers of observation; the women who gave their husbands a peck on the cheek before the car backed out of the driveway; those who never came out; the men who regularly cut the lawn and washed the cars and trimmed the hedges; the women who put out winter pansies in garden centre terracotta containers and planted aconite, snowdrops, anemones, grape hyacinth, tulips and daffodils along the path to the front door; the children who greeted the neighbours and those who stayed up late; those who had cats and those who had dogs; those who left Dairy Crest milk bottles outside their door and those who were disabled; those who left the black bins out too long and those who took them in early; those who recycled and those who did not; those who swept up the autumn leaves and weeded the flowerbeds; those who read the broadsheets and those who read the tabloids; those who bought DIY furniture and those who entertained; those who had attic conversions and those who had conservatories – and those who led happy lives.

Mr Chatterjee believed that the years devoted to the study of law and human nature had sharpened his faculties, and it was thus evident to him that Mary and David were a cultured elderly couple and ideal neighbours for the adjoining side of his semi-detached house. Even the dull, muffled sound on the stairs stopped after some years; David moved downstairs once he contracted Parkinson's disease. Mary was devoted and uncomplaining; she wheeled him out into the sun, a blanket over his knees, to cheerfully water the petunias. She began to suffer from migraine, a condition that made it difficult to tend to an ailing husband. Their two sons, who lived locally, made infrequent visits. Mr Chatterjee pursed his lips at their lack of filial devotion, while Swarnakumari wordlessly added Mary's Tesco and Sainsbury's shopping lists to her own. Soon David no longer left the house, and the sons no longer visited.

Returning from an afternoon in the Central Library, Mr Chatterjee was met by an excited Banerjee outside the lane. The neighbour, David, was dead. That was not all, said Banerjee, falling into step with Mr Chatterjee as he began to walk towards his home; it was murder.

Mr Chatterjee paused. *Murder*. The word reverberated in his head, growing louder until it was a horn blasting over the treetops and chimneys in the quiet square, flew over the Cherry Hinton Park, past the swans and over the railway and onto the speeding track, returning over the fields of Grantchester and along the ripples of the River Cam to the police car parked outside the house on Newton Square.

Arriving at his home, he noticed that an over-zealous police officer had extended the cordon to include the Chatterjee entrance, erroneously giving the impression of multiple crimes. Mr Chatterjee stared up at the house next door in disbelief as Banerjee narrated the succession of events. He felt betrayed. Had he not been reading the pages of the *Telegraph* at the library, he would have been at home; *he*, as Neighbourhood Watch Co-ordinator, would have been the one the police would have approached for assistance.

Perhaps it was still not too late. Striding up to the officer in the police car, he introduced himself, declaring himself ready for a lengthy interview on the neighbourhood and its inhabitants, but the officer merely had instructions to stay outside the house for a further hour. He knew nothing other than that there had been a murder, that the elderly lady had been taken away and that she was unharmed.

Mr Chatterjee walked up past the front lawn to his home along with Banerjee. Swarnakumari had little to add; she had been praying in her room, unaware of the commotion outside, and Mallika was away in London for the day. Mr Chatterjee sat still and small on his favourite leather armchair. He was afraid, and wondered whether he should write a note to the neighbours, but lacked the words. The motive for murder had to be burglary; the cold-blooded assassin had evidently noticed a helpless invalid and an elderly lady who stayed indoors and rarely received visitors. The man would have stood behind the privet hedge to observe the house at close quarters; indeed, he was lurking in the neighbourhood, waiting to strike again, and this time the target could be the Chatterjee household.

The presence of the police car was initially reassuring, but the officer drove off an hour later. Mr Chatterjee bolted every door and window in his house, placing chairs and tables and heavy objects against every exit. He wondered whether he should leave the lights on, but the electricity bill during Durga Puja and Diwali had been high, and prudence prevailed.

Long after Swarnakumari was asleep, Mr Chatterjee continued to sit upright in his bed, a torch and the cordless phone at his side, the cord from his pyjamas

72

dangling nervously as he trembled. He felt the warmth from Swarnakumari's soft folds touching his thigh. How peacefully she slept! The last words she uttered before she closed her eyes were that God and Guru Ma had taught her to fear nothing. He marvelled at his wife's composure; she squealed at the sight of a cockroach, but could be as steady as a lighthouse in a storm. Her faith in her mentor had been an irritant until this moment; perhaps it was time to test her Guru Ma's wisdom.

He leaned over and felt his way to the prayer book that he knew lay on her bedside table. Shining his torch low, he stared at the first page. Under the picture of a woman with streaming black hair was the blueprint for a spiritual life. He read Tagore's words from *Gitanjali*, and, inspired, decided he, too, would make his life simple and straight like a flute made of reed for the Divine One to fill with music.

Mr Chatterjee continued to read with increasing respect, discovering the philosophy of life that his wife attempted to adopt; it included purity of action and heart, compassion for those less fortunate, and a homily on health. The consumption of vegetables and fruit such as apple, pear, pineapple and melon was advocated to reduce the *tamasik* destructive forces in the body. Mr Chatterjee grimaced as he read the word 'pineapple'. He put away the torch, as worried about the life of the battery as his own, and lay next to Swarnakumari, inhaling her healing softness again. He extended a hesitant arm, his body cupping her back. Then he remembered; he had forgotten to find out what Guru Ma had to say about sex. As he groped in the dark for the light switch, there was a sudden thud and a crash. Mr

Chatterjee leaped out of bed in alarm, forgetting his arthritic knee, reached for the telephone and shakily called the police. A moment later he heard his daughter's incredulous voice calling. Mr Chatterjee had forgotten about Mallika's return that evening.

The police car he had summoned to his house woke the neighbourhood; those who had cats and those who had dogs; those who were elderly and those who were young; those who went to work and those who did not. The same officer emerged from his car. The Neighbourhood Watch Co-ordinator had been shamed.

Sitting upright on his leather sofa the next day, Mr Chatterjee answered the policewoman's questions about his neighbours Mary and David. When had he last seen David and Mary? How had Mary seemed to him? Had he ever overheard any disagreement between the couple? Did he know the nature of David's medication?

Prefacing his every reply with the words, 'As the Neighbourhood Watch Co-ordinator . . .' Mr Chatterjee proceeded to display his powers of observation and his legal competence to the young WPC. He inquired whether he should send a letter to the neighbourhood about the burglary. She raised her eyebrows. 'This was no burglary, it's fairly straightforward.'

Mr Chatterjee was perplexed; he decided to write a letter on the following Monday to Cambridgeshire Police on the public's right to know. A day later he had the distinction as the Neighbourhood Watch Co-ordinator of hearing the news first. Mary had killed David. She had poisoned him and confessed, ringing the police herself. She was in a low-security prison, and her lawyers felt that a reduced sentence could be obtained on account of the blinding headaches she had been suffering and for which she had received no medication.

Mr Chatterjee was appalled. Calculating the time of death, he realised that David had been murdered a few feet away from him at the very moment he was watching an adult film on the 'Mute' button. The body had lain in rigor mortis until the morning. It was said that Mary was clearly not in her right mind. She had told the police that she drew back the curtains to let in the sun, and brought David his morning cup of tea, placing the tray by his bedside. She had drunk her own before ringing the police to say that David did not want any more.

That evening Mr. Chatterjee felt nauseous and, for the first time since he could remember, was unable to eat Swarnakumari's macher jhol, dal and rice. He looked at his wife's plump form without comfort, and a dry fear invaded his being of ageing, waning life force, sense and faculty slipping away invisibly like the dew with the first warm rays of the sun, of burden and loss. It had been easy to be young, and it might be difficult to be old. The unformed questions hovered, taking voluminous shape as he looked at Swarnakumari's placid face. What were her unfathomable depths? Could she one day take on the aspect of Kali in a mood of vengeance, slashing his world with a word, a swoop, a sword? Could she dismember him in his sleep? He imagined the sheets covered in blood, his blood; afterwards, she would lovingly apply bandages to his body to stem the thickening flow.

He considered the large chopping knife lying in the kitchen drawer. Mrs Banerjee, after all, had been given to menopausal moods and had thrown objects in threatening rage, her large kohl-lined eyes flashing. Banerjee had told him so. It had happened almost fifteen years ago, he had added reassuringly, but Mr Chatterjee remained discomfited. Banerjee said he had simply stepped out of the way as an object whizzed past, and retirement had brought its own prudence; she would never hurl glass again. Men who had already lost their hair lost the last shreds of dignity at this age, mourned Banerjee. It was best to let women have their way; the alternatives were too dangerous, he joked seriously. His cousin Bikash's wife had trashed an entire collection of Matchbox Dinky cars painstakingly acquired by Bikash over thirty years. They would have been worth a small fortune, his son-in-law Heinz had lamented. Afraid he had revealed too much, Banerjee hurriedly changed the subject to the lack of kidney donors among South Asians in Britain.

Mr Chatterjee listened to Banerjee without his customary attentiveness. He was still deeply affected by the deaths of his neighbours, for Mary had died of natural causes in prison two weeks later. He could no longer be certain of his judgement, nor of his observations of human nature, but of one thing he was convinced: devotion came in several forms.

A year later, Mr Chatterjee was still deeply affected – by his new neighbours. Prior to Mary's funeral, there had been a flurry of activity from the two sons, who arrived in two matching self-drive vans and dismantled the home, piling the furniture and other items in the front garden as if for an auction. Peering through the net curtains, Mr Chatterjee witnessed the efficiency that could be produced by the equal distribution of blue and red sticky labels.

A *For Sale* sign had been stuck by a careless estate agent in the hedge on Mr Chatterjee's side of the house while he sank unsuspecting into his favourite armchair with his Bengali newspaper. The doorbell rang, a young couple brushed briskly past Swarnakumari, and Mr Chatterjee glanced up from the riveting results of the Mohan Bagan football game to find himself in the midst of an unorthodox inspection of his living room brick by brick, wall by wall. The woman even leaned over to examine a small discolouration in the paint on the wall directly behind his head. She wrote on a pad, noting the paint and the woodwork in a professional manner and stared disparagingly at the ceiling; the couple then proceeded through the conservatory and into the garden.

Mr Chatterjee followed, bewildered. The woman turned her gaze from the rock garden, the tinkling water fountain and goldfish to observe sternly that it would not do, it was not suitable as a play area for a young child. Mr Chatterjee meekly agreed, but demurred when she suggested the water fountain and goldfish be removed, and the rock garden covered. The couple returned to the hallway, sniffing appreciatively, their noses following the smells as they peeped into the kitchen and nodded at Swarnakumari with her floury hands.

'Can we go upstairs?' asked the man.

Tearing his gaze from the man's muddy boots poised on the first stair, Mr Chatterjee finally found his voice. 'Why?' he asked.

Three months later, as Mr Chatterjee was writing a

letter to the City Council about dog fouling at the lamp-post at the corner of Fendon Road, a large removal van drew up, followed by a car. Mr Chatterjee's curtains twitched. His new neighbours had arrived.

Mr Chatterjee heard the sound of laughter as he drank the tea that Swarnakumari had prepared for him that Thursday morning. It was that boy again, he thought angrily. That boy and Mallika together. He peered through the net curtains. They were outside his front gate.

The new family had bought a house where a life had been snuffed out, where memories swirled and fires of devotion still burned, and although he had refrained from comment he agreed with Swarnakumari that the new occupants should have performed a little ritual of prayer for the gentle departed souls of David and Mary, who might still want to linger. Perhaps even at this moment, their spirits were straying, seeking refuge in the Chatterjee side of the house, tinkling the Japanese wind chimes, swaying the curtains and dimming the lights.

The African family had spelled mystery. What business could possibly have brought the three of them all the way from Australia to Cambridge? wondered Mr Chatterjee. The talk of the Science Park and the Napp Laboratories was nonsense. What did the African man really do for a living?

Applying the strategies of deduction he had developed over the years, Mr Chatterjee concluded that, as his neighbour appeared to have unlimited funds for renovation of the house, there was an unambiguous trail of involvement in the illegal export of ivory. He knew that Portobello Road in London was awash with ivory of indeterminate age. Under British law, ivory had to be older than 1947 to be sold. The man had escaped to Australia from Nigeria, but when he found the police were on his heels he moved his family to the modest semi in Cambridge to provide a cover for his clandestine activities until he was exposed, for capture meant a maximum sentence of seven years of imprisonment. Mr Chatterjee was so convinced of the truth of his own speculation that he instructed Swarnakumari and Mallika to avoid contact with the family. Invited by his neighbours for an evening drink on a number of occasions, he had politely declined, recommending to Swarnakumari that she, too, find a suitable excuse. No member of the Chatterjee household was to be implicated in the trafficking of tusks.

Loud music, parties, overnight guests, carelessly parked cars, the slamming of doors and conversations in operatic tones next door obliged Mr Chatterjee to resort to longer daytime naps, and he spent waking moments in a state of roadside recovery, his wellbeing severely tested and threatened. He envied Swarnakumari her ability to sleep soundly.

Compounding his worries was the adverse impact he feared his new neighbours would have on the value of his property. He arranged a free annual valuation by a different Cambridge estate agent to proudly remind Swarnakumari of the wisdom of a profitable investment. He would have erupted in prickly indignation and incomprehension at the suggestion that his own move to Newton Square thirty years ago might have been a matter of similar concern to his neighbours.

Mr Chatterjee looked at the Nigerian teenager's

loose, fluid limbs, his low-slung jeans and hooded top and the grace rippling through his feet as he twisted effortlessly on his skateboard. Joseph was dangerous, even if he was only seventeen going on eighteen, he decided. He had caught Mallika listening to something she called 'gangster rap' and 'garage', and she had turned defiant. She no longer sang 'Rabindra Sangeet'. Banerjee was saddled with an Albanian son-in-law; who could foretell the frightening fate that might befall his own household?

Mr Chatterjee studied his neat list of errands for the morning. Driving out onto Queen Edith's Way, he stopped for Banerjee, who was rubbing his hands against the cold at the corner of Nightingale Avenue. They were on their way to buy fresh fish from the Bangladeshi shop off Mill Road, to make their selection from rui mach, ilish mach, koi mach, tangra mach and chingri mach. Mr Chatterjee believed that it took a Bengali to truly discern the freshness of a catch. He was not alone in this assumption.

As they loaded the fish into the car, Banerjee suggested they visit the charity shop. Mr Chatterjee looked surprised, but Banerjee was insistent; his wife had heard about Swarnakumari's legendary bargains, especially Mr Chatterjee's splendid grey Marks & Spencer cardigan. Banerjee's own maroon Debenhams cardigan had sprung two asymmetric holes, and he had been directed by his wife to procure an immediate and inexpensive replacement.

Mr Chatterjee would not be persuaded to visit the shop, and, loath to admit his reluctance either to Banerjee or to himself, he mumbled an excuse, but to his amazement Banerjee remained firm. It was either the charity shop or a confrontation with his wife. Any man in his situation would have chosen the former without a moment's hesitation.

Mr Chatterjee had no alternative but to acquiesce. It was his first visit to IndiaNeed, and he wished he were not attired in the ill-fitting grey Marks & Spencer cardigan, which made him appear meekly round-shouldered and small. He wished he were not smelling of fish, wished he could be alone and without Banerjee at the time of his introduction to the Honourable Mrs Wellington-Smythe.

# CHAPTER FIVE

# Charity begins at home

DIANA WELLINGTON-SMYTHE LIVED in England and dreamed of Tuscany. Summers were spent in their grape-laden villa outside Florence with her insolent daughter Imogen, silent son James and reticent husband Rupert. The Scrabble, draughts and chess were never unpacked, and returned to England in pristine condition during the last week of August. Imogen was growing breasts and James was growing restive, but Chianti at lunch and supper restored Diana's partial tolerance of Rupert, pale and city pink in short sleeves. As tall as her husband, she was imperious in classic Armani, her blond hair, too intimidated by its owner to be curly, swinging straight down her neck. Her features struggled between boredom and equine haughtiness.

Father and son, mother and daughter strolled in silence to the village piazza in the evenings as the sun glinted on the window shutters of the white-walled houses, setting the red geraniums ablaze. They stopped for ice cream at the local gelateria overlooking a narrow cobbled street. Human nature was like gelati, the elderly man told the signora; at its best when it had more flavours than one, the mellifluous pistacchio melting into the earthy brown of cioccolato, creamy vaniglia surrendering to the spicy strawberry red of fragola. It was the only counselling Diana would ever have.

On their way back to England from Florence, the family had dallied in Rome. Diana had shopped at Via Condotti; at Missoni, she abandoned the struggle into a size ten. Imogen, with her size six hips, swinging blond hair and pout, moodily twirled an orange and red flame-twisted scarf around her neck and stared challengingly at her mother in the mirror. They made their way to the Trevi Fountain. It had been drizzling, and the steps were wet as James and Imogen watched the scurrying tourists and their squealing slide toward the fountain, slippery peas posing in a pod. Imogen's lips curved mockingly as Diana impulsively asked Rupert for a coin.

'Euro or British, darling?' he asked, reaching into his trousers as an Asian man offered him a dozen roses *'per la bella donna'*. As Diana watched, Rupert waved him away indifferently. For one brief, mad moment, there was nothing in the world she wanted other than a single red rose.

Diana had recently joined a private class of Intermediate Italian learners who shunned the courses offered by the Sixth Form Colleges of Cambridge and met in an elegant home on Grange Road instead. 'Non parlo bene l'italiano,' she began with uncharacteristic hesitation, placing the mandatory bottle of Barolo on the table in front of the teacher, an Englishwoman who had lived in Florence as an artist for many years. The man next to Diana leaned over and smiled a crinkly, warm smile of wealthy cologne. 'Ma, Signora, non è vero,' he murmured. Diana had found a man to contradict her at last. Afterwards they talked of Tuscan painters' light, and the next evening they walked along Quayside, continuing into Midsummer Common, past the cows flicking their lazy tails, along the water and past the houseboats, returning to an Italian café and its red-checked tablecloth.

'Basta così stare insieme con te,' Philip had declared soulfully. Being with her was all he wanted, staring into her grey eyes after the macchiato. Diana melted quicker than the chocolate mint the waitress had placed on the saucer. Romancing in Italian in Cambridge led her three mornings later to perch among several Chinese vases in the living room of a Newnham home as Philip poured out the tea.

'Do you take sugar?' he asked.

'Don't you think I'm sweet enough?' was her arch reply.

The tray rattled. He trembled at the fires rising. 'Non c'è nessuno come te. There's no one like you,' he said unconvincingly, brushing her fragrant cheek and neck. She smiled faintly. He nuzzled her ear and drew closer. She was as soft as a giraffe on eggshells and smelled of lavender and a linen cupboard. Philip had warm memories of Wendy Barton's house in Hampshire. At seventeen he had stood with Wendy in her dark, fragrant linen cupboard lined with wooden shelves and piles of crisp white sheets and embroidered duvet covers. Wendy of the pert, round, shiny breasts; one silken orb had looked larger than the other in the dim golden light. He had wanted to ask her about the irregularity, bounce the weight of one and then the other, but her mother was laying out the tea and shortbread in the kitchen below, the radio rising in a ghostly murmur. Wendy must be all grown up out there somewhere in London, gym-slim, married to a banker, two children, St John's Wood, golden retriever, thought Philip, and he kissed Diana forcefully, sweeping her of all resistance.

The thought of wicked Wendy in London, still asymmetrically desirable, fanned his ardour. He continued to hold Diana in his arms, breathing endearments into her ear as he kissed her with increasing passion. He licked her earlobe and they subsided backwards onto the sofa where she was directly underneath his grandfather's portrait, which admonished the easy abandonment of Philip's green-checked boxer shorts.

Philip attempted to lift her, but she was rather more heavy-boned than he had anticipated, and they sank deeper into the sofa. As they kissed, Philip nibbled her earlobe again. Diana's skin felt warm and yielding. She unbuttoned herself swiftly out of her purple cashmere twinset and was in the act of unzipping her brown Italian boots when her mobile phone began to ring. It flashed the IndiaNeed number. Adroitly gathering her belongings and her control, she answered; she had never liked losing either.

Back in the shop, Swarnakumari hovered expectantly as Heera spoke. 'Oh, good morning, Mrs Wellington-Smythe, it's Heera from the shop. I'm sorry to disturb you, but it's important. That's why I'm ringing you. You see, we were just sorting the bags and we found—'

Heera turned to the others as she replaced the receiver. 'D'you know what that Diana ki bachi said?' She mimicked a clipped upperclass accent. 'I'm sorry,

Helen, shop matters will have to wait. I'm on my morning canter.'

'Lady God*i*va,' murmured Durga.

Diana had returned to Philip waiting unclothed and expectant on the sofa. He lay there patiently like a painter's sylvan Adonis sans woodland wreath. At the hint of steel in her voice as she spoke on the telephone, he had hastily draped his boxer shorts over his upper thighs. His grandfather's stern portrait relented, but the moment had clearly curdled. Philip had once been a King's College chorister, wearing the Etonian collar, singing in a pure, high voice at the Service of Nine Lessons and Carols on Christmas Eve. Then he sprouted hair on his chin and lost his voice, never to regain its power.

'You look ridiculous, get dressed!' Diana commanded in nursery nanny tones, and Philip obeyed, recalling his own nanny's reign and rein of terror. Philip was resigned; he knew when he had been given his marching orders.

Diana's grandfather had been given his marching orders after the Raj crumbled, and when he returned to England and to the impressive country manor in Berkshire, he had surrounded himself with antiques and artefacts acquired from India; a giant punkha fan of rosewood pinned to the wall, a peacock-shaped inlay table, figurines from Southern India, and the stuffed heads of tigers as sporting trophies. Diana's father had joined the Foreign Service and travelled with his wife and without his child to Nigeria. It was left to the grandfather and nanny to instruct and educate Diana, a task they performed with admirable resolve.

Diana travelled to India when she was twenty-four. She had originally planned a visit to Brazil, fired by a previous encounter in London with a man of mixed German and Amazon-Indian blood, who smoked thin, twirled cigarettes of dubious origin, brushed his teeth with bark and wore no underwear. She soon tired of his caveman looks, halting English and neat bottom shaking to the samba beat.

India and a people's raw display of emotions left her wary of the depths of dark, warm eyes. A hurried coupling with the Rajasthan tour guide would have been a mistake, and she had been wise to ignore his boyish charm and reject his gift of a sandalwood elephant, as she did the advances of the suave, handsome businessman at the Taj Hotel bar overlooking the Bombay harbour.

She had strolled out one evening from the air-conditioned splendour of the hotel lobby and into the world outside. A sticky blanket of heat had clung to her bare arms and legs as she walked under the arch of the Gateway of India, where King George and Queen Mary had once been welcomed with pomp and ceremony. Assailed by postcard-sellers, chattering footmen behind a queen's train, she finally sat on a parapet overlooking the harbour with its bobbing boats and grey water that never turned blue. Beside her was a family of Indian tourists, and the children chattered excitedly, pointing to various landmarks. A toddler in a woman's lap entwined his fingers into Diana's scarf, imprisoning the tassels in his little fist, and she stared solemnly into his brown eyes before disengaging her scarf. She rose and walked back to her air-conditioned room. Diana had learned at an early age that attachment, especially to pets and parents, led to heartbreak. IndiaNeed was born twenty years later as Diana's apology to the country of her father's birth.

'How many times have I told her my name's not "Helen",' stormed Heera, after Diana had abruptly terminated their conversation. 'You know, girls, I don't understand – what's this English problem with names? I have a cousin, Ashok Binani, who lives in Edgware. He's become quite fat now, but anyway, he used to be in the British Army – he was in the Falklands War – and d'you know what those English Army blokes called him?' She paused for dramatic effect. 'Bill.' She repeated, 'Bill. Now you tell me, d'you see any connection between "Ashok" and "Bill"?'

'Well, Army Bloke Ashok didn't have a choice, but what about the Asian population in Cambridge? Half of them call themselves Bill or Barry, Jill or Jane, and the other half's like me, putting up with ridiculous versions of our names. I'm Der-ger, Dugga, Dooga or Dergay, take your pick and mix,' laughed Durga, as she offered the other women a bar of Cadbury's.

'I just realised your husband's a plumber, Eileen, and his surname is Watts. He should have been an electrician,' teased Heera.

Eileen put away the basket of assorted skeins of wool and muttered as she munched a piece of milk chocolate, 'He should have been a lot of things.' She did not elaborate further on what might have been, nor on what might have been left.

'Except for Lady Di, no one has problems with my name. How about you, Swarna?' asked Heera.

'People usually call me "Sara"' admitted Swarnakumari. 'But what to do? If they can't say my name, they can't, *na?*'

'Or won't?' said Durga, licking her fingers. She loved chocolate with the passion that some women reserved for lipstick.

A name was nothing, thought Durga. She herself was nothing like her namesake in Hindu mythology – the Goddess Durga, protector of the good and the pure, and destroyer of the evil demon Mahishasura. According to legend, the combined energies of the gods created the feminine form of a ten-armed yellow-clad woman riding a lion. They hastily supplied her with weapons of destruction against the demon and she became Durgashtini or a mother goddess who destroyed evil and offered her devotees protection.

Names could be misleading; Durga's aunt, whose skin was the colour of milk with a spoonful of honey, had been superstitiously nicknamed Kaali, 'The Dark One', as the first surviving child after three stillbirths. Was a name an identity, an anonymous cloak or a terrifying emptying of self? The extra 'a' that her Gujarati neighbour Anal Shah had hastily inserted between the 'n' and 'l' of his name after receiving a scholarship to Harvard was the linchpin between respect and ridicule, but Ajay Dikshit at Trinity, a Cambridge friend, had succeeded in solemnising a marriage with Emma Cockburn in front of an audience too solemn to titter during the exchange of vows.

Durga said, 'So you mean Ashok is told, "Shoot the enemy, Bill!" and when the job is done and Ashok gets a medal, it's "Well done, Bill!" and pat, pat on the broad back.'

Heera continued, 'Exactly. I don't think I told you

about Seema Tipnis; she was a receptionist to an eye specialist called Ramsbottom. Poor thing, she was so embarrassed to say this man's name. After all, she's Hindu – how could she refer to Lord Rama's bottom fifty times a day? She told us his name was Dr Ramsey, but I found out, anyway.'

'Naturally,' said Durga.

'Talking of names, funny how Asians born here just can't pronounce Indian words the way we do,' remarked Heera. 'I once challenged a young Punjabi fellow to say "Pandit Ravi Shankar". And do you know – each and every word sounded so strange from his mouth. I said to him straight, "If you can say the 'a' in 'another', why do you have to say it like 'ant'?" ' Heera paused, puzzled. 'But *you* don't talk like that, Durga, and you have lived here all your life,' she remarked. Distracted by the sight of Eileen carrying a pair of longjohns, she continued, '*Arre*, I thought I asked you to throw this pair of men's thermals away. Why are they still here?'

'But they are new. Someone can use them, *na*,' protested Swarnakumari reasonably.

'Who do you have in mind? Darling Rupert? Have you seen how long the fork is? It can lift a truck,' observed Durga.

'I have a funny story to tell you about thermals, girls. My cousin Viju came to stay with us. Smart chap, he cracked the ticketing system of the London Underground by the second day, so he stopped buying a ticket. When his wife smiles, you see her large pink gums first, then her teeth. Anyway, you know how many of these first-time Indians are: he wore sweaters here even in the summer. Such a smell of mothballs! White thermals under his shiny suit on a Sunday, can you imagine, and we went to the Natural History Museum. I think the thermals had a very long fork, because it was looking so bunched up under his belt, I knew it couldn't be natural. Oh, and one trouser leg of his suit was longer than the other, so I asked him why. He said the Indian tailor told him he should continue wearing the trousers and it would be all right in time. *Arre*, what a funny thing for the tailor to say!' roared Heera.

Durga interrupted, 'Viju could grow a longer leg. It's never too late.'

'Anyway, we saw specimens of those reptiles in the museum, and then his thermals started itching, so we couldn't go to the Imperial War Museum. We had to come back to Cambridge. I finally told him straight, "Enough of this nonsense!" I made him change into a white kurta pyjama and Bata rubber flip-flops, and he was so happy. I saw his suitcase later. My God, so many Ludhiana Mill woollies, strips of Saridon, Vicks inhaler, cough drops, Johnson's turmeric bandaid, Madhiwala ointment, clove oil for toothache, Amrutanjan pain balm, Jeevdaya Netraprabha for sparkling eyes, safety pins and a bandage, even that anti-flatulence stuff, you know, Havabaan Harde. I just couldn't believe it. Was he preparing to go into an English jungle, or what? And when he was leaving to go back to Delhi, he gave me five packets of rose incense sticks. They are so strong, I get an instant headache.'

'Then you should have kept his Amrutanjan pain balm also, *na*,' advised Swarnakumari.

'What to do? I usually get very boring gifts from India,' shrugged Heera.

'Like oil-shedding mango pickle,' contributed Durga moodily.

'Or twenty sandalwood paper cutters. I tell you, I have some strange guests in my house, and where they all come from, God only knows! I once came home to find strangers waiting outside my front door. He was a software consultant from Birmingham and his parents had just arrived from Delhi. They knew a friend of mine in Hyderabad, that's how they'd heard of me. They made themselves comfortable, drank my tea, ate my biscuits, but his ma was so tired, he said, jetlag continuing from two days ago, could she lie down somewhere for a few minutes, so I showed her to the guest room. Then he said, Ma and Baba must be so hungry, not used to this cold, could I suggest some place they could eat, but Ma was a pure vegetarian and already tired of eating bread. After her nap, Ma suddenly sprang up full of energy like a toddler with a dry nappy, and got busy in my kitchen, helping me cook rice and *dal*. Then the son announced he was on a carbohydrate-free meat diet to control his diabetes without medicine, did I have any lamb or chicken, and look how Ma is shivering, how is she going to make it back to Birmingham, it is already so dark, and she had wanted to see Cambridge. As soon as he said that, his mother immediately went all floppy. So they stayed the night. On top of that, I had to lend the whole family their nightclothes. The son is a little taller than Bob, and he complained, "Oh look, these pyjamas of your husband are too short for me." *Arre*, was he waiting for designer Burberry made to his size, or what? I told him, "As long as Bob's pyjamas cover your bits, that's all that should matter." Then he asked if I had thought of breakfast, because Ma liked apple juice, orange juice was too sharp for her teeth, and Baba liked white bread for toast, and did I have enough milk? Ma awoke at five and started moving around noisily, so I had to get up too. She asked me when I went downstairs, *bete*, how do you boil the water here, I want to make chai, and can Baba do his yoga asanas on your carpet – no hurry, whenever you are ready. Can you believe this behaviour? And no Diwali card, no thank you letter from these strangers afterwards,' concluded Heera indignantly as the shop bell tinkled.

A toddler on a leash dragged his mother towards a Lego helicopter that he instantly dismantled while she looked apologetic. An expensively dressed woman entered a moment later with a tiny shaggy dog clinging to her bosom.

'Where's Diana?' she demanded sharply.

'Mrs Wellington-Smythe is not here, she has gone riding,' answered Heera. 'I'm sorry, but no pets are allowed in the shop.'

'Don't be ridiculous. Phoebe wouldn't hurt a flea or a fly. She stays right here with me, and you may tell Diana I said so,' the visitor retorted firmly. 'Well, I haven't driven all the way from Latham Road for nothing. I'll give her a ring, but if she isn't going to show up, I'd better look round the shop myself.'

The woman advanced, tenderly stroking the pet with her red nails. Swarnakumari froze as she met the creature's penetrating eyes. Guru Ma's prayer book had contained no references to pets.

'I'm the manager. Why don't I show you around?' suggested Heera.

'Not much to show, is there?' said the woman.

'Who do you get in here, or daren't I ask? Let me guess – dear old ladies with their knitting needles, dirty men in raincoats, impecunious students, mothers looking for next year's Christmas presents in January?' The woman smoothed her hair thoughtfully. 'I'm amazed Diana has kept this outfit running so long. About two months, isn't it? She's right – it does need a complete makeover. She can't keep asking Board members to send in the stock and buy it back, too. What do you get in here?' She stopped at the window display. 'I mean, *really!* An assortment of Wedgwood teacups and saucers, Indian trinkets, wine glasses, Jane Shilton handbags, Crabtree and Evelyn bath salts, lavender-scented candles, a china plate, the Queen's framed photograph. What is this, a shop for geriatrics?'

She looked disdainfully at the shelves and the racks. 'Where is your designer collection? Jaeger, Betty Barclay, Krizia? Handbags, shoes? Prada, Gucci, Fendi, Burberry? I thought not. Absolute rubbish in here. I'd say those Indian beaded necklaces are pretty, and the scarves and bags too, but this shop needs quality. It has to be trendy, chic.' As she turned, she tripped on a piece of Lego that had detached itself from the child's fingers. She ignored the mother's hasty apology and wagged a stern finger at the boy. 'That's very dangerous, young man! Your mother should really keep you – oh, I see, you already have a leash.'

She turned to Swarnakumari. 'Well, clearly, even if you did run an upmarket charity shop, it's in the wrong location. Ideally, you should be somewhere like Rose Crescent. And it is absolutely pointless having Postman Pat and hot-water bottles in here; you are simply turning away the well-heeled clientele you need.'

Swarnakumari agreed, nodding her head in bewilderment.

'Did Diana tell you about the new animal charity she wants to set up here? We are going to protect a rare species of Indonesian fox. It really is a most amazing animal, and it is being hunted for its fur, but anyway, I'm trying to convince Diana that this place would be just as marvellous as a trendy little French coffee shop instead. Monet, Manet, Matisse on the walls, croissants, pain au chocolat, café au lait – that sort of thing. It's a good size of room, bigger than the Salvation Army shop,' she said consideringly. 'It would be an excellent place for the school mothers to meet. Parking is such a chore outside Browns – I'm always afraid I'll get my wheels stuck in those ridiculous gutters of Hobson's Conduit. It's an absolute nightmare. Not that you have a great deal of parking here, either. None, in fact, as far as I can see. Anyway, I suppose Diana will explain it all to you. Now I simply must give her a call.'

The woman rummaged in her handbag for her mobile and placed the dog on the floor. 'Di? Vicky Bartlett. Where *are* you? I thought we were meeting at your shop. Anyway, I'm here, and I'm through, so if you want to meet up after lunch instead . . . Not Browns again, sweetie . . . Oh well, all right, I suppose we could collect the children directly afterwards. See you in twenty minutes? Ciao.'

It happened very quickly. The dog, unaccustomed to exercise away from Victoria Bartlett's sedentary breast, took a wobbly step forward. The child stamped on its paw. The dog yelped, Victoria Bartlett screamed and bent to scoop up the dog and glared into the child's eyes, and the child screamed back and threw up over

95

her Prada shoes. Victoria Bartlett left holding her dog and her temper.

'What a time we have had, *baba*. That naughty child, the dirty vomit, cleaning,' sighed Swarnakumari, a quarter of an hour later.

'*You* didn't clean up the mess, Eileen did,' contradicted Heera. 'And I could have kissed that child, if he hadn't thrown up. I gave him a free lolly from the till,' she confessed.

'I slipped him one, too,' confided Durga. 'Three, actually. I hope he does throw up again; that child will go far. If his mother gets rid of the leash first, that is. He's a strategist displaying precision timing.'

'How come I never see *you* doing any cleaning up, Durga?' Heera asked suddenly. 'Too many posh madams in this shop?'

'Forget it, *na*, Heera. The truth is the truth: we all know that Indians from good families are not used to cleaning up the vomit of strangers,' appeased Swarnakumari. 'Now tell me, what was the friend of Mrs Wellington-Smythe saying about the fox she was carrying?'

'She wants to save it. Lady Di, not the friend. The fox, not IndiaNeed. The friend wants a coffee shop, not a charity shop, and it was a dog she was smothering like an asp to Cleopatra's breast, not a fox,' explained Durga.

'It was not a fox,' confirmed Eileen. Negation came easily.

'Oh, I was wondering, because of course I knew it was a dog, but then I started thinking maybe it was a fox, because otherwise why would the poor child be so scared, *na*?'

'*Arre*, dog, fox, does it matter? That La Di Da woman is going to shut this place down and doesn't have the courtesy, the decency, to tell me?' raged Heera.

'You don't have to believe what the friend says,' said Durga comfortingly. 'She could be as truthful as her blond streaks.'

'What is going to happen to those villagers?' asked Eileen, turning to the photograph behind them.

'They're so last season, darling! Not in fashion any more. Next, please,' said Durga.

'The friend wants a coffee shop here. For what? As a meeting place for private school mothers to chit chat and find out if the other brats are doing more classes after school than their own. Ballet, martial arts, piano, swimming, drama, tennis, chess and Kumon Maths aren't enough, you see,' informed Heera. 'Don't think I don't know about all these things just because I don't have any children. I know many of these independent school mothers who drive up and down in big four-wheel-drive cars; they are on duty even on weekends for more lessons and sleepovers. On top of that they bake cakes for the school fairs and sew costumes for the plays. *Arre*, the poor things are so slim watching the League Tables and their own diets of ambition through the wind-screens of their shiny cars, they live in a different world.'

Italian opera soothed Diana's nerves as she drove into Cambridge every morning from the countryside surrounding Haslingfield. Imogen was hunched, silent, on the seat. She would go clubbing and stay over at Izzie's, and she didn't care what her mother said about Izzie's brother David not being a Perse or Leys or King's boy. She was fourteen and old enough, and he was seventeen and old enough. Her silence grew, swelled until it was a crashing cacophonous wave, beating a plaintive crescendo of rage. It was the hormones, soothed Diana's mother.

Rupert stared out of the first-class window as the train sped past Stevenage to King's Cross. He took a sip of Perrier to calm his dry mouth, dabbed at the tiny egg stain on his crisp Paul Smith shirt inside his navy Paul Smith suit and arranged the papers in his monogrammed leather briefcase. A knot of tension gathered in the pit of his stomach and spread down to his brown Hackett shoes as he thought ahead to the takeover bid and the auction in the afternoon at Sotheby's, but instead of the old surge of excitement all he felt was dread. Each day hammered the same dull beat of predictability.

She had sentenced him to slow torture more surely than pins bludgeoned into his extremities or slivers of wood slid under his nails. He was disintegrating into chalk and dust, severing his life force against the sharp, hysterical edge of her voice. The bloodless holidays with her were the worst; every year he wanted to tell her he was going to trek in the Brazilian rainforest or in the Australian outback, free to roam while she stayed at home alone.

Soon it would be Christmas and they would play charades, gaze at the roaring fire and roast memories and chestnuts, and jingle, jingle the bells until the blood rushed out of his head, leaving him a dry riverbed caked with cracks of longing. Unwrapping the decorated present, he would find last year's past; pulling the silent cracker, he ached to leave before he choked, spewing the miles of gold and red ribbon from his engorged lungs. Santa never came down the chimney, the partridge had never liked being in the pear tree, the world wasn't joyful and triumphant even when it snowed with eight milking maids, he never went to church in the silent night, and his mother-in-law would come up from Berkshire to stay and treat him like a little boy and insist he ate his Brussels sprouts, but his mother didn't when she should have, and would stay away.

He would grow his thinning hair into a ponytail and sideburns, wear flared studded jeans and a shirt unbuttoned to his waist, a black leather jacket, heavy leather boots, smoke pot, ride his Harley Davidson into the wind and not only to Harston village on Sundays past the church and the graveyard; there would be a girl waiting on the highway to heaven and she would ride pillion to San Francisco in a leather jacket with flowers in her hair and she would ask for nothing. Everybody had a hungry heart. He would be a rider on the storm.

Rupert was going through mid-life angst; it was the hormones, said Diana's mother.

# CHAPTER SIX

# Fools rush in where angels fear to tread

THE MID-MORNING TRAFFIC dawdled through narrow Mill Road, past the solicitor's firm, the bakery, the Indian curry houses, the Internet café and the grinning drunk lurching against the windows of the Chinese supermarket. A young man in T-shirt, jeans and black slippers pounded the pavement with urgent steps past the fish shop at the moment when Mr Chatterjee and Banerjee passed through its entrance. He looked over his shoulder in panic. The wind tickled the banner proclaiming *The Lord is Your Guiding Light* outside the church at the corner, before whisking away the hat of an elderly man and crushing it under the wheels of an indifferent car.

The young man continued to run, desperately seeking refuge. Only minutes ago he had been sniffing his mother's fragrant saffron rice, wondering how many of his annoying cousins would stay to lunch; now he was a fugitive, lungs bursting, legs racing for life. Too late, he saw a large woman in a blue sari leave a shop door to bend over a black bag on the pavement.

He collided with Swarnakumari, and the impact lost him a slipper, but he dashed wildly through the entrance. The young man's breathless tale as he was hustled behind the curtain to the Staff Area at his request was garbled: his sister had eloped with her English boyfriend to get married in Ireland and was on her way to Stansted. Although the rest of the family was distraught, it was his uncle who had exploded in rage, swearing retribution. His own father had been placatory; such a violent response was hardly appropriate. His son would follow the pair, he soothed, and use his powers of persuasion to prevent their departure. The apoplectic uncle nevertheless insisted on accompanying the young man, who quailed at the words; he had been his sister's confidant, assisting in the online ticket reservations. A sly, fat cousin sounded the alarm as he fled down the stairs. Three burly young neighbourhood thugs, eager to teach him a lesson on cowardice, followed in vengeful pursuit.

'Durga, quick, bring out that Roman robe and the woman's veil!' commanded Heera. 'They're both in that old cupboard there, along with the kimono that those drama students gave us.'

The young man was hustled into the shapeless robe, and a lady's veil of indeterminate cultural origin placed over his head. Durga suggested kitten heels. He stared at his feet in dismay, increasingly agitated as he realised he had lost a slipper in his haste to find refuge.

Heera was soothingly maternal as she imparted her instructions. She had taken command, driven by compassionate empathy to aid the fleeing pair. He was to remain in the main shop area and act like a customer, she warned. Durga suggested crutches to lend authenticity to his veiled and robed disguise. Eileen was directed by Heera to retrieve the telltale slipper from outside the shop, but she was blocked at the entrance by the elderly customer returning from Catnap.

Outside, the three burly young men giving chase met in simultaneous impact, subsiding in a heap of arms and legs. They plucked themselves free, straightening their collars with a scowl. The slipper lay humble and telltale, pointing truthfully towards the shop. A thug wordlessly held it aloft as he entered, and like gangsters in a film, the trio moved warily sideways through the clothes racks, awaiting the bullet that could whistle through the thermal socks and teddy bears or even the net curtains at any instant. The leader ordered his companions to their hands and knees to search under the clothes racks and in the wardrobes.

'Oh, hello there again,' twittered the elderly lady to Swarnakumari at the till. 'Oh, these poor wee cats, someone has to look after them! I couldn't have any cats in me own home, my Arthur said . . . Sorry I've popped in again, but I've remembered what I'd forgotten. I still have to get Dorothy a birthday present, you see! It's her eightieth; she's as spry as anything, still lives in her own home, you know. I'll just have a little wander and let you know if I find something, dear.'

She headed for the commemorative china plates as a chic young blonde turned to Heera. 'I was in the shop yesterday, and I think I lost a diamond earring in here,' she cried. 'Did you find it?'

Heera moved away with the blonde customer at the moment when Mr Chatterjee and Banerjee entered. Javed arrived a moment later, pausing to look at the golf set near the window, momentarily delaying the desire to see the love of his life as he flexed a golf club and tested its quality.

'Nice big place,' said Banerjee.

'I do not see Mrs Wellington-Smythe,' Mr Chatterjee fretted.

'Oh, there she is!' said Banerjee obligingly.

Mr Chatterjee straightened imperceptibly.

'Your wife, over there,' said Banerjee.

As he followed Banerjee's pointing finger, Swarnakumari emerged from the Staff Area, wet and flushed from repeated handwashing. It was Eileen who had noticed the bird droppings on the sari. Swarnakumari had already spotted her husband, but the sight of the shapely young blonde on her knees had initially distracted Mr Chatterjee's attention from his wife. Like bunnies in a china shop, the blonde and the three thugs hopped by on all fours, searching under the voluminous dresses trailing to the floor from the clothes racks. Eileen stood, arms folded, lips pursed, surveying the steady destruction of order.

'Nice big shop,' repeated Banerjee. Swarnakumari approached her husband, who remained taciturn.

Javed looked past Eileen at Swarnakumari, and at Durga, his gaze moving to settle on Heera and registering shock. He reminded himself fiercely that she had changed, but not beyond recognition; she had aged, but not to his dislike; he would be Hafiz, the Persian Sufi mystic seeking beauty of the soul, not of the flesh.

'Can I help?' asked Heera.

Javed continued to stare without speaking.

'I'll leave you to it,' she shrugged, and walked away.

The elderly customer approached a shelf of hats while the young man draped in robe and veil stared at the wall. 'Ooh, isn't that china plate nice! Dorothy likes the Royal Family, she does, got the Jubilee collection, too. If it's not too difficult, luv, could you use one of your crutches and pass me that pink hat on the shelf? The one with the flower, luv, that's it. Mebbe I could give her a hat instead of the dictionary, though she loves doing the crossword, she does.'

The young man obliged, and the robe fell away, revealing a hairy wrist. Mr Chatterjee stared, while his friend Banerjee was still absorbed in a book on German baking in ten easy steps. Javed followed Heera with his eyes; Mr Chatterjee watched Javed watching Heera.

'Ooh, wool and made in Italy, too! That's posh. Dorothy will like that. Poor Edith, went to Italy, quite rude and nasty they was with her, poor thing, but I like Italians, so friendly, never heard of anyone's bottom being pinched, have you? Come to think of it, I wouldn't have minded someone whistling at me or pinching me bottom, but they never did. I knew a nice Italian family on Neville Road, can't remember the name now. You looking for something special, dear?' asked the elderly customer kindly.

Heera rushed to the defence of the silent young man. 'She's deaf-mute, poor thing.'

'Oh goodness! And crutches, too! Some people have such rotten luck, don't they? I mean, look at poor Edith. She had that cancer scare, then the heart and the pacemaker, and going so quickly, too. Oh well, that's life for you. Oh, there aren't any electric ones, if you're looking for those, dear,' said the elderly customer help-fully, spotting one of the pursuers. 'I already been in here half an hour ago, and I was looking for electric blankets, and I didn't find any, but this nice lady here said there were some new Edinburgh ones. The thing is,' she leaned over confidentially, 'my Arthur used to say—'

The thug pushed her roughly aside, tripping over the blonde making a desperate bid to find her earring. Shocked, the young man in disguise moved jerkily forward with his crutches, inadvertently knocking Heera on her thigh. She tottered and Javed rushed solicitously forward, helping her to a chair.

Eileen was silently observing the wanton destruction of a morning's work. She disappeared into the Staff Area, returning a minute later carrying the toy gun partially concealed by an apron. She stood in front of a thug, her grim face a terrifying, shadow-ridden mask as she recalled an assailant's attack on her brother in a Belfast alleyway. There could be no doubt that she would pull the trigger, and a silent agreement passed between the thug and Eileen. The three men vanished. There had been no witnesses.

'The coast is clear,' announced Eileen, satisfied.

The young man flung back his veil. 'Phew, that was close!' he exclaimed. Mr Chatterjee scrutinised his face in stunned silence.

'Wait, isn't he one of them, too?' Heera, struggling to stand, pointed at Javed.

'Who?'

'Him,' accused Heera. Everyone turned to stare at Javed in suspicion.

'Who is he?' asked the young man, bewildered.

'I don't know. I thought he was one of your chaps,' replied Heera.

'Who is this person?' scolded Swarnakumari in a

loud voice for her husband's benefit. 'Who were those three men?'

'Looking for a man,' supplied Durga.

'Aren't we all?' contributed the chic young blonde sourly on her way out. 'I was hoping I'd find the earring, but it's not here, or maybe it's just too busy on the shop floor today.'

'Yes, there were three men looking for something they could never find,' agreed Heera hastily.

The blonde left. Banerjee was gazing speculatively at Javed's maroon Pringle pullover. Javed glanced at the motley group. He had not been expecting privacy, but the presence of so many staring Asians at the shop was intimidating. Blotting them out of his vision, he whispered tenderly to Heera, 'I'm Javed.'

She looked at him in disbelief, and her eyes changed first, turning moist, brimming as her chin and lips trembled, buckling under a torrent.

'Javed?'

He was wordless.

'My Jav—?' She recovered swiftly. 'I mean . . . Javed. I didn't recognise you!'

'I would have recognised you anywhere,' he murmured. 'Still the same Heera, not a day older, you look just the same.'

Mr Chatterjee hovered within earshot.

'I found just the thing for Dorothy. She'll love this vase, but mebbe I should have got her a cardie instead. She feels the cold through her bones, poor thing, not much hair on her head now, you know, but she'll still get her hair done on Wulfstan Way every week. Wants to look her best, and why not? A woman's got a right to look her best at any age, but between you and me I

106

wouldn't bother any more if I were her. I mean, it's not as if anyone visits her, is it? It's not right when children abandon their old parents like that, is it?' quavered the elderly customer to Mr Chatterjee, who did not respond.

'You look shocked, Heera. I'm sorry I frightened you by landing up like this,' apologised Javed.

'I'd better be off. I need to make sure my sis is all right.' The young man absently surrendered the borrowed disguise to a startled Banerjee and commenced a search for the missing slipper. Eileen's tart observation that he ought to be grateful he had survived to wear the one he still owned led him to tearfully thank Heera and the others. Immediately after his departure, Banerjee asked Swarnakumari for assistance in the search for a leather jacket and a Marks & Spencer cardigan.

'Where is Mrs Wellington-Smythe?' was Mr Chatterjee's renewed query.

Heera stared up at Javed. The tumbling waters foamed and crashed into cliffs and crevices of worn memory; her heart pounded as she gazed into his warm brown eyes.

Javed could never have imagined a reunion in a charity shop amid customers whose motives would remain a mystery. There were two men smelling faintly of fish, and why was one staring at his cardigan and the other at his face?

He had cherished a burning flame, but time had flown; he was no longer the moony, besotted youth of three decades ago penning poems to her eyes and hair. Her hair was a shock. He remembered long, luxuriant black tresses in which he had buried his head and entwined his fingers, not the henna-tinged hair limp around her neck.

Guilt-ridden and ashamed of his abandonment of Heera, he had swallowed his cowardice and carried his unease to his relationship with Shabana, finally surrendering to the forces of darkness pinning him into inaction and a dull acceptance of his fate. All he needed to know was whether she echoed his own yearning and longing, and if by some wild chance she was as unhappily married as he had been. Middle age was not so ridiculous that it precluded desire and spontaneity, banishing impetuosity. Passion did not belong only to the young, who knew not the value of what they held, and the mature vine glinting in the mellow autumn rays and burdened with the sweetness of ripened grapes was no less worthy than the young fruit that awakened eager and early to greet the morning sun.

Javed was suffused with poetry amid the clothes racks and shelves of the charity shop; it had become a rosy-hued paradise in which Eileen, Durga and Swarnakumari were the houris as he and Heera strolled in gardens of scented blooms. Heera, too, had forgotten her surroundings, transported back to the tiny bedroom in her parents' old Hyderabadi haveli overlooking her neighbour's mansion. As she leaned her arms over the rail, face upturned amid the garden scents of jasmine and rajnigandha, Javed would appear on the terrace a few feet away, unfold his latest poem and bequeath it to the dying rays of the sun, persuading them to linger until he had declared his love. She had laughed at the more extravagant phrases; surely she was not to be likened to a graceful swan, her face no rising moon, her powdered arms no more perfumed than the scent of a thousand petals?

A single candle glowing on his terrace and the mandolin strings spoke eloquently of his love, and on her eighteenth birthday she had returned to her room to behold a hundred winking candles ablaze on his terrace; lit by their flame, he had placed a thumping hand on his heart as he fell to his knees.

Did such a love last, she wondered, and did the flame burn brightly only because it never lit the darkness but for an instant? Was it better to have loved and lost, but then why was he in the charity shop, was it a sign? Was there a divine design to which she should surrender, recalling the countless times she had whispered his name across the oceans?

She must look ridiculous to him in her black work trousers and shabby blouse and with her sagging bosom and chin, big hips and hairy arms and unplucked eyebrows. Her hair needed a wash and her roots showed, age showed. What was she thinking, sitting here with him in front of all these people, and she had not even offered Swarnakumari's husband and his friend a cup of tea. All this love-shove business she had harboured all these years was silly, like the disguise she had given the young man – it was time to discard it without regret. She rose with determination at the moment when five middle-aged women entered the shop.

'Guten Tag, wir wollen nicht stören, aber dürfen wir . . . ?' A woman apologised in German for the interruption, switching to halting English; they were a delegation of German charity officials on a visit to Cambridge to observe the functioning of an English hospice. After an additional round of other charity shops in the area, they had been directed to IndiaNeed. The woman was apologetic; they had arrived unannounced. Durga stepped forward, introducing herself in fluent German to their delight, and they followed eagerly as she led them through the shop to describe the various village projects in Rajasthan.

'Swarna, Eileen,' hissed Heera. 'Help me make tea for everybody.'

'Allow me,' offered Javed gallantly, following her behind the curtain into the Staff Area. They found tea-cups with matching saucers as the kettle boiled. Heera darted quick, shy glances at him – they were making tea together. The vapour from the kettle rose, warming her heart.

The German women chatted companionably while sipping their tea, and Frau Inge Hartmann proudly displayed a handbag photograph of her son, Thai daughter-in-law and their two children. Banerjee was emboldened. It was time to come out of the closet; he had a son-in-law of German origin called Heinz, he confessed shyly. The women squealed and pumped his hand vigorously.

The shop emptied as the elderly customer left clutching a hat and a vase for Dorothy, followed by the German women crying out a fond 'Wiedersehen'. Banerjee had been defeated in his quest for a Marks & Spencer cardigan; he would now commence a search for Diwali cards. Swarnakumari showed him the cards produced by the Rajasthan project; Banerjee knew instantly his wife would appreciate neither the upturned faces of the villagers on the cards nor the price, and desisted from a purchase. Her disappointment would be difficult to bear, but her wrath would be far worse.

After her initial dazed and delighted response, Heera had appeared withdrawn and tense. Javed gathered that her husband was away. He wondered if there was something amiss despite her ready acceptance of his invitation to dinner, but as he left he had a spring and bounce in his step. He felt only release and liberation. So this was what it felt like to be born again, to be given another chance. Life wasn't supposed to send in a second monsoon shower moistening the baked, cracked earth, and if it did, surely it meant that he had to dare to be different, leap where he never would have trod. If he tripped and tumbled, dived and drowned, what would it matter, for he would have heard his heart as surely as if he had kicked the camel hard on its bottom, and if the camel wouldn't move, why then he would be fanciful, think he had laughed with the crowd, confess he was sitting on an obstinate, scheming creature as wilful as a new wife, and did they know what it felt like to please a wife who wouldn't be moved, and what could he do if cajoling and pleading didn't work, and begging only made her more obdurate? What could a man do but sit there, wait patiently until the new moon had made his young wife mellow and pliant? And then the crowd would have laughed with him and understood and melted away.

He stopped impulsively at the florists; the blonde woman appeared wistful as he ordered a dozen perfect red blooms to be sent to the charity shop to Heera. He penned an Urdu couplet; the words had reappeared from thin air, were perfectly timed and rhymed. He signed dramatically on the card, an elongated 'J' distinguishing the drab white envelope. The florist was impressed by his Porsche fountain pen.

He bought a packet of roasted peanuts from the shop next door and inhaled their nutty, salty smell. The crowd had sent peanuts whizzing past his nose at the camel that day; now it was time for the fizz, to celebrate as surely as if the peanuts were the glass of champagne from which he would abstain.

The four women rearranged the shop; clothes hangers had unhooked themselves from the racks, long dresses and coats had been flung over the rails, and everything that had lain in the storm path of the three thugs overturned in callous haste. A pile of blankets lay in a crumpled heap on the floor, and Eileen mumbled under her breath as Banerjee glanced at his watch and exclaimed at the lateness of the hour. His good humour had deserted him; he would return empty-handed except for the fish, still lying in the boot of the car, that would no longer be as fresh as when first purchased. There might be trouble ahead.

Mr Chatterjee had questions queuing in his head, bursting like a thousand noisy firecrackers. He was uncertain of what he had witnessed at IndiaNeed, the shop where his wife worked every Thursday as a volunteer. Swarnakumari's sari had been wet, clinging to her back, and she had looked like a curvy Southern belle emerging from a waterfall in an Indian film, stepping out in embarrassment from behind the curtain. His curiosity had led him to wander into the Staff Area. The sight of a blond wig, handcuffs, transparent lingerie and a pair of tiny white knickers with *Punish Me* embroidered in black lying on a table in the back of the shop was unnerving. It was the note pinned to the knickers, however, that was by far the most disturbing:

MRS W-S, WHAT DO YOU WANT TO DO WITH THESE? The query had been penned in capital letters; his legal training had taught him that, without further evidence to the contrary, he could not preclude the possiblity, however unlikely, that the note had been written by his wife.

Preparing for departure, Mr Chatterjee attempted for the last time to garner information on Mrs Wellington-Smythe's whereabouts. She was out on her morning ride, supplied a brusque woman with an Irish accent. He hid his disappointment well. He had always known aristocrats were thoroughbreds.

## CHAPTER SEVEN

# Birds of a feather flock together

BOB HEARD THE gushing of the bathwater; it was a gurgling, luxurious sound. Soon he would hear a light swish, a slap of water against a yellow rubber duck before a Beethoven sonata slipped teasing and seductive under the door. Resistance was no longer a choice, and he undressed reluctantly, his clothes falling in a heap outside the bathroom door as he walked inside to join Adam.

Cleverly concealed lighting shone softly on the gleaming chrome taps, glass basins and the rails with their fluffy black and cream towels; designer toiletries were arranged next to a DVD and CD player, and the Jacuzzi bubbled invitingly. Bob paused to look at himself in the Italian mirror of Adam's marble-tiled bathroom. He felt utterly ridiculous.

That was not the way it had started with Adam. *Adam* – he had been consumed by that name, until it became as natural as a breath; without it he gasped for air, strangled by guilt and shame. As he slowly lowered himself into the slippery bathtub, Adam handed him the rubber duck. Bob dutifully squeezed until it squealed. Its red beak bobbed in the foamy lather in which Adam floated. Bob looked at the duck; unlike him, it would never drown. When Adam indicated he was ready, Bob reached for the loofah, scrubbed his back and exfoliated his feet with peppermint scrub.

'Do you think the merger will go ahead?' asked Adam lazily above the music. Bob nodded.

'Hard day, wasn't it? We'll go to Papa Donatello's for a bite, or do you prefer Thai?' Adam shrewdly never suggested an Indian curry, and in any case it gave him indigestion – and Bob guilt.

Adam went organic when he cooked; everything, from the salad to the dressing and the nuts and the wine, had to be sensitively grown. The kitchen gleamed with a silver Smeg refrigerator and French copper bain-marie and casseroles, Skeppshult cast iron pans, Yatagan knives, an Au Nain mezzaluna, Piazza ladles, Alessi kettle and Rowlett toaster. Adam tossed the salad with his home-made vinaigrette only seconds before serving. The trick, he explained, was to prepare it in French style; the dressing was poured into the bottom of the bowl and the freshly cut salad leaves arranged on top.

The glass-topped dining table for ten was immaculately laid out for two; a blue Kosta Boda candleholder swirled the light into shimmers of gold. There was seduction in the salad as Adam turned up the volume on the Bang & Olufsen speakers. Bob had found the Scandinavian influence on the house intriguing: Holmegaard and Royal Copenhagen, Ittala glassware and crystal, Poul Hennningsen lamps, Arne Jacobsen chairs and Aalvar Aalto sofa. Adam explained casually that it was Anders Pedersen who had left those behind. Who was Anders, and what had he meant to Adam? wondered Bob, jealously aflame. It could only be the act of a generous lover; he would find out more about the Great Dane, or go quietly insane.

Bob sensed he was the new concubine as he surveyed the bedroom inspired by the Far East. An enormous Chinese fan was pinned to a brocade wall-hanging behind the bed, which had a black satin coverlet embroidered with dragons; the bedside tables were carved red wooden boxes, and tasselled lamps lit the way to a delicate bamboo wardrobe. Adam had gifted Bob a pair of embroidered Chinese slippers. As his feet sank into their plush softness, he did not dare ask whose memory still lingered there. He padded obediently in the slippers, which were a size too small, obliging him to take smaller steps. He would not mince, he muttered fiercely to himself; he did not want to mince.

Searching for clues became Bob's magnificent obsession, self-revulsion oozing a boil in every pore as he scoured Adam's home for former loves and past lives. There were secrets in the engraved wooden box for Havana cigars and in the collection of Cuban music and books on New Zealand. The music in the bedroom was Brazilian, with Milton Nascimento, Maria Bethânia and Gilberto Gil given pride of place. A bold hand had scrawled *Beijos* and lipstick marks on the cover of each CD, and Bob's tortured dreams were now mocked by men with black locks and bronzed Latin skins. He was lying on Copacabana beach, suffocating in a black suit and tie, while their string-ringed bottoms shook moist sand onto his face. Adam towered over him, a caipirinha drink in one hand, the other skimming the sleek twisting hips. Bob looked up to see the Corcovado Christ figure, arms open wide. He tumbled down Rio's hill and was lifted into the statue's concrete embrace.

116

On Bob's first evening in the house Adam had prepared a celebratory meal accompanied by Bollinger champagne. Listlessly picking at the lettuce, Bob had played hockey with the porcini mushrooms and pushed the puy lentils to a corner of his plate as Pavarotti ascended a scale. Bob was nervous of the step he had taken, his boldest since proposing to Heera in Hyderabad. Submission and surrender to another man's choice of toothpaste, wine and medium roasted coffee was not easy, and, although the fact was well hidden from Adam, he never slept soundly away from his own bed. As Adam bent his head to look quizzically at him, Bob met his eyes and smiled, displaying an assurance that he did not feel.

Bob entered the room of Chinese dragons to the accompaniment of a loud squawk. It was his introduction to Noddy, Adam's yellow nape Amazon parrot. The bird had olive-green wings, a yellow patch at the back of his neck, a dark grey beak, light grey legs and orange eyes. A native of El Salvador, he had been sold to Adam for a thousand pounds by a pet shop. Noddy, who weighed four hundred grams, sat in a cage with perches, toys, an avian gym and food and water bowls. The cage was hung in the Chinese boudoir.

'You never told me you had a parrot,' said Bob wonderingly.

'Shhh . . . don't say it aloud. Noddy doesn't like being referred to as a parrot. He's human, aren't you, my love?' teased Adam.

There was another squawk and Bob stared, hypnotised, into little orange eyes on fire.

'Aren't you going to do something about the pa—

about Noddy?' protested Bob, trying to ignore the flames of distrust emanating from the bird.

'Noddy loves to watch,' replied Adam.

That night Bob sought his teddy, Charlie, but dreamed instead of a jungle filled with hanging vines and snake-like gnarled roots that he blindly pushed aside, escaping marauding humans with piercing beaks for mouths as he stumbled helplessly towards the light.

He awoke to Noddy's raucous shrieks and stared at the bird, engaging the beady, venom-filled eyes in battle. What a ridiculous name for a parrot, he thought. There was soon going to be trouble in Toyland, but for the moment Adam had arrived with shelled sunflower seeds, fresh sprouts and fruit for Noddy, who attacked his breakfast with relish. Bob wondered whether both the seeds and fruit were organic.

'Stay absolutely still! Don't move!' commanded Adam. It took a moment for Bob to realise Adam was talking to *him*. Adam opened the cage. 'Step up, spit spot!' he ordered, and Bob froze. Noddy hopped onto Adam's wrist, attempting to jump onto his shoulder. Adam coaxed the parrot down onto his wrist again and stared firmly into his eyes. Bob relived the image of a head teacher thundering to a thin boy in shorts.

'Good boy, Noddy,' said Adam approvingly and scratched the bird's head as it obeyed. 'Now get on the stick!' Noddy hopped on. 'Sing, my little songbird!'

As Bob watched in amazement, Noddy cocked his head adoringly and trilled in a man's voice, 'You are the wind beneath my wings'.

'You are an angel.' Adam rewarded him with another head scratch, and gently nudged him towards the cage.

118

'Got to go now, my little singing nun, or I'll be late for work.'

Noddy hopped in, as he sang in drunken-girls-night-out-karaoke-style, 'I will survive'. Adam peered into the cage and pleaded, 'Please understand, my featherbunch!' Noddy sang, 'Leave right now', and was silent.

Matters escalated that evening. Bob had been shopping, and as he unlocked the front door he heard a woman's voice coming from the direction of Adam's bedroom. 'Adam, darling, not now. Ooh, that tickles!' she said huskily. Black jealous rage overtook Bob as he dropped the carrier bags, hurried upstairs and burst, incandescent, into the bedroom to find Adam sitting calmly on the bed while Noddy was strutting on the floor. As soon as Noddy saw Bob, he made a guttural sound; his tail feathers flared and his pupils dilated menacingly.

'Stay!' said Adam firmly, his palm turned upwards.

Noddy stared at Bob, then suddenly flew at Adam and bit him hard on his arm. Bob stared helplessly at the sudden patch of blood forming on Adam's shirt.

'Bob, leave the room for a mo and shut the door, will you?' requested Adam.

Bob overheard Adam's murmured endearments to Noddy while he sat on the Aalvar Aalto sofa. Adam emerged calmly from the room half an hour later; he had managed to stem the blood and tie a clumsy bandage on the arm.

As they drove together to work on the A14 in Adam's car the next morning, it began to rain. Bob looked out on the dismal flat landscape near Huntingdon that he had passed every day for years, feeling he would be consumed by flatness his entire life – until he had met Adam, that is – but he realised Adam had tweaked the truth when he said he was not in a relationship. There were three of them now: two men and a parrot. A very dangerous, jealous parrot.

Adam patiently explained: the yellow nape Amazon bird was one of the best talkers in the bird world; it could learn tricks as early as four months. It could sing opera, whistle, and memorise whole songs, imitate the young and old, male and female, rollerskate, go down on a slide, roll over. It loved an audience. When it was around five years old – coincidentally, Noddy's age – the species became aggressive, especially in the breeding season. Noddy saw Adam as his mate, and would seriously harm anyone who was a threat, not afraid to teach its own carer a bitter lesson to boot. So, thought Bob, other men and women showed off tattoos, but Adam had love bites from an Amazonion parrot. All this was very entertaining and endearing, but what was he, Bob, supposed to do? Accept defeat and leave the parrot crowing in victory, squawking its little triumphs? Make way for Noddy?

The mystery of Anders was one no longer. Noddy had apparently flown at the Danish lover in bird wrath, and nearly gouged out an eye. Anders left in a hurry and flurry, but not before committing a wilful, cruel act, shuddered Adam, eyes turning moist at the memory. While Adam was in the shower, Anders had written a note in Danish beginning with the words *Øje for øje, An eye for an eye*, let Noddy out of the cage and escaped himself, without saying goodbye or why. When Adam emerged, fragrant from emollient and sensitive scalp detangling lotion, he found Noddy flying in shock around the house, and about to insert his beak into a wall socket. Noddy could have died, shuddered Adam. He could have bitten house wires, been poisoned from chewing house plants, hammered the ceiling while searching for the sky.

Adam advised Bob to be patient and read *The Companion Parrot Handbook* on parrot handling. *The Guide to a Well-Behaved Parrot* by Athan and Earl-Bridges was another useful reference for an understanding of the wonderful world of parrots. He should remember the cardinal rule: he was never *ever* to enter the room again when Noddy was out of the cage.

Adam took Bob to London the next day; it was a treat to obliterate the trauma of the introduction to Noddy. Bob felt like an East Anglian bumpkin as he was led through Harrods and Selfridges and New Bond Street, and accompanied Adam into bespoke tailor shops on Jermyn Street. Afterwards, they dined in a gentlemen's club behind the Ritz. Bob was bewildered. Adam was clearly a man of wealth, so why had he chosen to work in an architect's firm and live in the Shelfords?

They walked together into the lights of Soho and Madame JoJo's, and ambled arm-in-arm to their hotel on Shaftesbury Avenue in the early hours of Sunday. Returning to King's Cross Station that evening, they made their way to Platform Nine for the Cambridge train which, to their surprise, was nearly full. Adam spotted the last two empty seats and as they sat down Bob realised he was caught in the midst of a Cambridge group of Women Working for the World members – a few of whom he recognised as Heera's acquaintances. Bob wanted to flee, Adam wanted to stay, the train doors slammed shut, and they were on their way. The numerous tunnels darkening the carriages as the train sped toward Stevenage and the arrival of the refreshments trolley initially shielded Bob from discovery. It was in the vicinity of Hitchin Station that Janet Hewitt noticed Bob.

'Bob?' she asked tentatively, leaning over her neighbour. He straightened uncomfortably; there was no way out as the other women began to nod and smile. The questions fell thick and fast. Why had Heera not joined them on their outing to the Bramah Museum of Tea and Coffee? They would not forgive her for staying away, and could he tell Heera to call? She was to arrange the next guest speaker. As Bob searched for a response, Adam chose the moment to publicly cement their relationship. He leaned against Bob and dropped a casual arm over his shoulder, drawing him close.

Mrs Chakraborti's eloquent fish-shaped eyes grew even fishier; there was silence as the group turned away from the unmistakable intimacy on display, commencing an animated discussion of English teapots. Adam continued to rest his hand on Bob's thigh or arm as he chatted. Leaving the exit at Cambridge Station, Mrs Chakraborti hissed, eyes flashing, 'Shame on you, Bob. Shame on you!' She disappeared into the crowd and Adam threw back his head and laughed.

They had their first argument as they drove out of the station car park.

'How could you?' spluttered Bob.

'What?' countered Adam coolly.

'You know what I mean! In front of those women . . .'

'You'd better get used to it, Bob. Either you're with me, or you ain't. There's no two ways about it, you know,' said Adam calmly, as they drove over the bridge, past Homerton College and onto Hills Road.

'This is all too new. It's going to take some time. You're pushing it,' snapped Bob.

'It was those women who got to you, right? Because they know your wife. You wouldn't have minded if they'd been strangers on a train to Newcastle, or if we were cavorting in Ibiza.'

'It's not just that. I'm not comfortable yet. I don't know whether I ever will be. The physical stuff is not something to put on display. I didn't even do it with . . .' Bob paused.

'With your wife? Poor boring Bob,' mocked Adam. 'It's all right when there isn't anyone looking, is that it? You do like your dark closet an awful lot, don't you? Are you sure you've come out of it?'

'There's no need for sarcasm. I said I wasn't comfortable, so just drop it, will you? Can't you see I have a lot of issues to deal with, inside me, with the people who know me, who know me together with my wife? Do you know how difficult it is for me not to think about her at all? That woman just used the word "shame". Do you know what that means? Yes, I am feeling shame. I'm not ashamed, but I do feel shame. Does that make any sense to you at all? You don't know, do you, what it feels like to be split in two, down into your very guts, wanting to be true to what you feel inside but not knowing exactly what or why that is. I like you, Adam. I like being with you a lot, you know that, but there are big issues here. You've got to understand, be supportive, give me time.'

Bob glanced at the other man's hard profile as they drove round the Addenbrooke's roundabout. 'You really don't understand, do you?' he continued quietly. 'I can't figure you out. Who are you, Adam? You're suave and sexy. Why are you with a miserable git like me? I've got to know.'

'Can it wait until we get home? We're almost there. Let's do this properly. And I've got to meet Noddy first, sorry. It's very important to interact with these birds on a daily basis. They misbehave so easily if one doesn't. So can we talk afterwards?'

Bob waited impatiently on the Aalvar Aalto sofa for Adam. The image of the fiery ball of a woman spitting those words at him was indelible; he deserved every word, he thought. It was punishment for following his inner self; would he now never cease to be haunted by what he had done? The temple of Apollo at Delphi carried an inscription: *Gnothi seauton – Know thyself.* The familiar feelings of guilt took control, emotions that he tried desperately to erase, and when Adam emerged from his chat with Noddy it was to discover Bob holding his teddy, Charlie, fast asleep.

By the next weekend, Bob had begun to unravel the mystery surrounding Adam. The bell rang insistently, and Bob opened the door to find a solemn little girl and boy on the doorstep, as a woman moved forward. She was slim and blonde. 'You must be Bob. I've heard so much about you. All good things,' she smiled. 'I'm Saara, and I've come to drop off the children.' Before Bob could respond, she looked at her watch and jumped into her car and sped away, shouting instructions to the children. They looked at him without interest, moving past him into the home with an easy familiarity.

'Where's Daddy?' asked the girl.

'Where's Noddy?' asked the boy.

As Adam explained later to Bob, he had two children, and the blonde Finnish woman was Saara. They were not divorced, only separated. Under Bob's watchful gaze, Adam changed. Gone was the cool, sophisticated exterior; stripped, he was a father.

He asked Bob to join them in the park at Cherry Hinton overlooked by a row of houses. They walked past the ducks onto an open patch of green and Adam unpacked a large duffel bag. Bob thought his lungs would burst as he raced after the ball and tossed and caught the frisbee. Claire remained mutinous and refused to look at Bob, rejecting his offer of a sweet.

It all made sense. Saara and the children lived in Cambridge, and that was why Adam hadn't moved away. He needed to see his children, and still referred to Saara as his 'wife'. It was as simple as that. Bob watched him as he sprinted after Mark, hoisting him in the air, pummelling him until he squealed in delight, pushing the swings and pumping the see-saw, his arms ready to catch the little boy as he slid down the slide.

That night Bob lay on his bed staring at the ceiling, ignoring the parrot although Noddy did his best to engage him in battle. Adam with his hands full of flour, pounding the pizza dough, bathtime and the bedtime story . . . who was Adam?

Adam had explained later. He had wanted to be the perfect father to his children. His own father had died when he was two, and he had grown up with an indifferent stepfather. Bob thought he understood now why Adam had sought him out, and it was not flattering. He didn't want to be reassuring, responsible or reliable; he wanted angels to sing of passion, feel Adam's desire for him burn his flesh and soul. The years suddenly yawned ahead. Was he being groomed as a grandfather to Adam's children, to read a bedtime story every other weekend and tackle their future teenage tantrums?

He had thought he knew Adam and his essence when they first met; now he realised he didn't know him at all. Was he the ogre in the tower or the angel in the skies? Adam had become more and not less, and Bob less and not more than when they first met. Why did it feel as if Adam was the rising sun, and he the setting orb?

That night, the telephone woke Bob and Adam instantly. As Adam dressed hurriedly in the dim light, he explained. Saara was being taken to hospital with terrible pains. It was appendicitis. Could Bob take charge, look after the children while he was gone? Bob observed with petty satisfaction that Adam had omitted to mention Noddy.

It was three in the morning, and Bob wandered into the kitchen, pouring a large whisky before entering the room where the children lay sleeping. He looked down at Claire, at her rumpled sleeve, the brown hair framing her face, her drooping lips.

Bob was swept by a surfer's wave on a sandspun beach as he bent over the child. His shoulders hunched, preparing for an engulfing torrent as he stood, a timid boy of thirteen in a white shirt and grey school shorts while his father paced angrily. His mother had averted her face as his father's cane came crashing down on his knuckles, her mousy hair undone. His stern father had withdrawn into a dark silence and his classmate Peter now avoided his gaze under the watchful eye of the teacher.

As he turned away from the faces of Adam's sleeping children, the first sob contorted his stooping frame; his tears pitied the bewildered schoolboy beaten until he bled into denial of realms he could not fathom, the mother who had long passed into embarrassed, early oblivion and a father whose deathbed remained unflinching tombstone.

He fled to Adam's bedroom in anguished rage at his own foolish arrogance, at the years of confusion, for the children he would now never have, that *she* would never have. The tears welled and swelled, spilling into the bathtub until the duck began to bob merrily, flowing over the tub's sides onto the dark marbled floor. The flood seeped under the door into the rest of the house, gushing over the designer furniture and the crystal, dousing the light of the Swedish candles, quelling the rhapsody until there was only hollow silence in the darkness.

He held his head between his hands; a quiet, dull man perched on the edge of a satin-covered bed next to a shabby one-eyed teddy, watched balefully by a parrot. Perhaps he could only be the one or the other, black or white, and the shades of grey could never be his. He envied Adam his several worlds. He himself was solid and stolid, boorish and bookish. He was no Latin lover in the Chinese boudoir, and he hated tasselled slippers, organic broccoli and whitening toothpaste.

Noddy squawked warningly as Bob continued to weep. He hopped down from his perch and his tail flared. The low growl came again. Bob had forgotten about Noddy. He looked at the bird, approaching slowly, rapidly gulping his whisky.

'Now listen, you little birdbrain!' His steely voice startled him as well as the parrot, which emitted a loud screech of protest. Bob stood his ground. He stared eyeball to eyeball with Noddy. Volcanoes erupted from the parrot's eyes; molten lava of hate spilled over the slopes of his wings as he flew in anger at the bars of the cage.

'Shut up, bird. You'll wake everyone. Do you want to do that? I think not. Yes, bird, that's what you are, only a silly old bird. Did you hear what I said? Old bird. Old bird,' repeated Bob.

The whisky was taking effect. Bob jumped shakily, clumsily, onto the bed to peer into the cage. He executed a wobbly jig. 'Look, I've got a bird's-eye view up here! "Fly robin, fly, up, up, to the sky",' he sang tunelessly, squashing the embroidered satin cushions without alarm. The bird bristled, shooting fire through the cage.

'You think you're a singing nun in Salzburg, but you are nothing but a mean green bunch of feathers and you'll end up on an Ascot hat, without the sound of music,' warned Bob. 'There's no old age pension for birds, you know. Tough mean parrots don't even get eaten; they just get tossed into the bin along with the . . . er . . . potato peel.' Bob was inspired, viewing his glass through pleasantly blurred edges and his life with clarity. 'And, you little birdie dum dum num num, however much you may want Adam, he's not yours. He's *not* yours. He's not mine, either, I can see that now, but he's certainly not yours, so just eat up your sunflower seeds like a good bird. You are not *his* bird. You are only a *bird*. B-I-R-D.'

Noddy glared balefully but made no sound as he paced his cage.

'Shall I tell you something else? You have a really silly name. "Noddy". Ha! Noddy's not only the dumbest character in Toyland, he sings terribly out of key.' Bob took another large sip. 'I'm surprised you answer to it. No self-respecting yellow nape Amazon parrot from El Salvador would ever accept "Noddy". Where's your Latin machismo and pride? Speedy Gonzales. Guantanamera. "Yo soy un hombre sincero" and all that. Olé! Arriba! Paella! Marbella! That's all the Spanish I know, sorry. I'm English. Not supposed to speak any foreign languages. And I'm in foreign country at the moment. Hang on, there's a Spanish phrase book somewhere!' Bob lurched towards a bookcase and found an *AA Essential Spanish for Kids*.

'Ah, here it is. Now let's see. Yes. *Tengo novio*. Now that's a useful phrase. That means I have a boyfriend. *Vete a la porra!* I'm sure you know what that means: Sod off! *Buen viaje!* Have a good trip! So now you've heard it loud and clear in your own language, I'd suggest you shape up – spit spot – or ship out. If you're good, I'll put in a word for you to stay, El Salvio. If not, well, I just might want to find out what it's like to kill a bird with a stone. It would be a shame, wouldn't it, if someone left your cage unlocked for the second time? Pure accident, but this time you would be alone, all alone in this beautiful house. What could happen next? Ooh, I fear for you! You might swallow the poisonous sap from the dieffenbachia growing in the patio, or your beak could get stuck inside a socket and this time you would get electrocuted, but never mind, you'd still have the best parrot perm and stringy bottom this side of Latin America.'

Bob was exhausted. He felt an urge to talk to Heera. He reached for the telephone and passed out. The next morning, Adam returned home. He rushed to Noddy's cage.

'Hello, my love, my Noddy. Sorry I wasn't there last night.'

Noddy turned his back on Adam.

'I said I'm sorry. Noddy? Darling? Listen, let me get you some breakfast. Some fresh fruit and sunflower seed, how does that sound?'

The parrot remained silent.

'Say something, Noddy darling. You know I couldn't help it, I just had to go, but I did come home as quickly as I could. Saara was ill, and you know these things can happen.'

'El Salvio! El Salvio!' shrieked the parrot.

'I know I should've been there for you, darling, but do understand. I'll buy you a new perch, would that be nice? And I'll let you out of the cage for a whole hour tomorrow, how about that? I'll come home early if I can.'

'El Salvio! El Salvio!'

It took two days for Adam to understand. His parrot's new name was El Salvio. El Salvio had started singing 'La Bamba'. In an English accent.

# CHAPTER EIGHT

# Faint heart never won fair lady

AT THE MOMENT when the young man had been racing down Mill Road, hurtling into Swarnakumari's ample, bending body and slipping into IndiaNeed, a man in his mid-thirties embarked on a leisurely walk from the College Backs towards Mill Road. Dressed in brown chinos, a cream crew-necked pullover and a beige overcoat, he strode, a man who loved the outdoors, across Coe Fen. He was American, and his name was Roman Tempest.

Looking back twenty-four hours later on his casual expedition to Mill Road that morning, Roman was reminded of Horace Walpole. Reading the tales of *The Three Princes of Serendip*, Walpole had deduced that an accidental discovery by sagacity of things one did not seek was 'serendipity'. Serendipity as happy chance, accidental good fortune and wordless wisdom, then, had charted Roman's course when he might otherwise have visited the Sedgwick Museum and greeted the reconstructed iguanodon skeleton or an ichthyosaur or two. Perhaps it was Teresa who had impelled his steps away towards Mill Road.

Teresa was a helpful English colleague who blushed

rapidly, embarrassment staining her pale throat and cheeks. He imagined the nervous redness spreading through her until she was a blazing tomato, and had stared at her skin in amazement as the flush spread down her neck, a glance she had coyly misinterpreted. She unbuttoned her blouse further, retained a fluttering hand in the region and punctuated her conversation with high-pitched giggles. Actively seeking his company, she alternated between Pouty Pop Queen and Ice Maiden, a combination he found disconcerting while discussing Steven Greenblatt and the New Historicism of American literary theory. Once he had idly formed an image of her as Britney Spears in academic garb, it was far too entertaining to banish.

Early that morning he had explored a path beside the river with a view to the back of the Wren Library and of the Gothic New Court of St John's College, wondering if Wordsworth had wandered lonely there as an undergraduate at St John's, moody in the mellow autumnal moment. Roman then made a ritual visit to the Peterhouse memorial to Rev. Godfrey Washington bearing the Washington coat-of-arms, the precursor to the Stars and Stripes flag. He had returned to the river, and as he stopped to trace the veins of a russet leaf on the Fen path before continuing on his way, verse flooded his being. He, like Whitman, was free and healthy and light-hearted on the open road; the long brown path beckoned and he would choose where he would go. A man in an oilskin coat and wellingtons nodded politely at Roman as he walked by with his poodle on a leash. The poodle paused, and the man paused to remove a little plastic bag from his coat, and soon they were on their way again.

Roman halted to admire the majestic horse chestnut trees on Trumpington Road and the autumn foliage of the Botanic Garden before continuing up Bateman Street and into Station Road, turning left onto Devonshire Road. Teresa's directions to Mill Road had been hurried and not as the crow flew; he suspected that she had deliberately chosen a long and winding route, hoping to offer herself at an opportune moment in the role of tour guide. A student distracted her attention as they had talked outside the Porter's Lodge, and Roman had slipped away in relief.

He stood at the corner where Devonshire Road met Mill Road at the bridge. Teresa had informed him that Mill Road was 'an exemplification of the ancient quarrels between the townspeople and the University' that led to the coinage of the phrase 'town and gown'. The 'town' was still smarting from the insults of Henry III in 1231, when he forbade it to exact high rents from scholars, and at the same time gave the University powers to license the alehouses and supervise the markets, fairs, weights and measures. It was not until the Act of Parliament in 1856 that old disputes were settled, she had added knowledgeably.

Roman entered Mill Road through the tumbling October leaves, recalling Thoreau's autumnal sun and autumn gale. Roman experienced life through poetry, and effortlessly memorised large passages for every occasion. It impressed the students, was useful to tease women like Teresa, but he nevertheless genuinely loved great poetry, chiefly as he was unable to write any of his own.

At the moment when Roman Tempest set foot on Mill

Road, Durga was checking the new deliveries of puzzles. If the cover stated 250 pieces, but a piece was missing, the volunteers were not permitted to proceed with a sale; typically, a missing piece was usually the motive behind the generous donation to the charity. Fortunately, 'Sir Puzzle' offered to take away the incomplete puzzles and still pay full price.

A tall, hawk-nosed man in a grey woollen overcoat and felt hat entered, followed by a short middle-aged man. The tall man asked to see the collection of watches, and as Eileen unlocked the shelf and brought out the tray, he lifted his arm to reveal four watches on his right wrist; none showed the correct time. He scowled and pointed to two with broken dials, strapped them around his left wrist, paid and departed.

Swarnakumari was staring through the curtain at the short man inspecting the lingerie. 'Durga, go and help him. Your Uncle would not like it if I do such things.'

Pretending to check the window display, Durga strolled out to the front of the shop. The bespectacled man in his sixties resembled her neighbour Mr Beescroft, who tapped his cap every time they met with their rubbish at the communal black bins. The man rummaged through the undergarments and thrust his hands inside a blue brassière, brushing it against his chest before returning it to its original place. As Durga approached, he hastily chose a red brassière instead, producing a brown paper parcel he was carrying to bundle his purchase under his arm. As he left, a third customer emerged from behind the rack of nightgowns. 'Don't worry, luv, he's harmless. He goes to every charity shop down this road and does the same thing,' he bubbled.

'Your Uncle would not let me come here if he saw what that dirty man did, *hanh*' was Swarnakumari's comment afterwards.

'*Arre*, c'mon on, Swarna, tell the truth. You complain loudly, but actually you enjoy this khichdi pot of life bubbling in here, don't you?' teased Heera.

The florist's assistant crossed the road with Javed's bouquet; he was a freckled lad miscast as the happy bearer of floral tidings. As he darted in front of a speeding car, Javed's card fluttered away into the traffic. The assistant stood outside IndiaNeed with his flowers, intent on his mobile, his fingers working furiously. Roman Tempest was standing outside the shop, peering at the window display. The lad dropped the bouquet and Roman dived, catching it neatly, a baseball in his waiting glove.

'You nearly lost that bunch. Hold on tight, man!' warned Roman.

'Thanks, mate,' replied the lad without looking up. He jerked his thumb towards the shop. 'Got to do this delivery and me girlfriend's waiting down the road. She's going to kill me – says she won't be waiting longer than five minutes. Got to send her a message now. Can you help, mate? Just go in with the flowers, say they're from the Sunflowers Florists down the road, all right? She's going to kill me. Gotta run. Cheers, mate!' He sped away.

Roman entered the shop with the flowers. He paused, searching for a note from the florists among the blooms. As he slowly approached the counter, he saw her, slim in a cream turtleneck and denim jeans, her black hair untidily bunched around her shoulders, noticed the droop of her neck, the curve of generous lips as she mocked and teased a large Indian lady dressed in a sari. He paused again, considered for a brief, mad moment saying the flowers were from him, but was intercepted by a grey-haired woman.

'Sunflowers Florists delivery from across the road,' he revealed hastily.

'Who are they for? There's no card,' she accused as she peered into the bouquet of a dozen red roses. He shrugged apologetically.

'They couldn't be for me. They must be for one of them.' The stern woman carried the bouquet to the counter. He waited uncertainly.

The large woman in the sari gushed, 'Let me see! Let me see! Lovely roses! For whom?' Her curious eyes devoured the flowers. 'For whom?' she repeated. Not for a moment did she entertain the thought that she might be the lucky recipient. Mr Chatterjee was not given to frivolous gestures.

'If you think they could be yours, take them, there's no card,' suggested the grey-haired woman.

Another Asian woman looked at the blooms and declared, 'Must be for you, Durga.'

Durga. He memorised the name, sliding over its unfamiliar edges.

The large woman looked at her, avid eyes snapping. 'Who is this admirer of yours, *hanh*, Durga?' She wagged a finger. 'Trying to keep secrets from us, *na*?'

'They can't be for me, either. No one sends a rose to a cactus,' replied Durga. Her voice was attractive and low. He hated shrill voices. Kathy's had become very shrill in the end. Cactus. Had she just said *'cactus'*?

'Then for whom are these flowers? Durga says they

136

can't be for her, Swarna says they can't be for her, you say they can't be for you and I'm saying they can't be for me,' wondered Heera, turning to Eileen.

'Blimey, that's women for you. If you don't send 'em flowers, they complain. If you send 'em flowers, they complain. What's a man to do? What's all the fuss about? Share 'em three apiece and get on with it,' advised the customer who had previously been buried in the rack of nightgowns but had since moved on to the inspection of old record albums. He winked at Roman.

'Phone the florist,' suggested Eileen. 'That's the logical thing to do.'

Roman continued to stare at Durga. Instant attraction didn't happen in real life, it was the stuff of the chick films Kathy had dragged him to watch with a popcorn bag in one hand and a large Coke in the other. He couldn't remember the last time he had felt silly and weak at the sight of a woman, flames leaping, sending incoherent thoughts and snatches of poetry to his head. San Francisco, Kathy and the Arizona retreat were a fading drumbeat; he was mesmerised by the curve of a stranger's lips.

Heera returned to the group, embarrassed.

'Well?' said Eileen.

'They're for *me*. They're from Javed,' acknowledged Heera shyly. She stood holding the bouquet, lost in the perfection of the flowers, sniffing their fragrance and gently caressing the petals. With brimming eyes she hugged the blooms to her face, returning to breathe deep of their scent.

'Flowers from Javed?' There was a world of inflection in Swarnakumari's voice. A flame once extinguished was best forgotten, she brooded. Even if Javed had been Heera's young love, it was a long time ago. Her parents should have kept a strict watch, and then it would not have happened at all. Now that Heera was happily married to Bob, after saying, 'Hello, how are you?' there should be nothing more for her to say to another man who was not a blood relative, she decided, convinced Mr Chatterjee would not approve, either.

He had not spoken during his visit to the shop other than to inquire after Mrs Wellington-Smythe, she realised with a jolt. She did not understand why he had arrived there unannounced; he had appeared preoccupied and tense, giving her no opportunity to properly introduce her shop colleagues.

In truth, Mr Chatterjee's face as he wandered through IndiaNeed had registered not only incomprehension but also the unexpected entry into a brave new world that had made him feel irrelevant, as if the life he had lived had been revealed as no life at all.

'Heera, when you've finished, could you take a look at those old cigar boxes I found?' called Eileen.

Heera accompanied her behind the curtain, carefully holding the bouquet, as two burly men entered the shop, dragging a large, heavy object. 'Afternoon, got a delivery. Could you sign for it?' said the taller of the two, drumming his thigh impatiently. Swarnakumari was curious; the shop rarely took delivery of large items. 'Dunno. Just did what I were told. Cheers,' drawled the man on his way out in reply to her question.

As Roman watched, the group of women slowly encircled the object abandoned in the middle of the shop. Durga stood a few feet away and he stared at her, at her dark hair and eyes; she was a stranger who felt a mere breath away. He paused, overcome by self-irony; it was too soon after Kathy. He was already running from Teresa, and he should continue to be cautious and prudent, but once he had seen Durga, delicate as the leaf he had examined earlier, he sensed the image of her would be forever his to own and pin on the wing of a Petrarchan sonnet.

It had been different with Kathy. Kathy was not to blame, nor he; perhaps they would blame it on San Francisco. If they'd never moved to the Bay Area from the New England small town, why would he be here, in wind-swept Cambridge on a chill autumn day? It had been a Faustian bargain, unlike any at Macy's. A rueful smile chased his face, as he remembered his enthusiastic endorsement of Herb Caen's Baghdad by the Bay in the early days. No longer would he gaze up for the moon and settle for those towering confections of steel, enough of the cable cars and fire sirens, the plaintive foghorns and the Pyramid. No more eclectic bookstore, rollerblading in Golden Gate Park, mingling in the crowds on Labor Day weekend on the ferry to Angel Island or the Halloween party in the Castro, the sweating bearded Cinderellas and Tinkerbells at the Moby Dick or Twin Peaks, the lighting of the Christmas tree at Union Square. No more *Nutcracker* at the Opera House or envious amble past Neiman's and Saks, poetry at St Paul and Peter's Church, jazz in North Beach. No more cherry-tree blossoms in the Japanese Tea Garden; no longer would he allow himself to think of the Wharf and chowder and sourdough bread, Red's Java diner, nor the Anchor Steam beer straight from the source and the Farmer's Market at the Ferry Building. Nevermore did he want to read another *Chronicle* arts critique, nor a restaurant review, nevermore scurry for seductions by wine and books and food and the conversations of strangers.

Caught in the dance, they had failed to see they had toppled off the floor. When she argued for a new French-designed pre-heated toilet seat and ordered pre-wrapped counter pick-up presents for his friends, he should have seen that together they had already staled their infinite variety. He had wanted to read, write, teach, recite poetry, and Kathy, now as slim and indispensable to her interiors firm as dental floss to her teeth, hair burning brightly from lunch, talked with animation only of her therapist and wax, both Brazilian.

Her hysteria was timed to December, so inconvenient in the run-up to Christmas that, when she bravely continued to arrive at work, her employer increased her benefits package in gratitude. Roman obligingly timed his own less dramatic breakdown to the end of the semester, moving to a Buddhist retreat in Arizona.

'I go to the back of the shop only for two minutes and there is a problem already. Swarna, you should at least have asked what these men were delivering! What is this big thing lying here right in the middle?' asked Heera in exasperation as she poked at the object's edges. She tugged a lever, and with a loud groan it opened like an accordion and settled amicably with four spindly legs folding out underneath.

'Looks to me like a bed,' volunteered the customer, peering over an album of Diana and the Supremes. 'You know, one of those collapsible ones.'

'But what's this on the mattress? Some fool's written in ink, *Pamela and John forever*,' cried Heera, vexed.

'What are you going to do with it? It doesn't look new at all,' scoffed Swarnakumari.

'No, it doesn't. Pamela and John have spent forever on foam. And it will collapse if you sit on it,' warned Durga. 'It *is* a collapsible bed, though,' she added reasonably.

'Those are the same two names as on the sorting table,' said Eileen.

'That's so naughty,' admonished the customer, uneducated on either plot or characters, but keen to appear enlightened.

'Naughty'. The word smacked of the nursery and the smack, thought Roman. He would use it one of these days; shuffle from one foot to another, a leg crossed over the other, and with a pained expression on his face and clasped hands he would concede, confess, 'I'm naughty,' and await his punishment. He was also waiting for an opportunity to add 'Oops' to his vocabulary. After a year out in the West where men were wild, and the saguaros grew tall and strong, where the giant cactus lived for two hundred and fifty years and grew to seventy feet, where time and space rolled out into the desert, there had been no opportunity to say 'Oops'. Now he was ready. He would learn about civility and tea, crumpets and horses, rain and tweed, the grumble and apple crumble, ale and Britannia, conservatories and the colour magnolia, country rambles and brambles.

As Durga turned, her dark brown eyes met warm hazel eyes. 'What's so funny?' she demanded.

'It's unreal. I'd heard about English charity shops and sweet old ladies, but this place is weird,' Roman spluttered.

She looked at his springy dark hair, fresh, open face and rangy frame, at his mouth and tanned skin. Her smile widened and deepened, somersaulting over the collapsible bed, tumbling in the mattress, bouncing high on its springs and vaulting gracefully back.

'I'm Roman Tempest,' he said, offering a hand.

'Then I must be Indian Storm,' she replied, feeling the firm warmth of his grasp spreading into her own. 'Why Roman?'

'My parents loved *Roman Holiday*. Isn't it a cool name?'

'Yes. But it's also cheesy – Mills and Boonish. Like a tall, dark, handsome stranger in a romantic novel.'

'I *am* a tall, dark handsome stranger,' he replied. 'And romantic.'

'I'm Durga,' she said.

'I'm Visiting Faculty, teaching an MPhil course in American Literature. Who are you?'

'I'm a Townie now, but I did an MPhil in Modern Society and Global Transformation, Social and Political Sciences. Starting a researcher's job in television in London in a fortnight,' she answered.

'Aren't you the florist?' interrupted Eileen suspiciously.

'I'm Hermes at your service, madam. Messenger of Zeus. Or rather, of Sunflowers Florists, Mill Road. Behold my invisible cap, winged boots and caduceus. It's a long story,' he continued, but it was too late. Eileen shook her head dolefully and marched away.

Turning to Durga, he chuckled gleefully, 'She thinks I'm nuts, doesn't she?'

'She thinks everyone is nuts,' replied Durga. 'What is a caduceus?'

142

'The rod that Hermes carried, entwined by two serpents. He received it as a gift from Zeus when he invented the lyre. He used the shell of a tortoise for the lyre, by the way.'

'Now *I* think you're nuts,' she confessed.

'But nice? Please say I'm nice. You British love the word "nice", don't you? It covers everything, just like a tablecloth, or should I say "sari"? Hey, do you think I'm "interesting", too? Because that's not good,' he said, reprovingly. "Interesting" is dangerous,' he concluded.

'Are you like this all the time?' she asked.

'I wasn't before. Now I know it's as important as carrying a dozen red roses.'

She laughed, and he felt he had always known the sound.

'I get the feeling folks around here think Americans are brash and pushy, but I'm acting on impulse – I don't usually do this – could I take you out to dinner and tell you all about the florist? It's a riveting story, I promise, and will last until dessert,' he pleaded.

She was silent. Sensing her hesitation, he retreated, 'Okay, got the message. Step back, Roman, step well back. Naughty, naughty boy. That was too brash, too pushy. I'll back off before I do something stupid. I've already been stupid, haven't I, but I've also been nice, so there is something you could do for me, now that I'm here. Could you direct me to an old bookshop that's supposed to be on this road somewhere?'

'You must mean Browne's,' she said, trying to suppress her smile. 'Turn left when you come out. It's a few doors down, you can't miss it.'

He was forced to move closer to her, as Swarnaku-mari brushed past, intent on fetching a measuring tape for the bed. 'Do you have a picture of a desert, or a cactus?'

'In here?' she asked incredulously.

'Well, why not? If you can have a collapsible bed, why not a cactus? Sounds reasonable to me.'

'Why don't you just go to a garden centre and buy a real one?'

'The sensible solution. Of course!' He smacked his forehead in a mocking gesture. 'Why didn't I think of that? Sure, I can do that, but I want a picture. Is that too much to ask? Can't I have a look, no, what's the right word, can't I take a "little peek" among these cups and saucers, anyway? How about a guided tour of Buckingham Palace?'

Pausing in front of the men's winter coats, he confided, 'Have you ever felt so lonely for what you think you might lose that you think you need something tangible to remind you of it?'

'You mean like crutches?' she asked.

'Crutches?' He looked startled before recovering. 'Never thought of it that way, but if you desperately want to talk about crutches, then I guess I need them, or maybe I just think I do. I'm from the East Coast. A smalltown boy who singed his soul in the big city, born again. Sounds very Jehovah's Witness, doesn't it? How interesting! My life was deadlines and dates and publishing papers. I was Icarus, flew too close. I also lost Kathy. We went to the School Prom together, that's how long I've been with her. She told me in the end that I made her unhappy every single day, and I thought all I was doing was loving her. That was the shock that shook the pear tree. Something was very wrong with my life, and I had to take it apart. I spent a year in a Tibetan Buddhist retreat in Arizona, and I found silence and space. Sounds very New Age-ish, and it was only a year, but it *has* changed my life. Anyway, back to Cambridge. It's driving me crazy. I want a desert outside. I need those crutches – a picture, something, anything that helps me meditate on the colours of the desert. Do you understand?'

'Yes, I think I do, but I'm not sure I can help. I don't think you will find anything in here.'

They wandered through the clothes racks, unconsciously distancing themselves from the others.

'A picture of an *Echinomastus erectocentrus var. erectocentrus* would do just fine,' he said humbly, enjoying the bizarre intimacy of standing close to her next to a shelf of leather handbags while the rest were discussing the bed resting like a sleepy pregnant elephant in the centre of the shop.

'That sounds obscene. Is it?'

'That's a needle-shaped pineapple cactus,' he continued with a pained expression. 'Me? Obscene? Haven't you ever seen a barrel cactus? It's an amazing flame of orange. Or a fish-hook, hedgehog, rainbow, the prickly pear and cholla, the night-blooming cereus, Arizona Turk's head, golden beehive, pima pineapple, the organ pipe?'

'I think that's called showing off.'

'I'm trying to show you that a man so desperately homesick for a cactus can be a safe dinner companion,' he wheedled as they passed the china plates. 'And scintillating company, too.'

145

'That's it, tour over. As you can see, no desert, no cactus.'

'I thought you said you were a cactus.' He regretted his runaway tongue.

'What? Did I say that? When?'

Roman decided not to pursue the subject. There was something about her softness surrounded by prickles that *was* like a cactus.

'Do you think they need some help?' He watched Heera attempting to fold the bed, and strode forward. 'I guess no one wants bedtime stories just yet. Where's this Sleeping Beauty going?' he asked, as he pulled the lever.

'There is really no space in the shop,' observed Eileen disapprovingly.

'Precisely. We'll put it outside,' decided Heera.

'Outside the shop?' asked Swarnakumari, alarmed. 'Someone might take it away.'

The idea had crossed Heera's mind, and was in fact part of a plan. It was an easy – if illegal – way to dispose of unwanted items, for even the charity shop did have to reject and eject on occasion. Roman called on the male customer to assist in the removal of the bed; together they placed it slyly to partially conceal the Catnap window next door, and leave the IndiaNeed display visible. Unlike the vinyl-loving customer, Roman felt this was his cue to leave, but it was no ordinary departure; he no longer felt like the same man of the morning. He had something urgent to say to her, but it was too soon. He was reluctant to have her eyes spell a cool goodbye to the cactus-crazy American searching for a bookshop on Mill Road. Her indifference would be hard to carry away in the wind.

146

Roman noticed it was a changed wind, giving direction, no longer scattering the leaves into the cracks in the pavement. Pablo Neruda knew what he was feeling, and had said it so much better than he ever could. She and he were together in the autumn. He could not merely vanish; a tempest did not go quietly. 'Tempest' was 'tempestas'; 'tempus' was time, and he would be Prospero, stirring up a storm into something 'rich and strange'.

Durga wondered why she had agreed to go out with Roman Tempest. He had returned after propping the bed along the wall outside the shop. Running his fingers uncertainly through his hair, he waited for her response to his invitation, his eyes soft and warm, the accidental brush of their hands leaving them both awkward. They had arranged to meet the next day; she would accompany him to the American Cemetery at Madingley, and show him the Eagle pub, where wartime American pilots waiting for sorties had etched their names with cigarette lighters and their girlfriends' lipsticks on the ceiling. Then they would go out for dinner. Another time they would visit the Samuel Pepys library at Magdalene College, the Whipple Museum of the History of Science, the Scott Polar Research Institute and the Fitzwilliam Museum. In the spring, they would visit the Botanic Gardens and walk in the Backs to admire the crocuses, daffodils, tulips and bluebells.

There was an important detail she had omitted to mention, did not see the need to mention: she was married.

# CHAPTER NINE

# Home is where the heart is

DURGA STOOD RUEFUL after Roman had left, a quiet tempest brewing. It had been stardust and shooting stars, she had met the stranger whose locked glance she had coveted in her dreams like a romantic fool, but he had been a pleasant interlude, nothing more. She would retreat.

It had been a spring day in South Kensington; the magnolia blossoms in the communal gardens were bursting into velvety bloom, and Durga was thirteen. Her parents informed her over lunch: her father, the manager of a leading Indian bank, was being transferred back to Bombay. The move had been premeditated; Durga was being whisked away from the temptations of drugs, cigarettes, sex and rock 'n' roll in time for a dose of roadtested middle-class Indian values.

At the age of twelve Durga had sung and pirouetted in her room in their South Kensington flat overlooking the French café, reed-thin arms and legs, gawky in a short skirt. Pop would ruin Durga's voice, argued Durga's mother; Indian classical singing came from the pit of the stomach. Soon after their arrival in Bombay, Joshiji had been summoned for Hindustani classical music lessons. He waddled in every week, his dhoti revealing smooth, hairless calves. Fondness for paan led him to clear his throat often as he transferred the sodden red wad to another cheek in order to teach Durga a simple taan. Reaching for her father's old Time-Life books on the coffee table, he would dictate notation and hum the unfolding of a raag. Durga observed his fascination with the page displaying Sophia Loren in the famous black and flesh-striped transparent garment. She would deliberately pause and ask a question as his little eyes feasted and fastened on forbidden flesh, returning with reluctance to the musical composition.

A few months later, Joshiji was knocked down by a taxi during an act of worship at a roadside temple, and, shocked by the inexplicable interruption of his prayers, he became a recluse within the four walls of his Borivli home. Durga was merely relieved at the cessation of lessons, and the tanpura's strings broke over time.

Mishraji was recruited to teach Hindi, and he arrived every Wednesday wearing a worn but spotless white shirt and trousers, travelling from his home in Kurla, high on a hill near a buffalo milk dairy, to leafy Malabar Hill for the tuition. Durga hated the lessons, demonstrating her contempt for her circumstances, the language and the country to which she had been unceremoniously transplanted by blotting the seat of his pristine trousers with ink. He merely smiled and proceeded with the lessons. Over time, his son and daughter-in-law commandeered his rooms in the humble tenement building, feeding him meagre leftovers; it was a cruel fate for such a mild-mannered man.

Miss Noronha, Year Nine teacher, was the school's unofficial guide to puberty and adolescence; between lessons there had been homilies on the evils of sitting on the floor and eating bananas during menstruation as both affected the flow, as well as the optimum angle of hygienic suspension over a public seat. Good things came to girls who waited before marriage, but Miss Noronha omitted to mention to her class that she had waited far too long. Durga's marriage invitation to Miss Noronha was returned as *Addressee Unknown*. She heard two conflicting stories: Miss Noronha had left for Australia, and Miss Noronha was dead.

Miss Sathe was hired for Marathi lessons. She wore starched Finlay saris and lived in a tiny flat behind a temple ruin at Walkeshwar. A mousy, diminutive woman, she puckered her lips and emitted kissing sounds to denote assent and consent. It was one of life's little ironies that she herself remained unkissed, although it was rumoured there had once been a middle-aged suitor in her life, a Hindi teacher called Mr Doot. On his first visit to her home he had found her ministering with clicking, puckered sounds to a cantankerous mother. His ardour cooled rapidly, but he tenderly left her his copy of a story by Munshi Premchand.

Durga's new friend Anita was dismissive about the extra tuition, urging her to focus on the development of the body instead. She enjoined flat-chested Durga to follow a daily regimen of throwing her arms wide to the front and back to the accompaniment of the rhyme *I must and I must and I must and I must, I must and I must increase my bust.*

At thirteen, Anita was already buxom in her too-tight PE shirt, drawing sly glances from the school caretakers. She loved erasers of every kind. The Indian ones were boring, had no smell, so she bought imported Japanese ones by the dozen; her favourites were square and white with a green border carrying a letter of the alphabet and a picture. She perched them between her nose and lips to sniff their scent during lessons as she rocked on her chair. Anita had merely laughed when Durga asked if increased bust size was linked to the sniffing of erasers, making no denial. Anita did not attend Durga's wedding either; she was erasing a messy divorce.

Durga remained unresponsive and sullen; on her aunt's advice, an astrologer was summoned to her father's executive flat near the Hanging Gardens. Poring over her horoscope, he had turned silent. Whatever the stars were planning for her future, champagne corks weren't going to be popped.

'But what about marriage?' asked her mother, an academic, who had bestirred herself reluctantly from a scholarly essay on Vinoba Bhave to await the verdict on her daughter's destiny. Displaying a deep scepticism towards astrologers, she demanded from their findings a scientific approach far more rigorous than they were willing to display.

'Difficult. *Beti*, your life is a struggle. You will encounter bad luck after bad luck all the way through,' he had announced to Durga between greedy slurps from the saucer of ginger tea. 'You will also suffer from women's problems,' he pointed vaguely in the direction of Durga's abdomen, 'but later, much later, maybe at thirty, thirty-five.' His baleful owl eyes gleamed as her mother slipped him an extra hundred rupees toward the dilution of planetary harm to the refined Maharashtrian family.

151

A stern, scholarly woman, she was happiest among her books. Durga remembered her seated at a little desk, head bowed nightly in a lamp's glow, an avid expression on her face as she turned the pages, her tongue darting between her lips in fierce concentration. She ceaselessly fed her daughter the texts of the Vedas, Sri Aurobindo, Ramana Maharshi, Vivekananda, Mahatma Gandhi, Sant Tukaram and Sant Gnyaneshwar, demanding nothing short of excellence from Durga, who dutifully collected the form's silver badge every year. The school badges soon began to be made of a dull tin-like metal, evidence of the school's declining moral standards.

Durga witnessed violent arguments between her parents as her ambitious father rebelled. Entertaining at home was an essential part of climbing the corporate ladder, he protested, but Durga's mother stayed firmly on the ground. The only exceptions, she said, were relatives, whose frequent interruptions had to be borne with equanimity.

Under her mother's influence, the family embraced asceticism; it was the poor and downtrodden who would receive its compassion. The modest approach of 'simple living and high thinking' was at odds with the new residences on Malabar Hill, where sprawling old bungalows and tree-lined grounds were being rapidly replaced by luxury high-rise duplex apartments overlooking the sea, and whose nouveau riche inhabitants roamed fearlessly in tooting cars.

Eighteen-year-old Durga took the single-decker bus from Hanging Gardens, rumbling slowly down from Malabar Hill past the dense trees of the Governor's mansion, the flame of the forest trees and their incandescent rain-drenched blossoms pierced by the rare shriek of a roaming peacock in the dense undergrowth. Reaching Chowpatty Beach, she would look across the bay and Marine Drive with its Art Deco buildings, and the Manhattan-like skyline beyond. Staring into the murky water, she wondered if she would ever return to England.

Durga had soon realised that her parents were loosely bound by convention in a relationship vitiating both as they struggled for independence. She came to the conclusion that they should never have married. In the meanwhile, her father watched the promotion of his colleagues with bitter dismay, convinced that his hermit wife was the cause of his own stagnation.

'You know what your colleague Verma does, don't you?' her mother erupted in self-defence. 'He is always putting an arm around the ladies, and there is also something going on between his wife and your boss, as if you didn't know. Did you think they were patiently counting bundles of five hundred rupee banknotes together every night?' As Durga's father remonstrated, she raged, 'Why should we adopt their pretence and loose morals? For a career? Money? Will you be able to live with yourself if we do the same? *Aho*, do you remember where you have come from?'

Durga's father was from a poor coastal Brahmin family. As a schoolboy, he had studied under the light of oil lamps; following a charitable system practised for centuries in the community, he was sent to a different household on a nominated day of the week for a free meal. A car once passed through the small dusty village with its magnificent mango groves, and an industrialist stopped to ask his way to a religious shrine. The boy

153

had been concise and clear in his directions, his eyes snapping with intelligence without fear. The industrialist had him transferred to a city school and paid for the family to move to Bombay.

Verma was undoubtedly popular with the ladies at the parties. His compliments on their saris and jewellery led to coy giggles over the risqué jokes as he moved closer to drop an arm around a waist, lightly tap a neck, or lean over to inhale a favourite perfume.

'Well, well, what do we have here?' he asked interestedly, roaming Durga's small breasts and narrow waist with his gaze. 'You have grown into a real beauty.' When she failed to respond, he laughed, 'Don't you recognise your Uncle Verma? Come, give me a hug, *bete*!' He enveloped her in a tight embrace and guffawed as she fled.

The director, a balding man from Jullunder, asked Verma's wife to carry one of her husband's ties to every assignation. She chose a different one each time, but either Verma's collection was too modest or the trysts with the director too many, for Verma was obliged to hurriedly purchase a fresh stock of striped, checked and polka-dotted ties from the Akbarally's at Flora Fountain. So strong were the ties of the Verma union that he was subsequently promoted to manager at the Delhi office while she remained in a Colaba flat, but a year later he was found hanging from the ceiling – by a tie his wife had never seen.

Durga could not have been more ripe for rebellion, a tomato ready to spew angry seeded pulp, but while her female friends flirted with male classmates in the college library and in the chapel and smoked cigarettes in the canteen or perched on the benches under the college

154

hostel trees, she remained protected by her mother's idealism and the fiery reformist texts of the thinkers and educationists who had been her spiritual guides. She had also inherited her mother's naiveté and trust.

At the age of twenty, Durga caught a chest infection. She visited a laboratory to collect an X-ray report. The grey-haired pathologist beckoned. Had she been examined recently? he asked. She should have a second opinion. The diagnosis was often wrong, he added jocularly. She should lie down, relax and let him reassure her. He asked her to undo her blouse, and stared at her small pert breasts, breathing noisily, his stethoscope dangling from his neck. He had straightened suddenly, and ordered her off the table. It was the equivalent of intoxication without the drink. It never occurred to Durga to complain; years later she heard the pathologist was under review for indecent conduct with a number of women.

Durga attracted the attention of several amiable young men; it was her classmate Vibhuti, striking a provocative pose in tight jeans and blouse, who told her about the 'Durga Virginity Challenge'. The rich son of a Bollywood music producer had even offered free canteen batata wadas and chutney sandwiches for all if declared the winner. Who would have thought a swot would be such a draw? spat Vibhuti grudgingly, leaving Durga bewildered and angry. Difference was a terrible burden. So was conformity.

She met a young British backpacker roaming the back streets of Colaba behind the Taj Hotel. Her nostalgia for London and untried rebellion led her to agree to accompany him to the Elephanta Caves on the island across the harbour. As she waited at the Reception of

155

the Presto Hotel while he changed for the trip, two large cockroaches scurried up the peeling, damp walls latticed with the stench of stale onions. He returned from his room clad in denim shorts. The sight of his wobbly pale pink thighs unleashed a rising, bilious wave as she imagined she saw the two cockroaches climbing his flesh instead. She fled, leaving a bus ticket fluttering to the ground, one that he collected and carried home to Nottingham as a souvenir to show his mates. She was a dark-eyed beauty, he had said with the air of a conquest over the Balti meal; she had sobbed when he left for England, begging him to stay and be hers.

The day she developed the mandatory infatuation for her French teacher at the Alliance Française, Durga met Vivek Thadani. An overcrowded bus had failed to stop; at the sight of another overflowing bus approaching, a young man suddenly detached himself from the impatient queue to lie supine on the road. The bus stopped. The young man winked at Durga as the passengers swarmed of single mind up the steps of the bus. He arose, nimbly joining the last eager passengers as they boarded.

'What's happening? Why have we stopped suddenly?' asked a woman anxiously, looking out of the window.

'Accident,' replied another succinctly.

'Who?' quavered a fearful elderly man, trembling as he held his newspaper and his breath.

'A young man,' contributed a passenger in the front seat near the exit.

'But I can't see anything,' sulked a plaintive voice from the rear. 'Can't you move your head?'

'Do you think this is the cinema?' another said reproachfully. 'Next you'll want popcorn.'

'*Arre*, she can't see anything because he's dead,' announced a peering passenger. 'He's under the wheels.'

'*Hai!*' screamed a few voices in panic, and a large, perspiring woman burst into tears that fell on her basket of spinach, giving it a fresh, dewy appearance.

'Calm yourself. These things happen,' murmured a stranger gently.

'It is in the hands of God. Time and place decide everyone's fate,' agreed a hard-faced woman in a snug salwar kameez.

'But what a place to choose to read!' exclaimed another woman.

'What? He was reading? In the middle of the road? These students of today ...' The hard-faced woman clicked her tongue disapprovingly. Several passengers followed suit until the bus reverberated with a click, click, click.

'What was he reading?' inquired an eager voice.

'*Arre*, does it matter whether it was a book or a bus ticket? He has gone to heaven now.'

'I think he was lying down,' confided an elderly passenger.

'*Hai!* Suicide?' shrieked a woman attempting to peer over the oily heads of her companions.

'The driver is looking under the bus,' reported a man in a vantage position.

As several passengers rushed for a better view, the young man slipped into a vacant seat and winked cheekily at Durga. As she subsided beside him, he buried his face in the pages of a newspaper.

'He must be a jilted lover,' concluded the hard-faced woman. 'He must have decided to end his life in a dramatic way to show her how much he loves her.'

'But then she should have been there to see it, otherwise what's the use? His life will have been wasted for nothing. Where is she? Could she be on the bus?' asked an agitated voice at the rear of the bus.

Several sharp eyes roamed the bus, pausing momentarily over Durga's wooden face.

'Maybe his girl is under the bus, too?' suggested a new, unseen voice.

The women looked as if they would burst into fresh tears, until a calm voice in the front said that was unlikely. That only happened in television soaps.

'*Arre, chalo, chalo*, come on, we are getting late,' shouted a man impatiently to the bus driver.

The large woman had a renewed bout of tears.

'A young man has died, and you are bothered about being late?' yelled the hard-faced woman. 'He is someone's son, someone's brother, and now he will never have a wife, or bear children. Shame on you!'

The man subsided, embarrassed. The driver climbed back into the bus. He glanced at the tiny picture of Ganesha pasted to the corner of the windscreen and bowed his head in thankful prayer. He had been convinced there was a man lying on the road; now he could no longer be certain. 'It was only a goat, and it ran away,' he announced to the passenger in the first row.

The driver's verdict spread like bushfire. As the bus lurched forward, several passengers began to scramble for seats now as scarce as small change in the shops. A couple searched in vain, and the woman glared at Durga and the head buried in the newspaper. 'Look, they are nicely sitting in our seats,' she grumbled, but her meek husband ventured, 'Never mind, at least no one died under this bus.'

Everyone agreed. No one wanted a ride in a chariot of death. Durga saw the newspaper shake, hearing little snorts. Soon she was giggling, her face red and puffy. The hard-faced woman nudged her companion. 'Look at these youngsters, no respect for death.'

The bus emptied opposite the post office near the Hanging Gardens. The driver hurriedly lowered himself from the seat to stand outside the bus, mopping his brow. Fate had saved him this time, but it was a sign: there was danger lurking on the roads. He would take up a job in an office canteen instead. At least he would not mistake food for anything else.

The newspaper was lowered and a cheeky grin emerged. 'Hi, I'm Vivek!' he announced. 'Did you enjoy the ride?'

'That was a really stupid thing to do. You could have been killed.'

'But you noticed me, didn't you? And now you'll never forget me.'

Durga never forgot. Vivek was inseparable from his motorbike, calling it Moody Baby, and unknown to her mother Durga had soon travelled the length and breadth of Bombay. The lights of the Haji Ali Mosque in the middle of the sea twinkled as they sped towards Bandra, her hair a pennant in the wind. Durga's mother frowned; who could have imagined bus rides to college could cause such damage to her daughter's hair? She prepared herbal concoctions using areetha and shikakai as shampoo substitutes, and oiled her daughter's hair with angry tugs.

Two years later, Durga's mother found out, and her first question, fearing much worse, was whether Vivek had held Durga's hand. Vivek made her laugh, said Durga. Her mother was sufficiently alarmed to discuss the matter with her husband. 'I think Durga should settle down,' she said firmly.

He protested, 'But she's only twenty-four. She's just finished the double MA and she's applying for the scholarship to Cambridge.'

'Let her get married and continue her studies. We should start looking now,' insisted her mother, lips sewing a thin line. 'She should not get into the wrong company.'

Vivek, the son of a businessman who manufactured matchboxes, was not the right company, she asserted, and the nonsense about him making Durga laugh was just that – nonsense. He was hardly going to set her alight. She should find a life companion with an intellect to match. Durga's mother awaited the impending visit of Mrs Kamath, friend of Aunty Sarojini and community matchmaker.

Mrs Kamath was a florid woman with a heaving bosom that moved like a rusty pendulum; her large gold earrings and prominently displayed mangalsutra, a gold chain with black beads and gold pendant, were not only a symbol of her married status but a calling card. She settled down comfortably to 'ladies talk only'. As she bit appreciatively into the pohe snack prepared with reluctance by Durga's mother, she confided, 'I have "n" number of boys lined up for Durga. Just say the word.' She patted the sofa with a plump hand, inviting the mother to move closer.

'First of all,' began Durga's mother firmly to Mrs

Kamath, 'you should understand that my daughter is highly intelligent. She wants to study for many more years and we want a boy who understands that. We would like the two to get married first, and study together later. Durga would like to go abroad, so we are willing to wait until the right one comes along.'

'Of course, anyone who knows your cultured family would expect that only, no question. Best match will be found. Now can I have her horoscope?' humoured Mrs Kamath.

The family stood firm. Horoscopes would not be necessary. Mrs Kamath sensed steel; years of experience had taught her it would buckle and melt like butter.

Dressed in an orange silk sari for the occasion, Durga's mother stood uncertainly in front of her wardrobe mirror before dabbing *Chanel No. 5* on her wrist. The bottle had lain in pristine condition since they had left England eleven years earlier. It was a frivolous gesture for a serious business.

Sitting uncomfortably in the opulent living room, Durga and her mother were boldly examined by a middle-aged couple seated on a silk sofa across the room.

'Where is your son?' asked Durga's mother for the second time as a servant brought in silver glasses of rose sherbet on a silver tray. Ignoring her question, the man addressed Durga. 'As you know, we are a well-known industrialist family in Maharashtra. We believe that girls should be educated, of course, and it is commendable that you want to continue your studies, but our daughter-in-law is expected to look after this family first. It is a lot of responsibility, and she must be ready for this status and position.'

'How many in your family?' inquired Durga's

161

mother, directing the question at his wife. The husband answered proudly, 'We have three eligible sons.'

'But which princeling are we supposed to meet?' asked Durga's mother. 'You've seen my daughter, but not a single one of your sons is here. This is not a cattle fair.' She rose hastily to her feet. 'Enough of this nonsense! Come, Durga, let's go!'

Mrs Kamath meekly apologised as they drove away. Rich people were 'like that only', she prattled, but there was no need to fret, she had already found another, the 'best' match for Durga.

'The boy is from a good Saraswat Brahmin family. Engineer. Good-looking, tall, fair, very fair. Lives in America, New Jersey. Your Durga can continue studying there. These American universities are first-class. The boy has no sisters, no brothers. And on top of it, his parents live far away. Only slight problem and you know I am telling you honestly, I never hide anything, the boy is moody. You see, what happened is that he was married,' confided Mrs Kamath. She placed a warning hand on Durga's mother. 'No, no, just wait. I know what you must be thinking and what you are going to say, but he was married for a short time only. He is as good as new.'

'What was the problem, then?'

'Nothing much. He had a child, poor thing, dead at birth and then the wife had a nervous breakdown and she left him. These things happen, nobody's fault. Since a long time it is over. He is on his own. Only thing, he gets a little angry. Moody, shouts a little, but when he is married again, when there is another child, everything will be all right.'

Durga's mother terminated the conversation.

162

'Really, this Mr Fair-Very-Fair-Shouter needs professional help, not yours or ours. We send him our prayers and good wishes for his complete recovery.'

'Your mother knows what's best for you,' concluded Vivek when Durga described the meetings with Mrs Kamath.

'How can you be so sure?' she asked as they walked along Juhu Beach in the sunset. The sand was warm and sticky under her feet.

'Never mind that. When are you going to apply for the scholarship to Cambridge?'

'Soon, but what are you going to do with your life?' she wanted to know.

He grinned. 'Make bigger and better matchboxes, what else? You go ahead and do the fame thing for both of us. Remember, even if you do this marriage stuff, make sure you study and do something great with your life. Don't become a housewife buying brinjals in Dadar market, I'm counting on you.'

Durga had little time to pursue either the advice or the application; her father had a heart attack the next day. The doctor pronounced it mild, but Durga's mother abandoned her books and ministered to her husband with alternating panic and calm.

It was weeks since Mrs Kamath had successfully brokered a match; she planned her next visit to Durga's mother with care. Mrs Kamath was no longer her usual ebullient and persuasive self; her daughter's marriage had been under strain over a property wrangle, and she herself suffered from headaches and back pain. The doctor's diagnosis was bad for business; depression and matchmaking were an incompatible combination.

'I have come with five proposals, not one,' she

gurgled. 'This time you will not say "No", I know that. Your pretty daughter is in such demand, really!' Mrs Kamath shuffled the order of the 'proposals' with practised ease. 'See, the first one is a really good offer, but they insist the girl should be a computer engineer. That too, software, only. The second family wants blood tests after the boy and girl have decided, because nowadays, these modern people you know, they want to be sure the couple can have children. And healthy children, also. The third wants quick marriage, there are four brothers next in line. It is a joint family. The fourth is a college lecturer, he lives a little bit far away – in Mangalore.'

Mrs Kamath put down her teacup with finality. Satisfied with the results of her strategy, she said, 'So you didn't like the other four? Never mind. No problem, what is the hurry? Durga is young, beautiful and intelligent. We can wait two years, three years, five years, whatever you say. But I thought that with Bhausaheb's health problem, God grant him long life, but you know how these illnesses suddenly come upon us, you are so sensible, I know you will want to have everything settled at the right time. Now I have one last offer. Of course, I will have to see about this one if you like him, because the boy is very much in demand, but if you are keen I can give you the details. Chitpavan family. He is a doctor doing research in Cambridge. Parents and sister live in Pune. He will return after studies, that much I can tell you.' She paused. 'Also handsome.' It had been a masterstroke to pretend to gather her handbag in a hurry. Durga's mother asked her to stay for another cup of tea.

*

Dip dip. That was what the tea-seller at Nasik Station had said as Durga arrived from the riverbanks, the immersion of her parents' ashes over. She had asked for tea. 'Will a dip dip do?' He had mimicked the dunking of an imaginary teabag in the chipped white cup he slid under her nose.

Her cousin had unexpectedly found a quiet spot on the ghat behind a little marble temple and under a magnificent banyan, and he waded into the sunlit water with the urns. He had performed the last rites, accompanied by her silent resistance and welling anger; this should have been a daughter's right. There was also a distant memory of the same annoying cousin thrashing about in a Bombay swimming pool; he had caressed her teenage thighs before swiftly escaping in a noisy splash.

The tranquillity of the moment and the sweet chimes of the temple bell were replaced by the loud tones of a raunchy film song, 'Choli ke Peeche Kya Hai' (What's Behind the Blouse), streaming from a transistor held by a young man in an unbuttoned shirt and tight trousers ambling down the path above. It was a cruel, noisy requiem for the disjointed lives of her parents, crushed in a pilgrims' stampede. Durga's Aunty Sarojini offered consolation. At least the bodies had been recovered: other victims would be missing for ever.

Durga plunged into legalities and paperwork. Uncle Manohar shook his head sadly as he looked at the disarray of his brother's financial affairs. Still, there was a small retirement flat in Pune as Durga's inheritance; at least she had a roof over her head, and by God's grace it need not be his.

Mrs Kamath seized the opportunity to sway Durga's Aunty Sarojini; the girl was vulnerable to exploitation by unscrupulous sharks now that she was alone in the world. Besides, she added, embroidering past conversations without guilt, she could hear the mother's voice pleading: 'Only you can find me a good boy for Durga, I am counting on you.' Sarojini was moved as Mrs Kamath, dabbing her eyes, embellished stories of her visits to Durga's mother. There was no time to lose, said Mrs Kamath, with determination. It was in Durga's best interests to marry the doctor. He was also a gynaecologist, what more could a girl want? One way or another, exulted Aunty Sarojini later to her niece, she would be going to Cambridge.

When Durga and her husband returned home together after the wedding, his mother had greeted them at the door with a ceremonial thali for the ritual washing of Durga's feet, her silk blouse tight under armpits circled with sweat. The silver thali made a loud sharp *thak* sound as she placed it on the floor; Durga stepped into the thali, and her sister-in-law Archana reluctantly poured a few symbolic drops of water from a jug onto the bride's feet. The mother barked, 'Napkin, napkin, bring napkin!' berating the servant as Archana ordered him to take the 'dirty water' away, and Durga's feet left the thali cleansed for her new life. Both mother and daughter ignored the ceremonial coconut Durga was carrying, and as she entered the house the servant took it casually from her, as if she were a wordless postman expecting a Diwali tip. The family had green coconut chutney at dinner.

Atul's relatives were in attendance on her wedding night. A noisy card game coupled with intermittent desultory singing led the uncles to chorus their demands to Atul, who obligingly obtained whisky from his gynaecologist father, owner of Patwardhan's Maternity Clinic. The Johnnie Walker Black Label bottles were concealed behind the woollen suits smelling of mothballs in his steel Godrej cupboard with the cracked mirror. Atul's cousin, a fair, green-eyed woman with long, plaited brown hair, sent Durga a sullen, smouldering look. There was something proprietorial about the cousin, thought Durga. And his sister, his parents, the entire family. She was married to the mob.

The nuptial bed was bedecked with rajnigandha flowers and rose petals. Atul and Durga had made their way to his old bedroom accompanied by winks and jokes from the uncles. Minutes later, there was a knock on the door. It was his sister Archana. With only a token apology, she removed a hairbrush from Atul's wardrobe. Her sharp, satisfied eyes noted the couple's awkwardness.

'Didn't your mother teach you to cook?' reproached Atul's mother a week later. 'I have taught Archana everything. Studying is not an excuse. It is every woman's duty to learn these things, and you will be doing the cooking in Cambridge, anyway.' She placed the lid firmly on the pressure cooker. 'He loves vange-bhaji, it's his favourite dish. You must learn everything about our style of cooking, although I must say he will still miss my special touch.'

As if on cue, Atul walked into the kitchen, placing an arm around his mother's waist. 'Yes,' he said simply, 'and if only I could, I would have you in Cambridge with me.' She looked as if she would cry.

Durga's moments alone with her husband were hurried rather than intimate; both waited for the knock on the door. The days passed in the constant company of his relatives and friends, who saw little need for their privacy. Atul's light-eyed cousin Shreya developed a mysterious infection that she could only discuss in confidence, so they disappeared to talk in hushed tones on balconies with lush overhanging bougainvillaea, in rooms darkened against the midday sun.

Durga and Atul were awakened one night by a harsh, reedy wail from his parents' room. He hurried out, indicating that she should remain in bed, and did not return until the morning. As he explained to Durga later, his mother was suffering separation pangs again, as she had done when he had left for Cambridge for the first time. She experienced breathing difficulties, and complained of palpitations and impenetrable aches in the neck and limbs. He had stayed by her side, they had chatted late into the night, and he had finally lain across her lap in exhaustion. He would invite her to Cambridge next summer, he said; that would brighten her mood.

A professional family portrait was suggested before they left for England; there was excitement as Atul made an appointment with Patekar's Studios at Deccan Gymkhana. It was the equivalent of a family trip to Disneyland. His mother stood in front of her grey Godrej steel cupboard, searching endlessly among the piles of neatly folded saris, as his sister hovered to advise. Atul was handsome in his black wedding suit although it pinched at the elbows; he stole an appreciative glance at Durga in a purple and red Paithani sari that had belonged to her mother.

Atul's aunt and his cousin Shreya arrived unannounced. His mother stood in front of her cupboard again, calling out to them to select two saris: they had accepted the invitation to accompany the family to the studio. Fifteen minutes later they were waiting, stiff and starched, for his father, who had been delayed by the slow progress of a patient at Patwardhan's Maternity Clinic. 'Are you giving birth to a buffalo?' he asked in desperation, glancing at his watch. The sweating, heaving woman cast him a pleading look. He relented. 'Push harder!' he commanded.

He arrived at Patekar's Studio along with his family to find it changed. The big cameras and black cloth and popping flashbulbs were gone, and Patekar Senior had retired; his fingers were too unsteady. The son, a smart young man, was courteous, but the Pune air in the studio was one of efficiency, of the instant one-hour passport photo service, the multiplex cinema and the Barista coffee shop. The magician's curtained lair of mysterious dusty props and the world of quiet, leafy lanes were gone forever.

Patekar Senior would have slowly arranged the family members around the Patwardhan patriarch seated on a grand velvet chair, but his son Ravi was more hurried, now habituated to digital commercial photography. He had snappily assigned everyone their places, but there was a cousin who hovered unhappily on the periphery. With an intuition his father would have applauded, he subtly altered the arrangement; Atul now stood beaming – if a little squashed – between radiant cousin and wife.

Durga rang Vivek and her relatives from her new home in Pune; the conversations were stilted and guarded. Atul's mother and sister were watchful, displaying their displeasure at her continued links with

169

her old life. Durga had clung to her surname fiercely, unwilling to exchange 'Prabhu' for 'Patwardhan'. Atul's anorexic aunt, who lived in Florida and organised classical music soirées for visiting artistes from India, intervened with the persuasive vocabulary of a Sicilian warlord to announce closure on the matter: Durga was no longer a 'Prabhu'.

'Do you have any idea what a well-known family we are in Pune?' challenged Archana. 'Or is it because you think you are too good for us that you didn't want to change your name?' She had waited until Atul was out strolling with his parents in the University Gardens. 'And forget about all those fancy friends. Who is this Vivek I heard you phoning?'

'An old friend.'

'Oh? Does Atul know about this? What is the need to ring this friend from here?'

Durga had remained silent, unsurprised by the hostility, unwilling to talk about her loneliness, and Archana was satisfied she had found proof of Durga's guilt.

A week before her wedding in Pune, Durga had perched on Moody Baby near the quiet, leafy Afghan Church in Colaba.

'You will stay in touch, won't you?' asked Durga.

'What do you think? Who else is going to make you laugh out there in cold Cambridge?'

'I'm serious.'

'*Arre*, I laid down my life on the road for you once, and I would do it again, but don't tell anyone, it's bad for my reputation,' said Vivek with a tremor in his voice.

She looked at him, choked by a new realisation. 'Why didn't you say . . .'

'Not good enough. Not for you. Do great things with your life, Durga, as you were always meant to. Now enough! Moody Baby will cry in a minute, and you know how she hates ruining her mascara and leaving those black streaks on the road.'

Prior to her departure for Cambridge, Durga visited her parents' retirement flat for the last time. Standing in the hallway as the sun filtered through the rooms, her eyes lingered over the contents carefully transported from Mumbai. Her mother's books were piled high on a table, the reading spectacles neatly folded, the chair at a beckoning angle. Her father's liquor cabinet caught the afternoon light swirling in the wine, sherry, cognac and whisky glasses shipped with pride from England, the pub souvenirs, a model of a London bus, Durga's pop cassettes and teenage fiction spilling over the shelves, the broken tanpura and the Time-Life book so eagerly perused by Joshiji. She walked to the wardrobes, opening them in turn, burying her face in the soft folds of her mother's saris, as neat and fragrant as when last worn, running her fingers over her father's shirts from Marks & Spencer, labelled with lingering cologne. Durga wept.

Atul's mother wept until her son was no longer a speck in the private Pune luxury taxi bound for the airport. She leaned heavily on her husband for support, a cracked stalk in the wind. Rivulets snaked down her face, as her husband bravely blinked back his own tears. 'What do I have to look forward to, except my Atul's next visit?' she cried plaintively, prompting several female relatives to pull out tiny handkerchief squares in haste. Dab, dab, dab. Their sons and daughters, too, had left Pune for the winking lights of the West, never to return. The green-eyed cousin Shreya wept pitifully in glandular gasps, but Archana remained dry-eyed. 'That is enough, *Aai* – you will make yourself ill. Do you want Atul to drop everything he is doing there and come back just for you?' she rebuked her mother, planting a seed for slow germination.

The rotund man sitting next to Atul in the aisle seat on the flight to Heathrow confided his diabetic condition within minutes of being airborne. 'So which fruit is the highest in sugar content, Doctor? Which vegetables do you recommend I should avoid? Doctor, any suggestion on exercise?' he asked humbly, whipping out a large notepad and pen. A gynaecologist was still a doctor, and the advice was free.

Durga looked at her husband's profile. The days in Pune had passed in crumbling suffocation, and black, hate-filled mosquitoes had bitten through her limbs despite the window mesh. She wondered at Atul's desire to have an arranged marriage; his cousin and sister clearly felt he and Durga were ill-matched, and slyly influenced his mother to concur. Atul's father was a mild-mannered man who spoke little. Surrounded by female nurses and patients all day, over the past twenty years his vocabulary had dwindled to the injunction 'Push harder!' at the Maternity Clinic. He was an unlikely ally, despite the apparent feminist sentiment behind the two words.

Faced with baseless suspicion from strangers, Durga was initially optimistic; she would turn the other cheek, douse fire with love. A smuggled surfeit of Mills & Boon romances had led to her muddled view of love and marriage, and she was horrified to find a rewritten script; she was playing the role of Cinderella *after* she had married the prince. Was he a prince who had turned into a frog, or a princely frog? Durga had taken a bite of the apple, but instead of a gentle awakening from slumber in a glass casket, she was learning to iron the creaseless shirt.

She glanced frequently at Atul during the flight. He was a handsome man, and perhaps it was too soon for disillusionment; they had left India and his family behind, the future awaited. It would be different once they were on their own and in Cambridge, city of spires.

Durga waited at the luggage carousel at Heathrow as Atul struggled to heave a second heavy suitcase onto the trolley. He looked down in dismay at the spreading oil stains on his beige chinos, leaned forward and sniffed. 'It must be mango pickle – oh God, it has leaked!' he exclaimed. He looked crushed, as a red stain formed a symmetrically large triangle on his crotch, coupled with two vertical red streaks on his thighs; his mother's blessings had safely accompanied him to England. Had Durga laughed, the echo would have sneaked into the terminal, into the waiting coffee cups and steaming ears of the passengers and out onto the tarmac with the planes, steering upward into the open skies.

'Do something!' he ordered sharply, aware of the smirks and stares of the other passengers.

'You mean do something about the suitcase first, or you?'

Before he could respond, a man approached. 'Atul Patwardhan? I thought it was you! We met at the New Hall dinner two months ago. Richard Cartwright, obstetrics.'

The two men shook hands and Richard Cartwright's gaze travelled downward.

'He's in a bit of pickle, can you help?' asked Durga. 'These suitcases are rather heavy, and I need to open one to get some wet tissues.'

Richard Cartwright obliged and as Durga dabbed Atul's trousers a passing passenger quipped, 'Mind the Crown Jewels there, luv!' Richard began to chuckle, but Atul looked thunderous. 'I'd say your best bet is to find another pair of trousers,' commiserated Richard as he left, but they discovered that the mango pickle had spread in spurts over the entire contents of the suitcase zealously fingerprinted on the outside by Atul's father with two large, handwritten, heavily gummed labels PROPERTY OF DR PATWAR-DHAN. The Cambridge address was prominently displayed. It was as legible as an optician's sight-testing chart.

Durga rummaged through the clothing and beheld the stained portrait. The eyes of the Patwardhan family were red blobs of sorrow. The packet of his mother's home-made sweets was coated in oil. Durga suggested disposal, but Atul was reluctant. 'We can't throw anything away. My mother has made everything herself. But I don't understand, how could you pack edible things with my clothes? You should have had some sense at least.'

'Who said *I* packed them?'

'Then who?'

'Mommy dearest? Sister dearest?'

He was about to protest when she waved a pile of baby clothes in indignation under his nose. They were all postmarked in mango red.

'Yours, I presume?' she asked coldly.

He stared sheepishly at the accompanying envelope addressed to Mrs Aparna Achrekar of Milton Keynes. 'That's my cousin Shreya's sister-in-law. She's expecting a baby. Maybe she asked *Aai* to send the baby clothes through us,' he mumbled, as she continued to display several packages at random.

'And who is Kishori Chavate in London? Lucky, lucky girl! A kilo of laadu for her sweet tooth. And who is Mr Mystery-Man Madhav Mhatre? Life will be one long party for him once he receives your mother's eight-cassette pack of Marathi devotional songs mailed direct by us to the American address attached here,' declared Durga with increasing flourish.

Durga would have been surprised to hear that she had begun to sound like her mother.

'All right, stop it now. I get your point. We are late for the coach. If we miss it, we have a long wait, so just put it all back and we'll have to sort this out later,' he said irritably.

It was a morose journey on the airport coach to Cambridge's Drummer Street. The driver had asked, 'What happened, mate?' in horror, for the trousers now appeared to be covered with dried blood, pointing untruthfully to the dismemberment of a vital organ. The other passengers politely averted their eyes, but a man walking quickly past had sniggered, 'Lost your lunchbox, did yer?' Atul scowled. His gaze returned repeatedly and hypnotically to the stains during the journey. 'They were my best chinos,' he complained. 'I bought them in New York when I went there for a conference. Dry cleaning costs such a bomb here, I'll have to wait and see if I can send them back with someone. Actually, Nikhil is going to Delhi soon.' He brightened.

'You mean send them all the way to India?' she asked in disbelief.

'Why not? What did I tell you, every damn thing is so expensive in this country. Why do you think my mother was so keen for you to learn to cook? Who can afford to eat out at these prices? Listen, I really hope you brought everything you need, because we won't be running around in the shops as soon as we arrive.' He softened. 'See, it's not that there is no money, but it is not to be wasted on frivolous things. It is important to count every penny while we are here, and then we will have something to take back when we return.'

He had omitted to tell her that anything saved would be invested in Patwardhan's Maternity Clinic. Despite the future purchase of gleaming new machines, women would still have to push as they had through the ages.

Durga looked at the rain-streaked landscape and grey skies of her London childhood with increasing excitement. She was back in England, going to Cambridge and that was all that mattered. She would roam the colleges, see the fan-vaulted ceiling of King's College Chapel, the Fellows' Garden of Clare and Christ's, the Grecian buildings of Downing, the Wren Library, Trinity's Great Court. She was living a student's dream after years of crammed after-school coaching classes in rat-infested dank buildings, and nights of endless study leading to a single magical word: Oxbridge.

Atul shared none of the excitement she felt. He had not spoken to her on the flight or introduced her to Richard Cartwright, nor had he commented on her return to England after the long absence. He did not ask if this was home because it was the country of her birth and childhood, if home was what she had left behind in India, or was home wherever she was with him? On her first day back in England, Durga's suspicions were being speedily confirmed. It was about a boy, not a man.

As the taxi sped towards Hills Road from the coach station, Atul leaned over and asked the driver about the woody smell inside. 'I thought it was you, mate,' replied the driver sanguinely. 'Smells like an old lady with a cold in the back.'

Atul sniffed his way to the source of the odour and scrabbled frantically in his rucksack until his fingers made startled contact with a cracked bottle of Olesan eucalyptus oil and a hastily wrapped packet of incense sticks. As he searched further afield, he found a hot water bottle, herbal back-rub ointment and three pairs of thick hand-knitted men's socks.

'What have you been putting in here?' he asked in anger.

'Not *mea culpa*.'

'Then who?'

Durga thought it prudent not to point a finger in the same direction more than once, and did not reply.

As they entered the tiny flat, he snapped peevishly, 'What a bloody mess!'

It was not the welcome to Cambridge she had fondly imagined, but Durga could only concur.

# CHAPTER TEN

# All good things come to those who wait

SWARNAKUMARI HAD DISCOVERED something far more important missing in her life than a mere dozen roses. 'Any of you have seen my Guru Ma's prayer book lying anywhere?' she asked anxiously. 'I had it with me when I came in this morning. I must find my prayer book, must find it. It has her photo on it. She has long black hair, and she is sitting in a white robe in lotus pose, with one hand up.'

'What's she doing with the other, I'd like to know?' said Durga.

'Durga!' warned Heera.

'Where did I leave it, where could it be? Girls, help me! What if it has gone?' Swarnakumari wandered distractedly into the Staff Area.

'Did you hear about the book by that woman who hadn't had you-know-what for thirty-five years, and suddenly she was having lots of it, so she wrote about it?' asked Heera, standing by the shop window. 'She was American, I think. Anyway, she was sixty-five or something and she put an advert in the papers, saying all she wanted was you-know-what, and can you believe it, a lot of people answered.'

Eileen gave a disbelieving snort.

Durga turned to Swarnakumari as she returned through the curtains. 'Did you hear that, Swarna? This woman could be a role model for all those who think life's over at fifty.'

'Keep looking for the book,' urged Swarnakumari absently.

'Imagine, the youngest bloke to do you-know-what with her was thirty-two,' marvelled Heera.

'What?' mumbled Swarnakumari, barely listening.

'Why beat around the bush? Swarna, what would you say if a woman of sixty-five wanted sex? What would your Guru Ma say?' asked Durga.

'*Baba*, now you are teasing me again. What is there to say? At that age a woman should be thinking of nothing but spirituality, *na*. She should lead a simple, pure life. She must lose her attachment to all worldly things – all possessions, wealth, family, children. That is all,' concluded Swarnakumari firmly.

'Why not have fun in the years there are left?' suggested Durga.

'Is this the time to ask me such things?' barked Swarnakumari. 'Where could my prayer book be?'

'People do strange things at that age,' mused Heera. 'I know a woman called Sudha Barjotia. A little older than me, of course, she has a daughter-in-law now – they don't get along at all, in fact, they hardly talk to each other – but do you know what she puts on her face? That cream you get in India called Fair and Fine. As if it is going to make any difference to her now, after the age of forty-five. Both she and her daughter-in-

179

law use it, so at least they have something in common.'

Swarnakumari looked up with interest. 'What is this cream?'

'A cream called Fair and Fine to make the skin fair and fine. Honestly, Swarna, what else could it be?'

'If you are fair, you are fine,' observed Durga. 'Unless you mean the groom.'

'Does it work?' asked Swarnakumari, thinking of Mallika.

'Why don't you ask the men who use it?' countered Durga.

'You shouldn't make so much fun of her,' whispered Heera. 'Just help her find the book. She really believes in this Guru Ma, you know. These gurus are powerful people, and they can be quite inspiring.'

'That reminds me – when I was visiting Pune, I heard an amazing story,' Durga told her. 'There is a holy man, a baba, somewhere, who meditated in a pond for years. When he decided to emerge, his followers apparently discovered the fish in the pond had devoured his legs, so they carried him off on their shoulders. According to some reports, he's gung-ho about going back in again. I would fear for his arms this time, but then that's the power of faith for you.' She continued, 'And there's another baba who changes anything his followers offer him into something that tastes sweet. So let's say I give him a bitter veggie, it turns as sweet as honey.'

'What else does he do?' asked Eileen.

Durga looked puzzled.

'I mean, what's the point in trying to make other people's lives *taste* good?' Eileen persevered. 'The world needs other miracles.'

'Do you know, I heard a TV presenter the other day, who described Indian skin as mahogany,' interrupted Heera indignantly, still reflecting on creams and complexions.

'Are you sure he wasn't talking about furniture?' asked Durga.

Heera rushed to answer her mobile phone. 'Yes, Bob, it's me . . . I'm fine. Really . . . No, I don't think that's a good idea. I'm going out tonight. Can't we talk another time?' She silently returned to the counter, unnerved by the call. There was an unhappy edge to Bob's voice. He had been so insistent; was it about Adam?

No one spoke. Such moments were rare at India-Need, and did not last long. The shop bell soon tinkled, and a strapping young man entered, carrying a bulky shoulder bag.

'Hiya, Assistant Photographer, *Cambridge Evening News*,' he trumpeted. 'Which one of you is Diana Wallington-er-Smith?'

Durga mocked, 'Do you think any of us could be Diana Wellington-Smythe? Such a deliberate transposing of the postcolonial subject would not only be aesthetically unappealing but necessitate an inapposite dismantling of notions of self, ethnicity, race and class, thus bringing it into hybrid discontinuity.'

A faint smile hovered over Eileen's lips.

'Er . . .' responded the photographer.

'The director of the charity is out riding and won't be disturbed. And she won't like you messing with her name, by the way. It's Wellington-Smythe. Why do you want to know where she is?' asked Heera sharply.

The photographer turned to Heera, relieved at her

intervention. 'Well, she wanted to pose for the shop photo tomorrow afternoon with a toff, Lady something or other. It's some sort of Charities Special, but I've got to rush and do it now, or it won't get into the Saturday paper. Can't you ring her?'

Heera was emphatic in her refusal.

'Oh, all right then, why don't you lovely ladies line up there under the shop sign? Right there, yeah. Brilliant. Tell you what, display something from this shop, will yer?'

Swarnakumari and Heera both jostled for a central position, looking on in dismay as Durga mischievously slipped between the two. Swarnakumari held a teapot aloft, Heera a scarf and Durga a clock, and Eileen hovered uncertainly, displaying a child's mathematical set.

'C'mon loves, you can do better than that! Give us a smile, will yer?'

Durga murmured, 'Imagine Lady Di's face when she sees her little "Cambridge Curry Club" in the papers!'

'Yeah, that's it. Perfecto,' grinned the photographer.

As Swarnakumari coyly adjusted her sari over her shoulder, she spotted her prayer book nestling among a set of wine glasses in the shop window and leaned across the others, screaming, '*Who* put my Guru Ma prayer book for sale in the window?'

The photographer clicked. 'Lovely. Now ladies, if you'll excuse me, gotta rush, gotta get back to work. You'll tell Mrs er . . . Willington-Smith, won't yer? Any problems, ask her to contact me, she's got my number. Cheers, take care now, bye!'

Swarnakumari retrieved her prayer book, pressed it gratefully to her bosom, looked heavenward and mumbled reverently, 'How my prayer book landed up in the window God only knows, but I have got it back now, that is the main thing.'

'I thought the jolly Germans had nicked it,' said Durga. 'Come to think of it, we had so many odd characters in the shop today, it could have been anyone. Anyway, I'm off to get myself something to drink. I'll get the milk, too.'

'But Heera, what if Mrs Wellington-Smythe gets angry because we did not ring to tell her the photographer had come early?' asked Swarnakumari as the door swung shut behind Durga.

Heera inspected a lime-green cardigan lying on a chair. 'Let's have lunch first. She could still be riding that stallion of hers in a mucky field. I don't want her telling me off again. I'll ring later.'

Swarnakumari hastily discarded the prayer book. 'Let me see that cardigan. Oh, Laura Ashley. Good quality. My Mallika does not like that colour, otherwise I would have bought it. Give it to me, I will put a price tag and hanger. Oh, it's size eight, it would never have fitted her. We only have size sixteen and size eighteen hangers left. Never mind, who is going to notice in the window? Heera, you must tell Mrs Wellington-Smythe we must have correct size hangers. We are facing such a big shortage. It was so embarrassing last week, *na*?'

The previous Thursday had passed uneventfully except for an incident at closing time. A tall, broad-shouldered woman had approached Swarnakumari while the others were at the back of the shop.

'It says size fourteen on the hanger, but it's not a fourteen.'

'Yes, madam,' agreed Swarnakumari.

'No, it isn't.'

183

'Yes, madam.'

'Do you think I'm lying?'

'No, madam.'

The customer had raised her voice, and Heera ran out. Noticing the green stubble marks on the upper lip and chin, the broomstick eyebrows, and hearing a manly voice, Heera was flustered.

'Can I help you, sir?' she said.

'You may call me madam, or I am leaving this minute.'

'Yes, madam.'

The confusion over the customer's gender was never satisfactorily resolved, and Swarnakumari blamed it on the hangers. As she scribbled a price on a label and placed the lime-green cardigan in the window display, she continued, 'You know, my Mallika is very choosy about her clothes. She's put on a lot of weight, *na*. But what to do? She tells me, "Ma, I feel very hungry when I study." I think she is not happy about the way she looks, but she does not talk to me about it, so how to help her?'

Heera moved to the small table and chairs in the Staff Area as Swarnakumari followed. 'If you want Mallika to stop looking like a rosogulla, don't feed her rosogulla!' she said plainly. 'Stop feeding her so much food. Simple. Look, there's a story about Kabir – you know the famous poet, right? A woman asked him how she could stop her child eating too much sugar. He asked her to return after a few days for the answer. When she came back, he simply told her that she should tell her child to stop eating sugar because it was no good for her. The woman agreed, but was surprised, and asked Kabir why he hadn't said so in the

184

first place. He told her he had to go away and stop eating sugar himself to see what it felt like before he could advise. *Arre*, what I'm saying is: practise what you preach. If you yourself are eating too much – of course, I'm not saying you are – but if you are, then how will Mallika stop?'

Mallika was battling more than the bathroom scales; she was breaking out, and not just in spots. Her parents had been indulgent, for Mallika had been prematurely born. Swarnakumari had desperately wanted a son, but once she had suffered two miscarriages after Mallika's birth, she had submitted to a humble acceptance of God's plan and turned to prayer. In the meanwhile, her culinary efforts had harvested happy results: the frail baby had become a plump, dimpled girl with stubby legs bursting out of her frocks. At school, Mallika was teased and bullied, and during PE lessons it was evident that forward and backward rolls would pose a grave challenge.

Coupled with the excess weight was the problem of hirsutism, leading to concealment of more than one kind. The hair on her head tumbled thick around her shoulders, her eyebrows met above her nose, the thick downy hair on her arms, back, stomach and legs triggered school nightmares. She squeezed her underarms together during gym lessons, tugged the swimsuit desperately over her thighs, but Swarnakumari appeared not to notice the severity of her ordeal. Her response was to buy Mallika a pumice stone, put chickpea flour mixed with turmeric in a bath bottle for application as a body paste, and instruct her to rub her skin harder. Fluffy English towels were discarded, and special thin white towels available only at the Khadi Gram Udyog emporium were sent for the purpose by an aunt from India. As time went by, Mallika developed a hairy upper lip and sideburns, too. She was eventually left to her own devices; experiments with the pumice stone left her in a dotted rash like a Madhubani painting, and she reached for her father's blunt razor instead.

Growing up on Newton Square, Mallika, like her father, had stared furtively at the covers of magazines. She longed to have the pale, translucent skin, pinched, aquiline noses, light eyes and long, fair legs, not only of the models but of her own classmates. Mallika stopped looking in the mirror; she was convinced it would crack. Black, black hair and skin, she wept as she contemplated a life of unremitting ugliness.

An English friend had once stayed the night when Mallika was eight. Swarnakumari had run the bath, and the two girls had splashed happily with their Barbie dolls. As Emma rose to dry herself, Mallika had stared at her friend's hairless, pale body and the velvet sheen of her skin, the golden curls of her shoulder-length hair clinging damply to her flushed neck.

Mallika's spots soon followed, dotting her face, competing with her eyes for size and luminosity. They never arrived singly, only in hordes, unannounced and inopportune, always staying the night, littering her forehead and both cheeks. If squeezed, an exposed spot like a lone student demonstrator resorted to angry retaliation, rallying support until it was a red army of protest.

While the boys were merely bullying Mallika, three of her classmates in Year 11 had become pregnant. To the proud approval of her parents, Mallika, the 'boffin' and 'swot', topped the school and Sixth Form College, breezing into Cambridge University. She had dutifully followed her parents' advice and earned the respect of her peers; the rest, thought Swarnakumari, was best left in the hands of God, although of late she had been wondering whether Weight Watchers could accelerate the divine pace.

The arrival of the African family next door was the opening of a new world for Mallika, piercing the boredom of her cottonwool existence. Joseph had lived outside Sydney, and he described Bondi Beach and the surf, the Blue Mountains and the colours of the sunset, Australian dreaming and four thousand years of aboriginal history, the Great Spirit, the Wandjina and Ngalyod, the Rainbow Serpent, and the sun as a woman wandering across the sky spreading light and warmth. He told her of the legends of the lizards, wombats and emus, of waratah stems and watering-holes, of desert oaks and manburrangkali lily roots and the aboriginal belief that all life, whether human, animal, fish or bird, is deeply connected to a vast, unchanging web of relationship through the universe.

The discovery of a stubby funnelweb spider in his mother's slipper on a wet day precipitated the family's hasty departure from the continent. Mallika had listened open-mouthed in Joseph's bedroom decorated with boomerangs and aboriginal and African paintings and a didgeridoo and African drum.

It was an innocent friendship whose beat slithered its insistent way in colours of red ochre and white pipeclay into her modest, neat room a few feet away. A torrent of yearning to discover new worlds took hold, refusing to shake and fall to the ground like the graceful yellowed leaves of the lilac outside her window. Mr Chatterjee had been right: Joseph was a danger to Mallika; but not in the way he had imagined.

Swarnakumari was still lost in thought as Heera unpacked her lunch at the table and observed, 'You know, Swarna, every day we eat cold lunch just because Lady Di says the shop should not have food smells. We are not allowed to eat warmed-up Indian food in here. *Arre*, what nonsense! Such a bloody hypocrite, setting up this shop to impress her fancy friends like that Vicky woman and calling it IndiaNeed! Tell me, does India need her? What feeling does she have for India? The only connection is that her father was born in some cavalry cantonment in Shimla in 1933. So what? He's not bloody Rudyard Kipling, is he?'

Durga entered with the milk and flipped the shop sign to *Closed* as Heera continued, 'And why does she call her Siamese cats "Jaipur" and "Udaipur"? D'you think I will ever name my goldfish "Manchester"? Anyway, it's a big name discussion again, so forget it.'

'Raj nostalgia,' ventured Durga.

'You know, I was just telling Swarna, it's so stupid that Lady Di doesn't allow us to heat up our food here. All that nonsense about Indian food smells! I know I should have told her right away from the beginning, but from next week we'll use a hot-plate, all right? I'll tell her straight on her face if she says anything, "You call us your 'Curry Club', don't you, so then we *are* going to eat our Indian food." Let it smell, who cares? *Arre*, in fact, if we started serving Indian snacks in here, the customers would come running *because* of the smells.'

'Including those on crutches.' Durga set the milk on

the tea tray. 'The natives are getting restless. Mutiny. The subaltern speaks.'

'Where did you get the milk from? I hope you went to the Co-op. Lady Di knows it's cheapest there. I can see your guilty face – why didn't you walk that bit extra? Anyway, put the receipt at the till before you forget. Now have some samosas, girls. I got them from Sangeeta Chopra on the way here. I've not been feeling that well, but never mind, can't resist. Did you see her photograph in the paper yesterday? She was standing next to the Mayor at some college do, posing in front of the big samosa she had made. It was twenty-seven inches long. How she made it, I don't know.'

'Or why,' said Durga.

'She does the catering for many Cambridge colleges, and she makes those children of hers roll out the pastry – small kitchen. I think her husband has gone for good; someone saw him at Yarmouth sitting in a car with an English girl. Why are you not eating? There's chutney too.'

'I am fasting – my Guru Ma's birthday, *na* – but I am just thinking, could it be this Sangeeta has sold you some part of the same big samosa? It could be so stale, *na*?'

Heera considered the possibility while sniffing a samosa. 'Hmm, all right, don't eat it, girls, you never know. I tell you, no offence, but we clever Indians are like spring water in a well. The deeper you dig, the more you find. By the way, I was thinking we should meet outside the shop sometime. We should all get to know each other better. Durga, I know nothing about you. You never talk about yourself, and Eileen, you're always rushing about. So I was thinking, why don't we have a Diwali get-together? I would have invited you to my place, but it's in a mess. Shall we go out? Any suggestions?'

'What type of food? Indian?' asked Eileen.

'*Arre* no, are you mad, or what? What sort of treat would that be? D'you know, the other day some of us neighbours met for dinner at an Indian place near Castle Street. The food was not bad, I must admit, but I spent the evening thinking how much better my own cooking is.' Heera chortled.

'And cheaper, too,' Durga reminded her.

'You know how I am, girls. I have to talk, so I told the meek little waiter he must be shivering in his pants when he sees Indian customers like me, because he must know we won't like the dishes or the prices. Poor chap, what could he say – he just smiled politely.'

'I never eat out,' said Durga.

'*Arre*, you're not missing anything. I once went with the Essex wife of Bob's colleague, you know how these goras are – they always want to go for an Indian – we were in London and we went to a place called "Curry in a Hurry". First of all, what a name! *Arre*, how can you have curry in a hurry? And that in a place looking like All Bar One? I ordered special Kashmiri dal, and I'm not joking, girls, the waiter brought a huge white plate with dal put only in the middle – the same size as a doughnut. There was a big coriander leaf stuck on top, and paprika sprinkled all around the empty sides of the plate.'

'What did you do?' asked Swarnakumari, her curiosity aroused.

'I ate it, of course. Jacqui was tucking into her tikkas and korma, but I felt like a fool because I was thinking of my mother and my childhood. The pot of dal at home used to be huge, and my mother always made extra in case guests dropped in. She loved to cook lots of good food for everyone. That's the way we Sindhis are, you know.' Heera blinked furiously and her voice faltered. 'Sorry, girls, I'm just remembering my mother. I never knew the last time I saw her that it would be the last time.'

There was silence; sharp, fragile, a laden cloud threatening to burst sutured skin.

Swarnakumari said with finality, 'Dal is dal.'

The others nodded.

'Shall we try the noodle bar on Mill Road, then?' asked Eileen.

Heera spoke slowly, ignoring Eileen's question. 'You know, girls, there is a big difference between being an Asian born here, coming from East Africa and coming from India out of choice and free will. When you come here from India, even if you try, India doesn't let you go. It's funny, but after all these years I still automatically convert English money into rupees sometimes.' She chuckled. 'And I keep a rupee coin in my purse for good luck. Shall I tell you something else? Sometimes I go into the Grafton Centre on a Saturday just to be in a crowd again. Not for shopping. I want to be pushed and shoved by everyone, but then I start searching for the old faces that I know I will never find there. And in any case, no one pushes me, and if I push them by mistake, *they* say "Sorry" to *me*! It must be the same for you, Swarna, we both came here only because of our husbands – but maybe it's difficult for Durga to understand.'

Had Durga spoken, the words would have stretched

all the way round the room, each letter bold on a fluttering white square, boxed row upon row until, forming a chain, they seized an open window and trailed behind a plane soaring in the distance. Letters in the sky appeared smaller, but lived longer.

'So when are we going out?' persisted Eileen.

'I will ask Your Uncle and let you know, *hanh*. Lunchtime will be good, evening time is difficult for me.'

'Before I forget, anyone interested in buying my friend Rama Prasanna's book on South Indian cooking? She's giving a discount – normally it is £6.99. If you buy two, then it'll be £5.99 for each,' said Heera.

'Why to take two? It's the same book, *na?*' Swarnakumari was puzzled.

'Like crutches,' said Durga helpfully.

'*Arre* no, what's this nonsense about crutches all the time, Durga? I mean two copies in case you want to give someone else a Diwali or Christmas present. I promised her I would ask you girls, but I also told her straight, no Asian will spend money on cooking books. At the most, one *bakra* – one sucker – will buy and then everyone else will borrow. A friend of hers called Aparna even bought the book and then gave it back and coolly took a refund the next day. What a cheeky monkey! Poor Rama was quite upset, but I told her, "Straight case of book photocopying by Aparna's husband in the office. Nothing you can do about it." Eileen, you must be thinking we are all mad. Even when we're not eating, we still talk about food.'

Diana had previously attempted to manoeuvre Eileen out of the Thursday shift and into the Monday slot with Betty and Mary, but Eileen had refused, a steely edge to her voice. She would work on a Thursday, or not at all.

'Has Mrs Wellington-Smythe said anything about the Christmas decorations for the shop? We must start soon, *na*.' Swarnakumari deflected the conversation away from the cookery book she did not plan to purchase.

'Relax, it's only October. What's your hurry? Who feels Christmassy in the wind and autumn leaves? *Arre*, let Diwali come first. Why would anyone want to buy Christmas wrap just now?' Heera paused. 'Actually, I could be wrong. A cheap and cheerful nine-metre roll might interest a few early birds,' she said meaningfully.

'Present company excluded, of course,' retaliated Durga.

'We should be the first with the Christmas window display,' continued Swarnakumari earnestly.

'By the way, I put the blond wig in the window on the way out, Swarna. Don't worry, it won't disturb your display,' said Durga reassuringly, as they cleared the lunch table.

'No prizes for guessing who it is this time,' laughed Heera as the telephone rang. 'IndiaNeed, good afternoon ... Yes, Mrs Wellington-Smythe, it's Heera here ... Yes, we just had a photograph taken for the paper ... But you told me not to disturb you and that's why I didn't ring ... You've already told the photographer not to use it? Yes, I understand ... Yes, I've been here all the time during shop hours ... Yes, I've locked up every Thursday this month ... Yes, *of course*, I'm here all the time, and the rest of the volunteers come and go ... Yes, sometimes I *do* buy things from the shop, but I always ... *I always pay*. Yes, I remember we talked about those thefts . . . No, I didn't realise it was always on a Thursday . . . Yes, I know it's a Thursday today . . . Yes, I will tell everyone to look out for anything unusual today . . . Yes, *of course* I'm closing at five . . . No, I'm not leaving early. Yes, I will call if . . .' She replaced the receiver in a daze, turning to the three women. 'Did you hear that? Did you hear that? She thinks I'm the thief.'

Swarnakumari asked, 'What are you saying?'

Heera's voice rose. 'She thinks I'm a bloody thief! You heard, didn't you, just now? Girls, she is saying I am a thief!'

'Are you sure?' asked Swarnakumari.

'Yes. You know how she is. First she ticked me off *again* for opening the shop ten minutes late. It was only ten minutes. You three were standing outside waiting for me and you didn't complain, so what's her problem? Then she changed the subject, talking about the thief and Thursdays, so smooth, and she said, "Do be extra careful, watch the customers today, and don't forget to report anything unusual," but girls, I know she meant me.' Tears of outrage shimmered in her eyes.

Swarnakumari trembled. 'A thief in the shop today? What will he do to me?'

'Let's see, the thief could be male or female, of any age, size, shape, weight or colour, shabby or well-dressed, a batty old man, a student, young mother, anyone at all. Or maybe there's a whole gang out there. But I doubt anyone would want to attack you, Swarna, for reasons that I won't go into now,' said Durga comfortingly.

Heera called out impatiently, 'Girls, girls, aren't you listening? What d'you think I'm telling you? She suspects me! Who the hell does she think she is? I'm telling you, I've had enough now. I live a comfortable life, and I am not doing this for the money. I took this job only because I needed to sort something for myself in my mind. Looks like I made the wrong choice, didn't I? I ended up sorting other people's rejects instead. What's a charity shop, after all?'

'A symbol of the Diaspora, failed dreams and of what we can't have or hold any more, a domain of collective hope and renewed, recycled life,' said Durga.

'I come here for a laugh, the customers give me respect and I help deserving people in India, but now this is a question of my reputation. I'm not leaving until I've cleared my name.'

There was silence in the shop as the women absorbed the significance of Heera's announcement.

'She hasn't exactly accused you—' began Durga, but Heera interrupted fiercely, 'You wouldn't be saying that if she had talked to you instead of me. And that thin, cutting voice of hers like sharp ice . . .'

Swarnakumari soothed, 'Heera, some people are like that only. You cannot change them, so you have to protect yourself. What is the point of getting angry? Guru Ma says anger always destroys. It will eat and eat inside, and you will be the one to suffer. And in every situation you must always think of why the other person is acting like that, *na*. Guru Ma explains this very well in her chapter on understanding. You know the word "understand". It means to "stand under", to feel how it must be inside the other person's skin. We must try to understand Mrs Wellington-Smythe. I think she has some problems. She is not looking happy – something is wrong.'

'You could be right, Swarna,' Eileen admitted.

Heera was incensed. 'What? Are all three of you taking her side? All this Guru Ma stuff has made mango pickle out of your brain, Swarna. How can you feel sorry for Lady Di, of all people? I feel really let down, girls. What is this behaviour? If you were in my place, I would definitely support you.'

'We are supporting you, but what can we do?' asked Swarnakumari without conviction.

'*Chors*, bloody thieves run around in this world doing dishonest things, but no, that Lady Di has to catch me instead. I'm telling you, I'm going to do something about this. I'm wondering now – what if this thief really does come in on a Thursday, just after we close the shop at five, just so it doesn't look suspicious?'

Swarnakumari was sceptical. 'But how can a thief break in just like that? People would see, *na*.'

Heera silently absorbed the truth of Swarnakumari's words. Mill Road was unlike other roads in Cambridge in that there was life after dark; soon after the bookbinders had closed and the florist had stored away the buckets and unhooked the yellow and white striped awning, the pawnshop had reluctantly locked its doors and the charity shops had removed any precious items from their windows, the curry houses and restaurants rolled up their shutters, ready for the evening trade.

She spoke slowly, voicing her thoughts. 'Yes, but what if the thief is so clever he isn't breaking in? He must be coming in some other way, but how?' She continued, 'Tell you what, we are going to find out, girls. Today after we close the shop we'll stay on a little longer, and see what happens. And don't you dare say you're not going to wait; if you're my friends, you'll help me.'

It was Eileen who was the first to agree.

# CHAPTER ELEVEN

# What goes up must come down

EILEEN OPENED THE shop door on her way out to buy stamps at the local post office at the moment when a frail old lady entered, holding a large purse, and headed purposefully for the counter, settling on the chair at the till.

'Madam, you can't go there, that area is for staff only. May I help you?' asked Heera.

'Eh?' The elderly lady adjusted her hearing aid, and slowly removed several folded carrier bags from her purse. She set them out on the counter; each was meticulously flattened into a neat square.

Heera whispered to Durga, 'Why does she have so many carrier bags? D'you think she plans to steal something?'

'No, she looks plain batty to me. And too feeble to carry away the video recorder. She can't possibly be the thief.'

'Yeah, she looks like she's not wired right. She needs carrying herself. She reminds me of my Aunty Buddi Mai. D'you know what Aunty said to me when I got married? "Just make your home so happy that your man wants to come every night to your bed." Poor

Buddi Mai – they say she poisoned her husband's second wife,' confided Heera.

Durga was staring intently at the elderly lady. 'Was your Aunty Buddi Mai as dozy as this one?'

Heera shrugged her shoulders in incomprehension. 'Maybe it's a trick, and she'll suddenly wake up and start nicking things when we're not looking.'

Durga peered closer, giving the old lady a nudge. She slumped lower. Durga felt her pulse. 'She certainly won't need anything from the shop where she's going. Not even an old cardigan.'

'What?' asked Heera, startled.

'Well, it's not far, is it – six feet under.'

'Talk straight, Durga.' Heera walked away to a corner near the display window, beckoning. 'What are you saying?' she hissed.

'One could, of course, ignore random disruptions, refute the notion of finality and adopt a metaphysical determinant of consciousness. All right, she's dead,' said Durga.

'Dead? The old lady? Oh my God, what a situation!' Heera pulled herself together. 'All right, so we ring. Who do we ring first? Lady Di or the police? Should we call an ambulance? But what about Swarna?' She paused before continuing briskly, 'The thing is, sales have been slow all day, and this old lady, bless her soul, is already dead, so we could wait a bit before we tell anyone, right? Or does that sound too mean?'

Durga shook her head.

'So then, let Eileen and Swarna just carry on as usual. We need them to act normally.' Heera was thinking rapidly. 'But what if Swarna sees the old lady? She'll either scream for England or wash her hands ten times.

No, Durga. You and I will have to put the old lady somewhere out of sight for now.' Heera cast a desperate glance around the shop. 'It will be safe in the changing room. C'mon.'

The two swiftly heaved the body onto the wheelchair and propelled it into the changing room, zigzagging their way through the clothes racks, and then returned to the till. Meanwhile, Swarnakumari turned to another customer and asked, 'Tell me, do you come in on a Thursday only, or other days also? What about this coat – you like it? Nice colour, *na*? Come with me, there are many more in this section. We have a changing room if you want to try on anything. We sold a new Marks & Spencer cardigan just last week, otherwise I could have shown it to you.'

Heera and Durga fled to the changing room to wheel the body out.

Heera warned, 'That silly Swarna is taking this whole thief thing so seriously she will send all the customers to the changing room just so that she can check their belongings. Such an *eediot*! She's ruining everything. Maybe we should tell Eileen when she returns. That way at least she can stop Swarna messing up.'

'Too late for all that,' said Durga. 'Let's just take the old lady to the window.'

'Brilliant. Yeah, let's do that,' agreed Heera in relief.

They wheeled the body into the display area while Swarnakumari attempted to interest the customer in a Royal Doulton figurine. Heera was panting as they reached the window, and fumbled with her free hand to retrieve a ringing mobile phone from her trouser pocket. 'Yes, Bob, what is it? *Jaan*, do you realise what a difficult position I'm in right now? I really can't talk now. Bye.'

She turned to Durga, still breathless. 'Sorry about that. It was Bob.'

'Men! They never get the timing right,' replied Durga.

'Here, pass me the blond wig,' urged Heera, and she placed it at a rakish angle on the elderly lady's head.

'I know blondes have more fun, but are you sure the timing's right for *her*?'

'Pass me the hat. Quickly, that long scarf too – it will be good for covering her face,' hissed Heera. 'And that cardie there. I'll drape it over her arms.'

Durga murmured as she bent over the corpse, 'Forgive me, for truly I know not what I do.'

Swarnakumari pointed to a porcelain shepherdess. 'What about something like this for your mother's next birthday? I know what you must be thinking, but do you know, you really can save a lot of money when you buy from here. We keep only quality things in this shop, and many times they are completely brand new. I would not work here otherwise, *na*.' She spotted the pram. 'Oh, nice large pram, you can put many things next to the baby. Can I just see how much space you have got inside?'

A well-dressed customer entered, along with Eileen, who began to shadow her, but the woman took a dislike to being trailed and left immediately.

Struggling with the body in the window, Durga cried indignantly, 'Hang on a sec, that's my cardigan! How did it get here? I left it right there on that chair when I went out for the milk.'

'Strange things happen. In this shop, in life and

death,' murmured Heera. 'We'll sort it out later, Durga. Let's just leave it on her for now.'

The two hastily left the window display area and returned to the till as the shop bell tinkled and Swarnakumari's customer departed. Swarnakumari was relieved. 'I checked. That customer was not the thief, *hanh*! We are safe.'

The shop bell tinkled again, and a dapper man entered, nursing an umbrella with a wooden handle. 'Oh hello,' he began nervously. 'I was just passing by the window when I saw . . . well, I was wondering if you could show me the binoculars you have there. And the blond wig too, if you please.'

'Yes,' replied Eileen.

'No. There is no wig there,' denied Durga.

'Oh, but there is! It's on your mannequin. Shall I show you?' asked the customer.

'Please don't, I'll get both for you. Kindly wait here. Durga, could you take the gentleman to the counter?' asked Heera hastily.

The wig was removed and brought to the counter along with the binoculars. Durga tenderly wrapped the wig in a carrier bag belonging to the elderly lady.

'Thank you so much for helping IndiaNeed today with your purchase,' chorused Heera and Durga, escorting him to the door.

'What was that all about?' demanded Eileen curiously. 'Why are you two behaving so strangely? Has everyone gone mad in the shop today?'

Heera stared meaningfully. As soon as the last customer had left, she snapped, 'Quick, Swarna, it's five! Turn the shop sign to *Closed*. Lock the door, Durga, and Eileen, turn down the blinds! Swarna and Eileen, switch off the lights and then go to the Staff Area, we're coming too, in just a minute.'

Swarnakumari looked bewildered, Eileen looked suspicous, but following Heera's instructions both obediently disappeared behind the curtain. Heera and Durga raced to the window and wheeled the elderly lady backwards, propping her frame upright in the centre of the shop. They followed Swarnakumari into the Staff Area and waited in the dark. Time passed.

'Heera, we have been just sitting for fifteen minutes already. What is this – how long are we to wait? I cannot even phone Your Uncle to tell him I will be late, because he will tell me to come home immediately. I always make hot food for him and Mallika, *na*. And Heera, now I am thinking, why did that customer want the blond wig? He had so much of his own hair. He was asking for the binoculars, but then why did he only buy the wig? Could it be *he* is the thief and it is his disguise?' Swarnakumari jumped, startled. 'What was that?'

'What?' asked Durga.

'That sound. At the back.'

Durga was reassuring. 'Only a ghost.'

Swarnakumari emitted a strangled sound. 'A ghost!'

'Oh, didn't I tell you? The charity shop has been erected on troubled ground. It was built at the very spot where a student was hanged for troublemaking in 1265 by order of the King's Justices. Up until the six-teenth century, several undergraduates were living in lodgings around the town. His wandering ghost is still seen in the shops of Mill Road. He has a frayed piece of noose around his neck,' explained Durga. 'Perhaps the thief is none other than the ghost? Incidentally, did you know Peterhouse had an eighteenth-century ghost? A Mr Dawes, the Bursar. Hanged himself.'

'I am not staying now. You are frightening me, Durga.'

There was a thud. Swarnakumari squealed.

'That must be a poltergeist,' said Durga.

'*Hanh?*'

'Haven't you ever heard of them, Swarna?' inquired Eileen.

'Peterhouse once had a poltergeist, too, apparently. They had to remove it from a student's room,' said Durga with relish.

'What's a polta-whatever?' inquired Heera.

'German word for noisy and troublesome spirits,' replied Durga.

'Oh, *those*, is that what they are called? D'you know, there were these polta-thingies in a house near us in Hyderabad. My mother's friend got married, and she lived there with her husband and his mother-in-law and his two brothers and three sisters. Poor thing, she was very young, and she had a terrible time there. Anyway, suddenly a lot of strange things started happening. When they woke up in the morning, each and every chair was smashed. Then all the clothes started getting holes. Can you imagine, all their clothes, even new ones in the wardrobe! They blamed it on the daughter-in-law,' said Heera.

'Naturally,' said Durga.

'But then they realised she couldn't be doing all those things by herself. In front of their eyes there were solid objects flying in the air. Once a heavy teak cabinet just lifted by itself and walked to the other end of the room. Then the dishes got smashed, and they heard loud bangs. The lamps used to swing, there were electrical fuses, and then the funny voices started. They heard male and female voices giving curses. The family got really frightened. The police didn't really believe these people, but then the policeman who stayed there the night got holes in his clothes too. So then they decided that my mother's friend must be a witch,' concluded Heera dramatically.

'Naturally,' repeated Durga.

'What happened next?' asked Eileen.

'One night those polta-thingies set fire to their clothes. My mother's friend rushed to try and save her husband's clothes from burning—'

'Not her own? How noble!' interrupted Durga.

'And a sister-in-law just pushed her onto the flames,' finished Heera.

There was silence as they digested the horror of the woman's plight. Heera's mobile rang, and Swarnakumari jumped.

'Yes, Bob . . . No, I think I'm busy tomorrow evening, too. The WI meeting – it gets over late. Tell you what, why don't you call sometime in the weekend? . . . Bye!'

Heera continued, 'Where was I? No, no, it's not a tragedy. It could have been, but my mother was there, and she was very brave. She pulled her friend out before she got badly burned. The funny thing is, my mother used to be very shy and meek, and now suddenly she just yelled at her friend's in-laws. Afterwards, she told everyone to keep quiet, and she began talking in a very calm voice; she was reaching out to those polta-thingy spirits. She kept telling them their work was done, and to leave everyone in peace. And suddenly the lamps stopped swinging and the fire burned out. The ashes made a very strange pattern, my mother said.'

'I'm feeling very cold,' confessed Swarnakumari in a small, shivering voice.

'Then there must certainly be a ghost around. Did you know the temperature is always lower when there's a ghost in the air? Cambridge, with all its fens and marshes, is an ideal breeding ground for them. They like the damp,' Durga added. 'I've got an idea – let's go on a Cambridge Ghost Walk, and then we'll all join the Ghost Club. A curry club is so predictable. Let's tell Lady Di to call us her little "Ghost Club" instead.'

Heera intervened. 'She's just winding you up. Relax, Swarna. The sound came from upstairs, can't you tell? It's the DIY bloke again.'

'If poltergeists were in here, would they make holes in the net curtains?' pondered Durga. 'What would you do if the net curtains looked the same from the inside and outside, Swarna?'

'*Baba*, enough, Durga! You don't know when to stop. I am really frightened. I don't like sitting here in the dark.' Swarnakumari screamed and pointed to a shadow on the wall. 'Look, there is a knife! Look . . . sticking out!'

'Give me your torch, Swarna!' commanded Heera. She shone it on the object. 'What a silly thing you are! How can you think the hanger was a knife, honestly!'

'Heera, conscience calls. Aren't you going to ring about the old lady?' warned Durga.

Eileen was suspicious. 'What old lady?'

'Ignore her. She's just winding us all up again.' Heera turned urgently to Durga. 'If I ring now, my plan will be ruined. The thief won't show up if there's a police car outside.'

Durga was insistent. 'You wouldn't leave your old Aunty Buddi Mai like that, now would you, Heera?'

Swarnakumari quavered. 'Police car? What are you talking about?'

'I suppose you're right. I'll ring,' agreed Heera.

She moved towards the telephone, and in the silence there was the sound of the unlocking of the shop door; the bell tinkled. The four women looked at each other in tacit agreement as Heera grabbed the torch and led them to the curtain. They saw a man bending over a box, and Heera moved forward with her torch as the others followed fearfully. The man turned, and Swarnakumari panicked, grabbed a saucepan and hit him on the head. As he tried to escape, there was the sound of something tearing, he tripped over an object in the centre of the room and there was a crash as he hit the floor. Heera switched on the lights.

'Well done, Swarna! Knocked him out! Your Guru Ma would be proud of you,' she cried.

Swarnakumari responded shakily, pleased. 'Really? But I hit one person only. How come two are there now? Heera, Durga, tell me. I hit one person, *na*? This same person. But why is he lying on top of this old lady?'

Durga explained, 'Two lovers with a single death wish.'

'What to do with this girl! Durga, do not tease me. I do not understand anything at all. Tell me first, are there two thieves or only one?'

'Look, the young man you knocked out is the thief. The old lady is dead. She's been dead for some time. Why they ended up in a passionate clinch on the floor is a long, long story. But anyway, well done, that was a nifty little blow you gave him,' said Durga.

'But . . .'

'Seriously, great job, Swarna. And look, you've ripped his jeans, too!'

Swarnakumari was bewildered. 'God and Guru Ma save me, *eita ki hochche*? What is happening?'

'Shouldn't we see who he is? C'mon, help me!' ordered Heera.

Heera and Eileen heaved him over as Swarnakumari looked on in horror, and Durga peered down at him. 'Young bloke, seen him before. Wait a minute, there's no need to call in the police just yet. Do you know who we've got here?'

'W-W-Who?' asked Swarnakumari.

'You'll never guess – it's Lady Di's son!' announced Durga.

'What?' Heera yelled.

'It's Lady Di's son,' repeated Durga.

Swarnakumari asked in hushed tones, 'Are you sure?'

'This Hugh Grant wannabe hangs about near the Mill pub at the river after school. He's in the Sixth Form. I know a student who is a friend of his,' replied Durga. 'What? Don't you believe me? Can't you see the spitting resemblance to his mother?'

'But how did he get in? We heard the sound of the key turning, didn't we?' asked Heera.

'His mother's, of course,' deduced Eileen.

'Anyway, terrific initiative, Swarna. You can explain to Lady Di you killed him in self-defence,' said Durga.

'What are you saying? Oh God, save me, how was I to know . . .'

208

Durga relented. 'I was only teasing, Swarna. You've only knocked him out, that's all. Serves him right.'

'He's breathing,' said Eileen.

'Oh, what a big scare I got, and my heart is beating so fast! Durga, you frightened me, but I forgive you. I am wondering, why does a boy from such a good family steal from this charity shop?'

'Drugs,' said Durga.

'Drugs?' Swarnakumari was speechless. 'But why? Must be these English boarding schools. Children are lonely without their parents, *na*. And by the time they are seventeen, eighteen, they have picked up all the bad habits. Smoking, drinking . . .'

'Wild sex.'

'All right – yes, Durga, that also. But you know, I am thinking now I know why Mrs Wellington-Smythe must be worried about this naughty boy. Now I know why she is looking upset all the time.'

'Perhaps he's only a harmless modern-day Samuel Coleridge – the poet was a colourful character in his undergraduate days at Jesus College, you know. Ran up a pile of debts, and had to leave.'

Heera thundered, 'What are you two on about? Don't you realise what this means, girls? We've caught the thief, and he's her son, of all people. Can you imagine her face when she sees it's her own little samosa?' She paused triumphantly. 'Girls, girls, oh what sweet revenge, what a day this has been!'

'Could he be wearing something he's stolen from the shop?' speculated Eileen.

Heera and Eileen inspected the young man while Swarnakumari paced the floor.

'Does this striped shirt look familiar to you, Durga?' asked Heera.

'Yes, it's a Paul Smith.'

Swarnakumari fretted, 'Such a good, aristocratic family, and poor boy, no one to give him proper guidance. If the parents are too busy, or not caring about the problem, at least there should be grandparents like in our Indian families, *na*, to advise this poor boy.'

'Do you have any idea how many young Asians do drugs?' asked Durga.

'*Hanh?*'

'And how many Asian parents deny the problem exists?'

'Girls, girls, we have caught the thief, and it's Lady Di's son. That's all that matters,' Heera reminded them.

'Will he return my reading glasses?' asked Swarnakumari hopefully.

'Come here, girls, I'm dialling Lady Di's number. Now just watch the fun.' They gathered near the till.

'Daina?' Heera said quickly, deliberately mispronouncing her employer's first name to dispense with protocol. 'Heera here – you know, you call me Helen – from the shop again. Yes, I'm sorry to disturb you . . . No, I didn't know you had important guests for dinner, but you told me to ring you . . . Yes, I will ring Sue Carter in the evenings from now on. Yes, I have her number . . . Yes, this *is* an emergency. You told me to call you about the burglary, and well, I now know who it is, and we have also caught him. He is right here in the shop . . . Yes, of course I can do that, but I think you should accompany the thief to the police station yourself along with the police.'

Heera was oblivious of the frantic signals from Swarnakumari and Durga as the young man raised himself in a daze and bolted out of the door, leaving it ajar. 'If you are there, who knows, maybe the *Evening News* will want a photograph of you.' She smiled, satisfied. 'You are coming in twenty minutes? Yes, I'll wait . . . Yes, actually we're all still here. It's past closing time, you know, it's nearly six o'clock . . . Yes, everything is under control, I am waiting in the shop for you . . . We are waiting, goodbye!'

'Heera, he's gone,' said Swarnakumari.

Heera looked in disbelief at the empty space on the floor. 'Oh my God! Gone! How could he just get up and run off like that? Swarna, you're useless. I thought you gave him a nasty blow, but I should've guessed, naturally you wouldn't do it properly. Why didn't you stop him? Durga, why didn't *you* stop him?'

Swarnakumari was relieved. '*Baba*, now what has happened has happened. It was good I didn't hurt him, *na*. After all, it is no less than the son of Mrs Wellington-Smythe. Guru Ma says violence . . .'

Heera raged. 'Pardon my language, but to hell with your Guru Ma, is she going to help us now? No. So, what are we going to do?'

'God will give us the strength to find the way,' said Eileen calmly.

Swarnakumari agreed, 'Yes, be calm, be calm. While you are thinking about what you are going to say to Mrs Wellington-Smythe, I am just going to wash my hands, *hanh*.'

'What d'you mean? You're not going anywhere, Swarna. No handwashing allowed. You stay right here. I'm not doing this alone. Let's think about what we are

211

going to say to her. We're in this together, and we're all going to wait for her to arrive. We were so close – we were *this* close to catching him.' Heera stepped on a set of keys. 'What's this? Keys to the shop? They must be the ones he took from his mother, and they dropped out of his pocket when he fell. Girls, now we have proof it was him. *Arre*, watch the fun when Lady Di arrives. She will have a lot of explaining to do.'

'But do you not think that Mrs Wellington-Smythe might say *you* stole her keys from her? How can you prove it was her boy?' asked Swarnakumari.

'You're right.' Heera was crestfallen.

'For once,' said Durga.

'What are we going to do?' despaired Heera.

Durga prodded, 'What are we going to do about the *old lady*?'

Heera and Durga heaved the body back onto the wheelchair. The handbag on the corpse fell open and a mirror and a pair of gloves tumbled to the floor.

'Swarna, gloves! Do you want them for sorting the bags?' cried Durga.

As she spoke, a man entered through the open door. 'Evenin'. Sorry I'm late,' he said. 'Traffic on Milton Road's shocking tonight. Got to collect a wheelchair for the Arthur Rank Hospice.'

Swarnakumari, Heera and Eileen froze, but Durga straightened and moved forward. 'Oh, there you are. She's been waiting for you.' She bent over the old lady solicitously. 'Haven't you, angel? Off you go, my dear. Now, take good care of yourself where you're going. Goodbye!' She turned to the man. 'She's all yours.'

'Got orders to pick up a wheelchair,' repeated the man, perplexed.

'A wheelchair. Yes, with her in it. She's taking a nap, the old dear. She's been travelling back and forth such a lot lately, poor thing. Let me help you wheel her out, that's it. Could you hold the door open for me? Easy does it . . . Right. Goodbye.'

'Wait, take her crutches too,' said Eileen, handing them abruptly to the man.

'Yes,' agreed Durga. 'Wouldn't want to leave them behind, would we?'

Still perplexed, the man left with the elderly lady in the wheelchair, the crutches placed neatly across her lap.

Swarnakumari spoke slowly. 'My heart is beating very fast, *baba*. What is all this happening? I need to sit down. Where did the young man go? Where did the old lady go? Where did this other man go?'

'Oh no, I forgot to tell the man the brake on the wheelchair isn't working. That was why some *eediot* had donated it to us in the first place,' lamented Heera.

'And I forgot to get my cardigan back,' added Durga regretfully.

Heera fumed, 'Forget the bloody cardigan. Lady Di will be here any minute. Girls, what are we going to do?'

The shop bell tinkled again, and before their worried eyes, the *Cambridge Evening News* photographer entered. 'Hiya, *Cambridge Evening News* again. How are the four lovely ladies? Got a call from your boss. She's coming down here. Had a lot of excitement lately, haven't yer? Where's the bloke you caught?'

Durga moved forward again. 'It frequently happens that the signifier slips and evades the grasp of the signified in a poststructuralist site of unintentional fallacy.

It must be remembered that we live in a society of simulacrum, free of connection to reality. One should therefore desist from further discourse.'

'Er . . .' mumbled the photographer, lost.

'Hang on, what's this?' she exclaimed as she spotted an object lying on the floor, and scooped it into her hands. 'A wallet. Whose?'

'Maybe a customer lost it?' suggested Swarnakumari.

'There's only one way to find out,' advised Eileen.

Durga flicked it open and paused for dramatic effect. 'We've got the proof although we don't have the pudding.'

'Talk straight!' commanded Heera.

'Is this a hanger I see before me? Nay, behold, 'tis the purse of the noble lord.'

Heera spluttered, 'You mean . . .? Oh my God, this is brilliant. Brilliant. It must have fallen, but how? When Swarna ripped his jeans? Oh my God. Yes!'

'Good "back pocket" job on the trousers, Swarna,' applauded Durga. 'Your people in Kolkata would be proud of you.'

Swarnakumari looked pleased. 'Really? You, and Mallika, you young girls are clever, but I am no less, *na*. But I still do not understand what is going on. First that young man falls on that poor lady, and then another man takes her away in the wheelchair. Who *are* these men?'

'Rivals, both, for her love,' quipped Durga.

'What a story I will have to tell Mallika and Your Uncle. He has already been in the shop today, and so much has happened, *na*. How is he going to believe that so much more happened in one single day? Actually I still do not understand what happened, but

214

anyway . . . Oh, I am so late! I have to make the dinner.' Swarnakumari paused. 'Never mind, they should wait this time, *na?*' she added, with a smile in Durga's direction.

Durga smiled back. She had a sudden thought, speaking decisively to the photographer. 'Mrs Wellington-Smythe would surely wish to capture this for posterity, since this is the moment we found proof of the thief's identity and guilt. We're ready for our photograph.' She mimicked the photographer's earlier instructions. 'We'll pose here, right under the shop sign *IndiaNeed*. Brilliant.'

When the phone rang, Heera hesitated. It finally hiccuped into silence as her mobile phone took over.

Durga urged, 'Heera, come on, in the centre, that's it. Now, why don't you three lovely ladies display something that doesn't belong to the shop? Ah, that's it, the wallet. Could you hold it up so Mr Photographer can get a good close-up?'

Mesmerised by her authoritative tone, the photographer clicked obediently.

'Did you get it, love? Now another one of the four of us. C'mon Swarna, heroine of the hour, c'mon Heera, Eileen, we can do better than that. We are the "Cambridge Curry Club". United we stand, though we may fall or fail. Right – we're ready.' They posed, beaming at the camera.

The photographer clicked again to the accompaniment of a thunderous crash upstairs. A shower of golden dust sprayed the group, followed by another and yet another, until they stood choking and gasping, ghostly apparitions – victims of DIY floor lamination.

A large, jagged hole had formed in the ceiling of the

charity shop. As they gazed upwards in mute horror, a fresh mound of rubble fell through, knocking the wallet out of Heera's hand and burying it beneath a pile of bricks and dust. A tousled head appeared directly above, and a Yorkshire-accented voice said cheerily, 'Eh oop! Sorry about that. Everyone down there all reet?'

The shop was plunged into darkness.

# Epilogue

SIX WEEKS LATER, spangled golden Christmas lights winked at the thronging shoppers in the city centre as the Salvation Army band struck up a carol outside Lion's Yard. Not far away, Mill Road carried its own festive look; bunting, miniature Christmas trees and snowmen decorated the shop windows, but the bookbinder was closed; Wright, the elderly owner, had an inflamed knee. The wistful blonde florist turned contemplative; the boyfriend had not proposed, but there was always next year. The grocers Veejay had artfully placed mulled wine sachets above the coriander and ginger. A brand-new pizza and kebab takeaway called Bytes4U was proving popular with the residents; a special promotion offered a large pizza at £9.99 with free fries and a Coke and a red-and-white candy stick that said *Xmas Xtra*. Its predecessor, IndiaNeed, could never have offered such inducements, and had humbly surrendered to the takeaway's gleaming ovens, chrome counters and sunshine teenagers in perky caps and aprons.

Swarnakumari and Mr Chatterjee were away, holidaying in Kolkata over Christmas. Their sudden decision to leave Cambridge could be traced to Mr Banerjee's brush with fate in early November. He had been walking along Queen Edith's Way on a Sunday afternoon in the fading light, admiring flowering winter jasmine in a passing garden when a sharp object was thrust into his back, and a voice commanded him to hand over his money without turning round. Banerjee froze before removing his wallet containing a pound in change and a smiling photograph of Heinz and Madhumita, and turned. The next moment he lay on the ground, writhing, as his attacker fled. A resident sounded the alarm, but Banerjee lay unconscious until the ambulance arrived. The young thug sped away, cursing as he found the meagre coins, flinging the wallet into thick shrubbery at the junction of the road. Unknown to Banerjee, the worn Indian leather wallet and the smiling photograph of Heinz and Madhumita were to nestle for several years among the leaves, along with an abandoned packet of salt and vinegar crisps, unnoticed by the human eye.

It was difficult to ascertain whether it was Banerjee or Mr Chatterjee who was left more shaken by the incident. But for an urgent letter to be written to the City Council complaining about a faulty streetlamp on Newton Square, Mr Chatterjee would have been Banerjee's companion on Sunday's fateful walk. Mr Chatterjee lay sleepless as tortured thoughts encircled his pillow; would the assailant have attacked two elderly men on a walk, or only one? Would the thug have targeted him more brutally than Banerjee for not carrying his wallet at all, and would he have been left to bleed, a cracked skull, life ebbing on the Cambridge pavement of a Neighbourhood Watch street?

Madhumita, Banerjee's daughter, was tearfully apologetic. She would have flown out immediately, but their schedules were 'real tough'; neither she nor Heinz had leave for the rest of the year. Mr Chatterjee had pursed his lips silently at the thought of the ketchup clown, although Banerjee was more understanding. Heinz was going to buy a new car next summer and the couple had planned a holiday to Europe, he explained. Banerjee was simply too blind to see how foolish it was to rely on offspring to sweeten old age, thought Mr Chatterjee with sudden insight. Children were like the books he borrowed from the Rock Road Library: to be kept only for a limited period. He nevertheless viewed Mallika's application to Stanford on the recommendation of her supervisors with anxiety; in geographical location, it was dangerously close to San Ramon.

Banerjee was in pain, and waiting for an operation on the National Health Service to his shoulder, but no date had been provided. The uncertainty was already taking its toll. Mrs Banerjee's military-style ministrations added to the general discomfort, and it was impossible to tell which was more intolerable. Banerjee's malt whisky had been banned and banished; medicine and alcohol were a lethal combination, bellowed his commanding officer.

A witness to Banerjee's tribulations, Mr Chatterjee was deeply alarmed on several counts. The assailant could still be concealed in the bushes, ready to pounce. In the meanwhile, Mr Chatterjee read about another attack, reported in the *Cambridge Evening News*, on a blind woman who was out walking. Two youths kicked away her cane and snatched her purse. Mr Chatterjee was shaken to the core, as he lay in his bed staring at the ceiling that night. This was not the Britain he had dreamed of as a boy growing up in Calcutta, this was not the country of Shakespeare and Keats and Shelley and Wordsworth. It was a wasteland, he thought. It had become a council estate wasteland and Hooligan's Choice – not Hobson's – before his very eyes.

Banerjee's NHS wait was deplorable; this could not be permitted to happen in the country that rationed his friend's pension and had swallowed his tax contributions. Mr Chatterjee felt unease, betrayal, and as a consequence the Neighbourhood Watch duties were no longer challenging; it seemed irrelevant and futile to invest in securing other homes with his own still at risk. Old age had always been a worry to Mr Chatterjee; now he was deeply troubled. For some days, he had not bothered to glance at the magazines on the top shelf at the newsagent, nor had he scanned the headlines in his Bengali paper with the same relish.

Returning late from a Diwali party in Girton two days after the Banerjee incident, he was surprised to see a police checkpoint on Trumpington Road. As he fearfully rolled down his car window, the officer inquired about the extent of his consumption of alcohol earlier that evening.

Unfamilarity with the situation made Mr Chatterjee, a man of legal precision, respond meekly and weakly, 'Not much.' He watched miserably as other cars were let through. Recovering his wits as the officer approached him with the breath-testing unit, he supplied quickly, 'I remember now. It was one glass of whisky.'

It was too late. The officer took no notice, proceeding with rapid instructions that left Mr Chatterjee trembling like the Japanese wind chimes in his conservatory. He blew into the tube, cupping it with both hands. The officer shook his head. 'That's no good, sir. Try again.' Mr Chatterjee continued to quiver while Swarnakumari sat wordlessly beside him. The second attempt failed. 'No, don't hold it sir. Just blow. Blow!' Mr Chatterjee humbly confessed that his nervousness prevented him from fully comprehending what he had to do. Could the officer explain slowly? he asked, whereupon the officer warned him that if he did not blow properly one last time, he would be under arrest.

Mr Chatterjee had spoken the truth about his intake that evening; the officer eventually let them pass. The couple did not speak as they negotiated the Long Road bridge. Mr Chatterjee's hands clutched his dignity on the steering wheel, as he drove steadily past the Sixth Form College and Tennis Centre.

He recalled an incident from the time his cousin Palash Ghosh was visiting from Jamshedpur. Mr Chatterjee had extolled the English way of life with enthusiasm. 'Observe the immaculate dress of the English. Even coach drivers wear black suits. Observe how respectful they are towards cultured Indians. My postman calls me "sir" just for giving me the post – the accountant, the busdriver, all of them say "sir" to me.' Ghosh had agreed; English civility was exemplary. Ghosh had been equally impressed by the English roundabout.

Swarnakumari looked ahead; her fingers unclenched eastward. Mr Chatterjee's fingers were perspiring over the wheel. He now sensed that 'sir' had more inflections than one.

Mr Chatterjee's changing moods mirrored the dreary

winter landscape. When he continued to stare at the leafless trees outside as he sat at his desk on a Monday, his Parker pen idle in his hands, Swarnakumari produced the telephone number of Heera's Essex travel agent who specialised in cheap fares to India. Mr Chatterjee protested over the stops at three Middle Eastern destinations en route, but the persuasive Gujarati man pointed out reasonably that it was high season with low availability. Mallika would invite an Indian friend to stay, and look after the house; the neighbours, including Joseph, had offered to keep an eye. Mr Chatterjee demurred but Swarnakumari, now calm, referred him to the chapter on parenting in the missing prayer book. When a bird was ready to fly, said Guru Ma, a sloping nest was never a deterrent.

Swarnakumari's skilful manoeuvres infused new vigour in Mr Chatterjee, who now believed that the holiday in India had always been his suggestion. He took enthusiastic control, checking the locks on windows and doors, pruning the bushes and clearing away the leaves, switching off the fountain feature and storing the garden Aphrodite in the garage. The neat bundles of junk mail in there reminded him to instruct Mallika to stack the post neatly on his desk during their absence. He organised the payment of the utility bills and discontinued the Bengali newspaper for a month, glancing only out of habit at the magazine covers turned upside down.

'Going home?' asked the envious newsagent.

It was eight years since the Patels had returned to Gujarat on holiday. The shop was only closed half-days on Sundays, and there was no one to take command if they went on holiday; the son was at university and had already expressed his lack of interest in his father's enterprise, and Mr Patel's brother and nephews ran shops of their own in Ealing and Wembley. Mr Chatterjee was startled by the newsagent's wistful reference to 'home'.

After the holiday in India with Swarnakumari, Mr Chatterjee's life would chart a different path. The passengers had arrived in Kolkata fifteen minutes ahead of schedule. The pilot had mentioned strong tail winds.

Bob was unlikely to patronise the Bytes4U takeaway. He was no lover of fast food. He was pining for Indian food, Heera's food. Repeated calls to her after the shop's closure traced her to a Tupperware demonstration in Farida Nayak's living room. Standing on a familiar doorstep a week later, he fumbled ruefully for his key before ringing the doorbell instead. The hallway still carried lingering odours of spice.

They sat at the kitchen table with a fruit bowl in its centre. El Salvio loved red seedless grapes, he thought, before realising he had transposed two realities and two households, two lives and a split existence. How easy it would have been not to leave at all, to share a convivial pot of Chinese green tea with Heera and put the rubbish out in the bin in the frost-covered patio, and climb the stairs to sleep and never have climbed down again.

He noticed, heart sinking, that she offered him the Wedgwood cup and saucer reserved for guests. She sat stiffly on the kitchen stool, regal and resolute in her shapeless kaftan. Staring at the turmeric stain below her shoulder, he was mesmerised by its yellowness as it engorged, swelling into a flame of orange hope. He began slowly in a quiet voice, telling her of his childhood in the dank cottage on the moor, the rooms filled with reproach, his confusion, the beatings and his cowed resistance, the city, the unending questions of who and what and why he was, and his fear of the ending of the world and his life without knowing, the struggle, the battle to find his self, himself. He loved her utterly, he knew that now.

Heera rose to fill the kettle and in the rising steam recalled her meeting with Javed in the cosy Turkish restaurant on King Street. The flickering candlelight had enacted a shadow dance on his face; the mystery of the missing card on the bouquet now solved, he recited the Urdu couplet, soft, baritone, seductive. He had penned additional lyrics for the occasion in praise of steadfastness, and she had listened spellbound. They had laughed at each other's slide into middle age; she patted the rolls of flesh around her hips and he pointed wryly to his chin and his protruding stomach. When she shut the door firmly later that evening, he lingered outside her house under the moonlight on the gravel path, looked up at the night sky and knew she had set him free.

Heera sat down at the kitchen table again. She told Bob that nothing had changed; she was still his wife, and he her husband. She had her self-esteem and dignity and her standing in the community, and just as a decision to leave had not been taken hastily, so was his desire to return to be weighed with care. If he returned, she said firmly, it would be on her terms. With a compassion that left him wordless, she said she knew he was not ready, whatever he might profess to the contrary, and the matter of the mortgage should be settled in the meanwhile; the house on Tenison Road would be sold, and she would move into a small flat. A small flat? he asked, dazed. It was not a split decision, she said, smiling. There was always a right action and a wrong one; the right action was the one that never seemed to be so at the time.

He stayed until midnight, boldly uncorking a Merlot from his wine rack. He narrated his battles with El Salvio, and she laughed, tears streaming. As he left, carrying the bunch of red seedless grapes she had hastily packed into a Tesco carrier bag, he turned to see her in the hallway, her reddish hair framed by its light. From where he was standing it looked like a halo.

The day after he first met Durga, Roman waited impatiently in the travel section at Heffers. It had been a mistake for him to suggest the bookshop, he realised. Teresa might be lurking behind the shelves, red and ready. He decided not to look at his watch again. It would only confirm one fact: Durga was not coming. She was already an hour and ten minutes late, and there could be no mistake about the place or time. Although he had supplied his telephone number, she had merely stated cryptically that she would be there.

He walked away, through All Saint's Passage, turning right onto Sidney Street, and up St Andrew's Street and Regent Street, turning left at Gonville Place, past the Parkside swimming pool and onto Mill Road, his steps treading a furious mile.

He stood speechless, staring at the exterior of the charity shop. A red and white ticker tape had been placed around the entrance, sealing all access. The ceiling appeared to have collapsed; all he could see was debris inside the shop. Fear seized him as he stared, all recrimination and reproach banished.

The blonde florist at Sunflowers was happy to tell him the sad news; the entire ceiling had caved in that morning, but the shop had already been closed. A small part of it had collapsed the previous evening while the volunteers were still inside, but they were unharmed. The police had already visited and so had the shop's director. The secretary at the solicitor's firm two doors down was of the opinion that IndiaNeed would not re-open, she added.

Roman was calming a thumping heart. Where were the volunteers? he asked. Were they operating out of other premises? Did she know the woman called Durga? He began to describe her – slim, tall, shiny shoulder-length hair, dark-brown eyes, full lips – and the blonde florist turned more wistful as she saw the soft light in his eyes matching the velvet of the scarlet blooms. He dashed out of the shop when she could help no further, having spotted her freckled assistant moodily scuffing a shoe against the pavement.

'Hi, remember me?' said Roman urgently. 'I delivered your roses for you to that shop over there. I met you yesterday. I delivered the bouquet for you, remember? You had to see your girlfriend. It was only yesterday. Wake up, man!' Roman smacked the lad's cheeks between his hands.

'She dumped me,' said the lad morosely.

'That's too bad. Listen, did you know Durga, who worked at IndiaNeed? She's Indian. Slim, beautiful, shoulder-length black hair? Did you know any of the people there? Do you know where they live – anything? Come on, man.'

The lad was unable to oblige, sinking into a witless stupor. Roman felt a sudden compassion for the woebegone Cupid. 'Listen, man, you've got to pull yourself together,' he advised. 'If you really love her, then you'll find a way. Give her a dozen red roses. Don't you get a discount? Plus chocolates and a heart-shaped card. Maybe a big red balloon too? You're a good-looking fella, bet you know what to do. Go for it.'

The freckled lad listened before slumping moodily again against the unforgiving wall as Roman returned to the blonde florist.

'Nick's a good lad, but a bit slow,' she said when he reported the failure of his efforts. 'Why did you ask him? He wouldn't know a thing. Oh, did I tell you the director's name was Diana Wellington-Smythe? Everyone's heard of her – maybe you should get in touch.'

Diana was at a trendy salon off Market Square, enjoying a vigorous Indian head massage to restore her jangled nerves. IndiaNeed was gone, had vanished in a little puff and cloud of dust. Immediately after the collapse of the ceiling the next day, she and other members of the Board of IndiaNeed had declared the items beyond recovery; salvage was too much trouble and money. An electrician surveying the damage had handed her a long-stemmed rose he had found nestling behind a twisted wooden rack. It was still a perfect bloom, he had said wonderingly. She twirled it for a moment and placed it on the debris as she left. The 'Cambridge Curry Club' had been disbanded without ceremony.

Rupert was away in London, as usual, staying overnight at the little flat in Chelsea, and James had not returned home, either; he was probably staying with his awful friend Henry. It was all so tiresome.

Her mobile rang and she answered, hair oily and wild, as the masseuse paused and stepped back respectfully. 'Diana Wellington-Smythe . . . Who? . . . Tempest? Dr Tempest? You are from where, did you say? . . . Oh, I see . . . No, that's all right, I like to leave my mobile number on the answerphone. People should feel they can reach me quickly, or what's the point . . . Yes, it was a disaster, quite appalling, very distressing indeed . . . In touch with whom? . . . Dewga? Dugga? No, I don't recall that name. Do you mean the Indian woman who was doing the research for a television company – the Cambridge graduate? Yes? In that case, Helen would know how to contact her – you know, my manager . . . *Her* home number? No, I'm afraid I can't remember. It would be in the files, but it's been such a dreadful business with the debris, can't find a thing . . . Her last name? I simply can't remember . . . You're welcome. Dr Tempest, you sound American. Are you? . . . How interesting! Are you staying over Christmas? If so, perhaps you would like to join us for dinner some day . . . We would love to have you at our table. Rupert and I regularly entertain Cambridge Faculty. Do give me a ring, won't you? Goodbye.'

Roman turned to the blonde florist in desperation. 'Do you know the shop manager Helen? What does she look like?'

'She's of South Asian origin, not tall, not slim, and the surname is Moore. An Asian gentleman sent her roses yesterday,' replied the politically correct florist. 'Helen . . . Funny, I'm sure her name was Heera,' she added.

'Heera, that's the one! Moore, did you say, as in M-o-o-r-e? That's an English surname.' Roman asked for the directory again.

There was something in his desperately seeking voice that prompted Heera to give him Durga's address.

'There's someone downstairs who wants to see you. He said his name was Dr Tempest. Shall I let him in?' asked Atul.

Durga dropped a startled ladle into the cooking pot. 'No, tell him to wait downstairs. He's . . . he's in a hurry. I've got to give him a message. I'll be right back.'

They met outside under a clear night sky near the neat lawn overlooked by the block of flats, camouflaged by the communal bins. They gazed at each other until he said, 'I guess you didn't want to be found.'

'No.'

'When I was a kid, I used to play detective. I had a rusty bunch of keys on a wire. They unravelled every mystery, and I solved every crime in the neighbourhood. My mom found them lying around one day and threw them away. They were just a bunch of old keys to her, but they were the shiniest, newest keys in the whole wide world to me. I should have found out where she got rid of them, and I should have kept looking.'

She remained silent.

'Well, anyway, here I am,' he said.

'Yes.'

'I need to get something straight. You didn't show up, and I've been through a helluva lot of trouble tracing you here. It's a long story, like the one with the florist, and I think that's two reasons to still meet for

dinner. I wasn't imagining it yesterday. There's something I felt that maybe you felt too . . .'

'Yes.'

He moved closer. 'Then why didn't you show up?
Cold feet? Did you look me up on the Internet and
discover my Cactus Cowboys Escorts Service? Damn, I
should've known you'd find out who I really am.' He
searched her face. 'Who's that guy who answered when
I buzzed you downstairs?'

'My husband.'

He stepped backwards with an exaggerated gesture
of disbelief. 'A husband?' He stood silent, considering.
'I'm okay with that, too. Things aren't going quite the
way I planned, but no problem. How about you, your
husband and me go out to dinner? A bit crowded at a
cosy table for two, but I think an extra chair just might
be arranged if we move the window.'

'I'm sorry.'

'Why? Because you didn't think it was important
enough to tell me? That you didn't tell me? No problem. How about I come up for dinner, then? What's
cooking?'

'Vangebhaji and amti and bhaat. Aubergines, dal and
rice.'

'This vangerber stuff sounds good to me. Is he good
to you?'

'Yes.'

'Why didn't you tell me?' he asked softly.

'I wanted to help you find a cactus.'

They spoke under a spell in the darkness.

'And I thought I'd found one, and didn't want to lose
it,' he said.

She shook her head, moving away.

'Do you always follow your head?'

She shook her head again. 'This is madness.'

'Have you never given in to the madness, the crazed dance, raced the rushing blood to the horizon?'

She looked away.

'Well, my speech is over, my lines are laid to rest. You have my number, coyote. If you want to, give me a call.' He strode away into the light.

Durga lay awake next to her husband, coiled in the memory of Roman and the burst of stars. She waited, still, in the silence. A plaintive saxophone played softly across from the apartment opposite. It was never the same sound every night and always the same sweet blue riff of curling desire.


The volunteers and the photographer had staggered out of the shop the previous evening, choking with dust, helped out by passersby. Swarnakumari had looked shocked, and the secretary at the solicitor's firm, staying late to type a client's will, offered tea in her office.

'First things first, girls: what did we lose? The Fire Brigade man said he would try to recover all the missing items I mentioned, but was there anything we forgot?' asked Heera later.

Swarnakumari was still in a daze, and Eileen whispered, 'Her Guru Ma prayer book.'

'Of course, I forgot all about it. She hasn't mentioned it, though. I think she's still in shock, poor thing. This time it might never be found,' replied Heera in a low voice. She looked at the three women. 'Cheer up, girls! At least the collapsible bed's gone as well. Someone's nicked it.'

'Shouldn't Mrs Wellington-Smythe be here by now?'

interrupted the solicitor's secretary sharply. 'I've got to lock up, it's getting late.'

'Yes, it's quite late. I think you should all go now. I'll wait outside until she arrives,' agreed Heera.

They put on their coats as the secretary tidied her desk.

'I'll wait with you,' offered Eileen. 'I only live round the corner.'

'What should I tell her?' asked Heera slowly. 'I mean about the wallet, and her son.'

'The truth, of course,' replied Eileen, puzzled. 'Why do you ask?'

'See, the thing is, the wallet is gone, right? It's somewhere under the debris. The ceiling's gone as well, and everything's a mess. It's going to take them a while to clear all that up – who's liable, who's going to pay for the damage, all that sort of thing. It's clear that we can't go back in to work for a long time, and who knows when that will be? Who knows what's going to happen to us, and to the shop? So what does it matter in the end?'

She turned to the others, pausing for breath. 'Girls, let's not tell Lady Di it was her son. We really can't prove it unless the wallet is found, in any case, and she's going to get a nasty shock seeing the shop, as it is. She had planned to have Lady What's-It come by tomorrow – it was going to be her big day. Maybe Swarna's right. Maybe she's having a rough time already, who knows? What if her son really is on drugs? Anyway, let's forget it, shall we? Simply drop the whole thing. I'll just say the thief ran away when the ceiling came down and that's that. Let it go.'

'No,' said Eileen forcefully. 'She should get what she deserves.'

232

The others digested her words in silence, surprised by their flinty weight.

Swarnakumari's stomach rumbled loudly. She had been fasting all day for Guru Ma's birthday. It had been one of the most eventful days of Swarnakumari's life; so coloured, it was now a white blur.

'What do you think, Swarna?' asked Heera.

'*Ami arr parchi na*,' croaked Swarnakumari fuzzily. 'I can't, I just can't cope . . .'

Durga was inclined to agree with Eileen; the wallet episode should not be dropped. To resolve the issue in democratic mode, Heera suggested a secret vote, much to the irritation of the solicitor's secretary, now regretting her impulsive gesture of goodwill. She would not be paid overtime for her Samaritan spirit. As Heera read the four hastily written slips a few minutes later, she beamed. 'We *are* a club. Unanimous vote not to tell Lady Di.'

The day after their meeting near the black bins in the darkness, Durga found Roman in the fading light and hushed leaves outside Darwin College. They walked through Malting Lane and Ridley Hall Road, turning right onto the Backs, stopping on Clare College Bridge. In the end, it was the most natural place, and a knowing of the place for the first time, for her to move closer into his arms.

At first he did not ask, nor did she want to talk about her life with her husband. It did not matter in the walks over the Grantchester fields and the Fens, or as they rummaged in Waterstone's and Heffers, or huddled in the cold of a college garden.

'Don't you read any poetry? Elizabeth Barrett

233

Browning, Christina Rossetti, Emily Dickinson? I thought you would go for Sylvia Plath,' he teased.

'I like to laugh,' she replied.

Atul was a good, upright man, said Durga, conscientious and competent in his work, respected by his colleagues, liked by his friends, and loved by his family. He was also handsome, she added. Roman waited patiently for her to continue, and as he held her hands firmly between his own, she spoke of her childhood in England, of India and her teachers, her spiteful schoolmates, of college, her parents and relatives, of Malabar Hill, the sea and Vivek. The sea was not a painter's sea, she reminisced, but magnificent in the monsoon when the tall waves crashed and pounded the rocks and shoreline, spraying the city's waterfront promenades and the flimsy stalls selling corn on the cob and coconut water. The monsoon was the time for romance, she said wistfully.

Vivek was no longer in the matchbox business; his family had acquired a chain of luxury hotels. He was married and had a baby. She had met him in London at a café overlooking Green Park. Roman watched her face closely as she said Vivek no longer did silly things, and was content. Life had moved them both along.

She talked of her research for the television documentary on charities and her role as a Thursday volunteer in the shop, marking time before the job in London. Her eyes glinted as she talked of the customer searching for electric blankets, and the bizarre death of an elderly lady who was to have been the shop's newest volunteer.

'What do you think it was Arthur always used to say?' she asked, waiting patiently for his reply.

'Is this a trick question? Somehow, I get the feeling my answer is important to you. I guess I should make Arthur say a whole bunch of witty stuff about kings and round tables, but basically, I think he used to say that the true love of a man or a woman was all the blanket anyone would ever need.'

She shot him a smile, and he felt he had passed a test as challenging as a driving test for British roads. He had a teaser of his own, he said, retaliating. A road sign near Stamford in Lincolnshire announced *St Martin's Without*. Without what? He chuckled and spluttered before she could answer.

'Oops, I've just thought of what St Martin could be without. How interesting. Roman, you naughty, naughty boy!' He slapped his wrist. 'Okay, drop that one. Tell me how to get off a roundabout.'

'You have to know where you're coming from. And you have to know where you are going,' she said slowly.

She drew sharp, witty portraits of Swarnakumari, Heera and Eileen, saying she would probably never meet them again once she started work, blinking fiercely, unwilling to let him see her face, but in the end the words tumbled in tearful laughter as she recounted the bizarre events of their last day at the shop. In the end it seemed as if her entire life was about letting go of everything, she said wryly, dust to dust, rot to rust, what must end must. *I must and I must increase my bust* had failed too. She spoke of Atul's family, of his mother, sister Archana and cloying cousin Shreya, and the time that had passed, sand in a glass between her and her husband, was the unease of strangers in a lift between floors.

'I wouldn't be so hard on your sister-in-law Archie,'

he said. 'Why should she be the one stuck holding the weepy Oedipal mother-in-law while you guys have fun in Cambridge? She just needs to get a life. What she really needs is a man. If Archie babe were back home, I'd fix her up, but say, why doesn't that woman you told me about, the fat scheming matchmaker, get her together with the moody guy in New Jersey who shouts and yells?'

He laughed at his own wit, and then quietened. 'I have a confession to make – I shouted and yelled a lot. At Kathy. I also yelled into the desert. It was ugly. *I* was ugly. Shouting is cowardice, isn't it? A fear of losing control, so you end up losing all control. But maybe Archie babe should still give it a shot with the New Jersey dude if she's got a pair of sturdy earplugs.' Roman continued, 'Sounds like the green-eyed cousin with the secret uterine infection needs a man too. Is she a first, second or third cousin? These things matter.'

'I'm not sure. I'm not sure he likes her that much, either,' Durga's tone was edgy.

'He does, but I guess it's just not the right time, right place.'

She had turned prickly, and Roman wondered why, and what he could do. He would always feel he had been to blame for what happened with Kathy, but he had laid his own demons to rest: they had been pulverised and scattered somewhere over San Francisco and Arizona. Atonement, repentance, penitence for all things past, he was going to Durga in wonder and in trust, and he could never have imagined that he would meet her, only known that when he did she was real. Nothing and everything was wrong about her marriage, but it was not for him to decide its thudding dullness or its sanity.

A month and a half later, Christmas shoppers thronged Market Square, hungrily sniffing the warm smell of doughnuts at a corner stall. Durga hurried towards Roman, who was waiting near a Guildhall festooned with golden lights.

'What's up?'

'How do you know something's up?' she replied.

'Whatever it is, I want to hold you and wish it away,' he said.

'This is too big. There was a phone call from his sister in the middle of the night. Atul's rushing back to India. His mother's unwell, and apparently she's been like this for a long, long time with a mysterious ailment, but Archana didn't tell him, and the mother's been having all sorts of tests and examinations, and the doctors there think it's time Atul should be with her for reassurance. I'm fine with him going to hold her hand, of course, but the thing is, Archana says his dad wants him to stay on and take over the Maternity Clinic and not return to Cambridge at all. Atul has finished his fieldwork and case studies, you see, so technically he could stay on in India and complete from there. It's all very confusing, a big mess. He's busy checking flights and packing.'

'What about you?'

'What about me? Got to go, too,' she said dully. 'He says I should follow after we've sorted out everything. There's the flat we're renting – we have to give notice. I was going to start my new job . . .' She looked at him, eyes moist. 'I'm such a loser. I've just drifted through

237

my life, a Peter Pan of academia. I've done nothing with my life but study one thing after another – foreign languages, English and German Literature, Political and Social Sciences. Even being at Cambridge was so weird. I thought it would be different, but I was never part of student life at all. And now, just when I thought I'd be doing something for myself in London, it's all changed. Back to Pune.'

He caught her wrist and stopped outside Great St Mary's Church, but she twisted free, eyes brimming. 'And you – what am I doing with you? My life's already complicated. I'm *married*. I'm supposed to be thinking of my querulous mother-in-law in a creepy ancestral house in Pune. Where does this thing with you lead? Nowhere.'

He held her close, speaking earnestly. 'As I see it, you've got a choice. Maybe for the first time in your life. You don't have to do what he wants you to do. He'll cope – the clan's there, and they need *him* right now, not you. And maybe he and they don't really need you in the long term, either, and maybe you don't need him? Think about it. You can choose to go or not go, you can choose to be or not be with him. As for this thing with me, if it bothers you that much, you can choose to end wherever and whatever you want. You don't *have* to do anything.'

Durga stood at the window of her flat, looking at the neatly parked cars in the street below. Despite Roman's stirring words, she would go to India, remain by Atul's side and nurse his mother. Roman belonged to a society that encouraged individuals to seek their own paths, one in which a path that did not lead anywhere could be dropped, she reasoned. But could a relationship, a marriage be dropped simply because it was dull? Her own parents had worked at staying together, and wasn't marriage about imperfections and warts and fissures and cracks and packs of Band Aid? It was ironic, deeply ironic, she thought, that it was she, not Swarnakumari, who had travelled across the world with a suitcase packed with tradition and values, too afraid to unlock and unpack its contents. And now it was to be carried back, handled with care across the Arabian Sea and over the craggy Deccan mountains to Pune, to be set down with an obedient sigh to mop a moping brow.

In the end she discovered it was quite simple. It was not about his family; it was Atul she found boring and boorish and not the man she thought he would be. Now that she had met Roman, she would no longer think miserably about the years and the life stretching ahead with Atul. Roman could not last, passion did not last; she would soon find something she didn't like about him. Perhaps he needed more space than she did, and in any case there were worlds to cross, and it was no longer easy to stay flippant – and what if he went away at Christmas, in the spring, one day, never to return? Far better to leave first, to hold on to the memory of him on a hot, hellish night in Pune when the mosquito bites and the angry red blisters on her skin became too much to bear. Then she would never let him go.

That evening she told her husband she could not leave Cambridge in a hurry. There was the flat to vacate, bank balances to be transferred, belongings to be shipped. They would understand in Pune, if he would. She needed time.

Atul left the next day, obediently following the

thoughts that had already arrived safely in India before him. His chinos were waiting in his father's cupboard on the shelf below the Johnnie Walker Black Label whisky. An unwilling Nikhil had carried them a year earlier to Delhi, from where they accompanied a Grant Medical College friend a month later to Pune, along with Atul's instructions to his mother to have them dry cleaned. His frugal sister gave them to the dhobi instead, who arrived every Monday with the bundle of the previous week's washed and ironed clothes. Squatting expectantly in the hallway, the wrinkled man looked expressionlessly at the pickle-stained chinos. Customers often expected miracles he could not deliver.

Upgraded to Business Class for his cleancut looks and air of authority, Dr Atul Patwardhan was seated next to an attractive, wealthy young woman with natural cleavage and symmetrical white teeth, the kind that bit into an apple or flesh leaving a perfect dent. She was from Goa, and suffered from chronic thyroid problems. She felt completely at ease discussing her condition with the polite, handsome doctor. She listened to his advice and fluttered near his shoulder.

He thought of Durga and the feel of her silky hair and the look on her solemn, puckered face. He thought of her with the sudden panic of having abandoned his hair-trimming scissors that he wished he could have carried on board, but should at least have packed into his luggage. His companion leaned over comfortingly. The French red wine had complemented her meal.

Roman chose the same day to place his hand over his heart and bend a knee on the cold stone floor of a college archway. He had prepared to recite a long passage from Thoreau, but in the end the words were his own. He shivered, but he would stay on that stone until he froze, he declared, the damp grey cold seeping into his bones, turning hot blood into icy deliberation; he would stay there on that stone and become a stalagmite, which was more or less the same shape as a cactus. The word 'stalagmite' was derived from the Greek *stalagmos* or 'something dropped', he told her with chattering teeth. Was she ready to drop something else and take his heart instead? His was a healthy heart, bronzed and glowing: would she hold his heart in hers and take both into the Mumbai monsoon?

He swore that he did not care if he never saw another cactus again, unless it was with her by his side, and a desert was only a desert unless he saw it with her colours, and what they really needed was a collapsible bed, because they would travel to the ends of the earth together for the rest of their married lives, because that was what he was proposing – marriage – or why would he be on his knees turning to stone on the stone, and he didn't care if the three Furies from Pune pursued him through tempest, wind and fire, if Tisiphone, Alecto and Megaera castrated him with their tongues for his abduction of Durga, his goddess whom he adored, his protector of the good and pure, destroyer of evil, destroyer of the demon Mahishasura, destroyer of negation, at whose feet he worshipped, humble and devout.

He paused for breath. His knee was soon going to be frost-bitten, he warned. He was no match for a dishy doctor, he admitted, but if she was going to choose, he thought she should know that he, Roman, was pure, delectable, melting, swirling, sinful, brownest of brown chocolate. She had laughed, heard the sound in the echoing courtyard, and her eyes were soft as she said she loved chocolate, how did he know, she needed time.

Eileen lived on David Street, an arterial road near the charity shops. She had witnessed the transformation of IndiaNeed into the pizza and kebab takeaway, Bytes4U, with loyal disapproval. The overpowering smell of charcoaled kebabs sent her scurrying to the newsagent to purchase her first lottery ticket – after apologising to the spirit of her Catholic mother.

She had stood in the shop, a wispy-haired woman lost in calculations before she carefully made her selection, and was only mildly surprised at the winnings of twenty thousand pounds. Danny Watts was delighted; it was a neat little sum for retirement, and they could even nip across to the Algarve every year, two weeks in the sun, quiet hotel by the beach, half-board. Her silent response was to seek an interview with the loans department of her local bank, where she impressed the manager with her figures and forecasts. Six months later, in the hall of the church round the corner, she was running a successful after-school club called Kids Love Maths with a year's waiting list. She had been saved by numbers.

The hairdresser James (Juan) had dreamed of the Costa del Sol every Christmas as he went home to his cantankerous mother in Glasgow instead. Then on another windy morning two days after IndiaNeed closed, a Spanish woman visited his salon; he carefully highlighted her blond hair as she chattered, and forgot his accent as he watched her smile in the mirror. Events moved along so rapidly that, shortly afterwards, he accompanied her to Barcelona, instructing the estate agent to advertise the sale of his salon.

Mr Khan of Waterford Way already owned two take-aways in Cambridge. He knew his neighbours resented the parked delivery van outside his residence, but Mr Khan had other things on his mind and his eye on Mill Road, and once the salon was on the market he lost no time in making a successful bid as a cash buyer. The salon space was ideally suited to an Indian restaurant.

Meticulous to the last detail, Mr Khan aimed to provide authentic cuisine; not for him new-fangled dishes such as Indian-style pasta, nor would he ever serve curries, burger and pizza under one roof. He carefully proofread the menu for errors, changing *motor panir* to read *matar panir* instead.

The name of the restaurant was initially a challenge; Mr Khan had proposed Koh-i-noor and The Taj, but these were already in existence, as were The Gandhi, Curry Palace, India Gate, India House, Indian Garden, Royal Tandoori, Raj Mahal, Raj Villa, The Mogul, Spice City, the Bottisham Tandoori, Downham Tandoori and Romano's Histon Village Tandoori Restaurant.

In an inspired moment while painting on top of a ladder in the restaurant, Mr Khan tumbled upon the name. He would call it The Cambridge, like the popular pub that went by the name of The Granta at Newnham. A day later, his uncle from London suggested he add the word 'club' for an air of exclusivity and refinement. It was to be The Cambridge Club until Mrs Khan insisted that no flavour was possible without the word 'curry'. She always had the last word.

The Cambridge Curry Club opened in early December

and was taking bookings for Christmas. A gust of wind almost unhooked the sign; Mr Khan had it firmly nailed back the next day. The telephone staff occasionally stumbled over the long name and privately thought The Taj would have been snappier, but The Cambridge Curry Club it remained.

In the concluding chapter of the prayer book, Swarnakumari's Guru Ma had succinctly elucidated the transmutation and transformation of all matter over time:

*Nothing ever died that had never lived, nothing lived that had never died, and nothing lived or died, that was not reborn.*

# THE HOUSE OF SUBADAR

## Vijay Medtia

Veer Subadar murdered a man, for family honour and the people of his rural community in northwest India. Upon their release from prison years later, Veer and his friend Mohan discover that the Subadars' farm has been repossessed by the bank, and any chance of a livelihood destroyed. Veer and his family seek work in Bombay, lured by the promise of a new life.

The impoverished Subadars are forced to travel across 1,000 miles of Indian countryside, from their home in the Punjab through Gujarat and Rajasthan. They trek through a landscape of weary campsites and despondent souls, a test of endurance and will set against the fury of religious intolerance and hostility between Hindus and Muslims.

Their dreams begin to dissolve around them as they are told that employment is scarce, and the new arrivals are treated with hostility. Can Veer control his passions, and can his family find stability and a better future? *The House of Subadar* is a vivid journey of chance and will, cruelty and tragedy, and of the perseverance of the human spirit – a modern-day *Grapes of Wrath*.

'A remarkable debut – a celebration of family and hope'
SUE BAKER, *Publishing News*

'Unpretentious and evocative, danger never far away' *Independent*

250pp
ISBN: 978–1–901969–27–6
RRP £11.99

# ANCESTORS

## Paul Crooks

### HOW A LOST FAMILY WAS FOUND

It is the late eighteenth century. Aboard a slave ship bound from West Africa to Jamaica, a terrified young boy is cared for by Ami, a fellow captive, who becomes his surrogate mother during that nightmare voyage. They are sold to separate owners, but their lives remain curiously intertwined, and the boy, now a man named August, marries Ami's daughter, Sarah. *Ancestors* tells the story of their lives, their part in the struggle for emancipation, and the hope and faith that sustains them.

At the age of ten, Paul Crooks' great-great-great-grandfather John Alexander Crooks was captured and put aboard a slave ship bound for Jamaica. *Ancestors* is the fictionalised account of John's experiences from 1798 to 1838, the year that slaves in the British West Indies were set free.

'A moving tale of a black British family that travels through the ages from slavery and beyond' BONNIE GREER, *Guardian*

'An inspiring piece of literature. You can also smell the sweat and blood, hear the cracking whips and bitter cries of a people thrust into bondage' *The Voice*

'An exceptional debut novel. It is rightly being hailed as the heir to Alex Haley's *Roots*... A highly recommended read for the entire family' *Woman to Woman*

308pp
ISBN: 978–1–901969–07–8
RRP £9.99

# Bahia Blues

Yasmina Traboulsi

Translated from the French by Polly McLean

SALVADOR DE BAHIA – AN ILL WIND IS BLOWING
THROUGH THE OLD QUARTER OF THE CITY. THIS
POWERFUL DEBUT HAS ALREADY EVOKED
COMPARISONS TO THE BRAZILIAN FILM
*CITY OF GOD*.

On a vibrant square in Salvador, a small community, although impoverished, lives in harmony: Maria Aparecida, former carnival queen; Ivone, the beautiful, naïve convent guardian who dreams of becoming an actress; Padre Denilson, full of compassion and understanding for his wretched pensioners; seven-year-old Sergio, who sells sweets and perfumed napkins to support his whole family; Zé and Manuel, two gay teenagers begging to survive. Despite the hardships they are forced to endure, it is their deep-rooted sense of community and positive outlook which protects them from the violent chaos that rules Brazil's two major metropoles. Suddenly a stranger called Gringa enters this small world, and everything starts to change: Maria has disappeared, one-eyed Tonio has stopped singing and Mama Lourdes foresees nothing but tragedy. One by one, the inhabitants of the Square, tired of their provincial existence and dazzled by the urban glamour portrayed on their favourite soap opera, depart for the cities of Rio and São Paulo. However, the reality of life in the cities' *favelas* is a bitter disappointment – a tough game of survival guaranteed to harden even the most tender of hearts.

'A very impressive and engaging first novel and Yasmina Traboulsi is unquestionably a writer to watch'
SALMAN RUSHDIE

'Traboulsi's tough, pungent prose works well in translation, and one never doubts the authenticity of her *favela* portraits' *Guardian*

220pp
ISBN: 978–1–905147–28–1
RRP £10.99

# MISTRESS

## Anita Nair

A SEARING NEW NOVEL OF ART AND ADULTERY
FROM THE BESTSELLING AUTHOR OF *LADIES COUPE*

When travel writer Christopher Stewart arrives at a riverside
resort in Kerala to meet Koman, Radha's uncle and a famous
kathakali dancer, he enters a world of masks and repressed emotions. From their first meeting, both Radha and her uncle are
drawn to the enigmatic young man with his cello and his inces-
sant questions about the past. The triangle quickly excludes
Hyam, Radha's husband, who can only watch helplessly as she
embraces Chris with a passion that he has never been able to draw
from her. Also playing the role of observer-participant is Koman;
his life story, as it unfolds, captures all the nuances and contradic-
tions of the relationship being made – and unmade – in front of
his eyes.

A brilliant blend of imaginative storytelling and deeply moving explorations into the search for meaning in art and life, *Mis-
tress* is a literary tour de force from one of India's most exciting
writers.

'A talent. . .She makes the closed world of the Kathakali perform-
ers come alive and paints a poignant picture of the segregated,
cloistered Muslim village' *Washington Post*

'Nair is a powerful writer. . .she has created what must be one of
the most important feminist novels to come out of South Asia'
*Daily Telegraph*

428pp
ISBN: 978–1–905147–30–4
RRP £11.99

# THE HOLY WOMAN

## Qaisra Shahraz

### A POWERFUL AND COMPELLING FAMILY DRAMA

A romantic story of love and betrayal set in a wealthy Muslim community, with all the pressures and conflicts that modern life and old traditions bring.

'A dramatic story of family intrigue, religious passions and riproaring romance' MICHÈLE ROBERTS

'A lean, lyrical meditation on tradition and independence, sensuality and sacrifice, set against the moral background of modern day Pakistan. Shahraz's debut beguiles throughout' *The Times*

'An international best-seller . . . an extraordinary story of love and betrayal in rural Pakistan' *Manchester Evening News*

'An intriguing tale of love, envy and jealousy . . . Compulsive reading' *Asian Times*

'A riveting family saga, where three young women are haunted by the events that occurred two decades earlier' *Bradford Telegraph & Argus*

'A very moving tale of love, passion and Islamic traditions . . . Difficult to put down' *BBC National Asian Network*

'Stunning debut novel. An intricate study of love, family, politics and sacrifice' *Eastern Eye*

'A real story-telling' SUE GEE

570pp
ISBN: 978–1–905147–63–2
RRP £8.99

# Typhoon

## Qaisra Shahraz

### Three women, one man, one night

*Typhoon* is a riveting family saga of deceit. The long-awaited second novel by the best-selling author of *The Holy Woman.*

Chiragpur is a traumatised village, warped in time and space. Haunted by what happened some twenty years earlier in a court-room, *Typhoon* is a tragic tale of three young women, each one demonised by her past.

'Full of vivid detail about the lives and loves, the duties and desires in Muslim life' Yasmin Alibhai-Brown

'Seamlessly takes her readers on a vivid journey exploring the lives of her Pakistani heroines' *Manchester Evening News*

'Gripping, involving and satisfying. Shahraz gives us a compelling insight into Pakistani village life' *Indie Magazine*

'Her long-awaited second novel about love, jealousy, adultery and rape – tells the tragic tale of three young women in Chiragpur, Sindh' *Asian News*

354pp
ISBN: 978–1–905147–62–7
RRP £7.99